man crush
MONDAY

KIRSTY MOSELEY

Copyright © 2020 Kirsty Moseley
All rights reserved.

The right of Kirsty Moseley to be identified as the Author of the Work has been asserted by her in accordance with the Copyright, Designs and Patents Act 1988.

No part of this publication may be reproduced, stored in a retrieval system, or transmitted, in any form or by any means without the prior written permission of the publisher, nor be otherwise circulated in any form of binding or cover other than that in which it is published and without a similar condition being imposed on the subsequent purchaser.

All characters in this publication are fictional and any resemblance to real persons, living or dead is purely coincidental.

Editor and Interior Designer: Jovana Shirley,
Unforeseen Editing, www.unforeseenediting.com

ISBN-13: 9781711201405

To Lee, for keeping us all alive and fed while I was trapped in the writing cave. I love you.

ONE

Guess what day it is!

*It's Man Crush Monday. *le sigh**

> *Are you going to speak to him today???*

YES!

> *More than just, "Ticket, please"?*

Well ... maybe.

> *That means no ...*

"**U**gh, Mondays!"

I glance up from my screen and slip my phone into my trouser pocket as a harassed-looking woman in a brown business suit climbs aboard the train, noisily bumping her briefcase on wheels up the step, almost dropping her coffee cup in the process.

"Good morning." I offer her a beaming smile, pressing back against the wall so she can pass me in the small corridor and get into the quiet carriage.

She gives me a grunt and slops some of her coffee over the side of her cup, narrowly missing my ugly black work shoes as she heads past without another word.

"Oh, well, good morning to you too, Amy," I chirp sarcastically to myself as the door slides closed behind her.

Everyone dislikes Mondays; it's ingrained in us to hate it on some primal level. Mondays signify the end of the weekend, going back to work, alarm clocks, and routine, so I can see why people detest it. But not me. It's actually my favourite day of the week. It never used to be. Up until five months ago, I was a normal Monday hater, just like everyone else, but then something happened. *He* happened.

Let me explain. I work as a ticket conductor on a busy train route. Every day, I squeeze my slightly-too-big bottom into my ugly uniform and tuck my pale candyfloss-pink hair up into a bun or Katniss Everdeen–style side plait and go to work, collecting tickets on the train from Cambridge to London. It's a mundane job, but it pays the bills and keeps me in hair dye, Dr Pepper, and Converse. A girl's gotta do what a girl's gotta do.

I'd been doing my boring, mundane job for almost two years when, one dreary Monday, I looked up, and *bam*, I caught the feels. It wasn't insta-love—this isn't one of those stories—but it was definitely insta-lust. That was almost five glorious months ago.

The guy in question—my dream guy and object of my unrequited crush—is tall. It's hard to judge with the train rocking and the amount of time I get to stand next to him, but I'd guess he's around six foot. His shoulders are broad, and he's lean and perfectly proportioned—I can tell this from the tailored suits he wears and how they narrow in at the hips and fit across his thighs in a way that sets my pulse racing. His brown hair is quite short on the sides and a bit longer on top, styled effortlessly. But it's his eyes that get me. The brown eyes the colour of single-malt whiskey with flecks of gold around the pupils. They're the type of eyes you want to stare into all day, the type of eyes you could lose time to. They're smiley eyes, if they can be such a thing. They exude warmth, and when paired with his killer smile, straight white teeth, and strong jaw, it makes me catch my breath and clench my thighs.

Now, don't get me wrong; it wasn't his looks that made me catch the feels. Yes, I'll admit, his looks were the cause of the insta-lust, and I'm not going to lie and say I don't want to climb him like a monkey climbs a tree because I do. But his looks weren't what made me fall in love with him. No, that was purely his personality.

You see, my Man Crush Monday is a geek. A one hundred percent bona fide geek. And it turns me on more than anything. Geeks and nerds have always been my thing. I've always been attracted to the smart, dorky guys who are into Star Wars or Dungeons & Dragons. If a guy talks to me about astrophysics or can tell me random facts about history or how they put the bubbles into cream soda, I'm putty in their hands. Hello, major Tony Stark fangirl here. And my crush, this hot dork who gets on my train every other Monday, is about as close to Tony Stark as I'll likely ever get.

I grip the handrail and lean out, scanning the platform. More hurried people jump on the train, and I anxiously scrutinise the crowd, looking for him. My eyes flick to the platform clock—8:07 a.m. The train is to depart at 8:09 sharp. He's cutting it close today.

A ball of disappointment settles in my chest when I realise with a jolt that he's not coming today.

Bugger.

I'm on holiday from the weekend, two blissful weeks of lie-ins and late nights. I prepared myself to not see my crush while I was off, but because he only boards the train every other week, if he doesn't turn up today, it will be pushing four weeks that I won't clap eyes on him. This is a disaster. It's 8:07 a.m., and my day is officially ruined.

As if my thinking about him makes him appear, he bursts through the ticket barrier at the end and runs, newspaper tucked under his arm, briefcase thumping wildly against his leg as he pelts towards the train. He looks up, his eyes meet mine, and he raises a hand in greeting—or maybe it's not a greeting; perhaps it's a *don't leave without me* gesture, but I take it the other way. Small wins.

I smile and playfully roll my eyes, and he grins the cutest smile ever and climbs on board at the other end of the long train just as my walkie crackles to life with instructions.

I sigh happily, my disappointment dispersed.

Day officially *un*ruined.

Once the train is safely on the move, I set about the other part of my job—ticket-collecting. I start at the front and work my way to the back—to him. The job is old hat now; I could do it in my sleep. When I first started, the motion of the train made me feel nauseous, and I'd wobble on my feet, almost falling over passengers' bags they'd carelessly left in the aisles. Not anymore though. I'm like a ballerina, traipsing down the carriage like a swan gliding on water. Practice makes perfect.

I greet the passengers with my usual cheery smile, a little bit of chitchat to the regulars, and a few snippets of information about London for the obvious tourists.

When I step into the last carriage, I see he's chosen a seat facing front at the far end. I chew on my lip, absentmindedly selling another ticket as I discreetly let my eyes glide over him. He's chatting to an older guy next to him, and I see he's already given away his newspaper. I smile to myself and hand a young teenage couple their change before moving on to the next passenger. The old guy seated next to him laughs at something, and I smile inwardly. My crush is one of those people you could drop into a room full of strangers, and within ten minutes, they'd be ordering a sharing platter, and he would be in their wedding.

The light slants in from the window, bouncing off his hair in a way that makes my fingers itch to reach out and run a hand through it. I bet it's soft, like silk. He shrugs and takes a gulp of the disgusting train tea he purchased from the refreshments cart. I watch his Adam's apple bob in his throat as he swallows.

Jeez, that throat! I would be perfectly content to do nothing other than run my tongue down that throat all day.

My greedy eyes drag over the rest of him. Today is a shirt-and-tie week. His grey suit is paired with a white shirt and blue-striped tie; it's stylish and hot as sin. Last time, he was distinctly more casual—a well-worn grey *Goonies Never Say Die* T-shirt under a fitted blue suit, and I swear it almost made me come. In fact, I did come later when I was alone and thinking about it.

I sigh as a wave of longing washes over me. *Why does he have to be so cute and so damn perfect for me?*

I'm done, and he's not even looked up at me yet.

Control yourself, Amy. You got this. Big-girl panties. Remember what Heather said: just talk to him like you would any other passenger.

I'm at the seats just in front of his now. With each passenger served, the anticipation builds. This is it, my favourite part of the week.

I hold my breath as I stop next to his seat but deliberately keep my eyes away from his face, dragging the moment out like a masochist. "Good morning, gentlemen. Tickets, please."

"Good morning." The old guy next to my crush smiles over at me and holds out a credit card. "Open return to London, please."

I nod and ring it through, conscious of how close I am to *him*. I can almost feel the soft brush of his knee against mine as I lean over the table with the card machine, watching as the old guy beeps his card to pay. I daren't look at him as his subtle yet decadent aftershave wafts up; mixed with the tones of his skin, it smells delicious and makes my mouth water.

It's so hard not to just jump the guy. The insta-lust is strong with this one.

On the table in front of him, his book sits, abandoned. It's facedown, so I tilt my head a little to see the title on the spine. We read the same books a lot, me and my crush. Sometimes, it's just a happy coincidence; sometimes, I pop into WHSmith on my way home and buy the book he's been reading, like the weird stalker that I am. We have similar tastes though; we both like crime and thrillers. Today's pick: C.J. Tudor's newest novel. I've already read it, so I smile in satisfaction.

When I can put it off no longer, I raise my eyes to his face, and it's like being sucker-punched right in the heart. His beautiful brown eyes meet mine, and his mouth pulls into that panty-wetting smile that exposes all his perfect teeth. My knees feel weak, and words just ... go. I'm struck dumb. This happens every time I try to talk to him. So much for all the practice my best friend, Heather, and I did on the phone last night; all the conversation starters she made me memorise have vanished into a puff of air.

"Morning."

Damn. That voice.

I clear my throat and force a smile. My gaze wanders to the tiny little freckle he has under one eye. It's the only thing that isn't flawless, industry-standard perfection about him, yet somehow, that little brown dot makes him even more beautiful to me. One of my secret fantasies is kissing that little freckle while he does sinful things to my naked body.

"Morning," I reply, trying not to let those sinful freckle fantasies show on my face.

"I almost didn't make it today—slept in," he says, reaching up to run a hand through his hair, the grin still paralysing me.

I long to say something witty, to say *anything* actually. But the ease of conversation I seem to be able to manage with everyone else is like a distant talent. Like him, I'm also one of those people who can make friends with strangers, and in fact, I *have* actually met someone on a plane and then stepped in to be a bridesmaid at their beach wedding less than twenty-four hours later. (It's a long story involving lots of cocktails, tall heels, a broken ankle, and a hospitalised should-be bridesmaid.) But around this guy, my brain just melts into a puddle. He makes me nervous; he's the only one who has ever made me nervous.

"I saw. A couple of minutes later, and you'd have been on the next train," I reply, my throat scratchy with the need to clear it again.

"That wouldn't do. Your train is my favourite."

Is he flirting with me? My whole face burns as my insides squirm with pleasure at the mere thought.

"Yes, this train does have the fewest stops and gets there the fastest." *What am I doing? Flirt back, Amy!*

He laughs, a throaty, almost-awkward laugh, and the hair at the nape of my neck prickles with sensation. Other than his voice, his laugh is my most favourite sound in the world. He looks down at the table and holds up his prepurchased ticket; I discreetly wipe my sweaty palm on my trouser leg before I take it, punch it, and hand it back.

"Thanks. Have a good day," I mutter.

"You too."

Disappointment settles over me. Our interaction is over, and now, because of my holiday, I won't get to see him for weeks. I open my mouth to say something, anything, just to snatch another precious few seconds of his time, but nothing comes out. I feel my face warm from my neck all the way up to my hairline, and I walk off, kicking myself because I wasted another perfectly good opportunity to talk to him.

I don't even know his name, for goodness' sake. Five months of seeing him twice a month, and I haven't even worked up the nerve to ask his name. I suck big time.

I walk to the end of the carriage and press the button on the door, hearing the whoosh as the door slides open. I step into the quiet corridor and close the door behind me, leaning against the wall, taking a couple of deep breaths. Maybe I'll get another chance today. Maybe I'll be lucky, and he will get one of my return-journey trains this afternoon. Sometimes he does, but more often than not, he doesn't, and some other lucky conductor gets to drool over him instead.

I look back through the glass window, seeing the back of his head. He is sitting to the side now and has picked up his book.

I let out a sigh of longing. I have it so bad that it's physically painful.

My friend Heather doesn't believe me that you can fall in love with someone you've never really spoken to, but she's wrong, dead wrong. I don't need to know his name or where he lives or what size shoe he wears or what his favourite dinner is to fall in love with him. All that stuff is somehow irrelevant. I know *him*. My soul knows his.

Over the last five months, I've learned a lot—stalker-style, of course. I know everything that is *important* to know about him. Like, how he smiles when he speaks to his mother on the phone or that he always gives up his seat when it is busy. And how he befriends strangers and always gives his newspaper away. I know he likes *Doctor Who* and Marvel movies. I know that his favourite snack from the refreshments cart is a custard cream biscuit and that he dunks those biscuits like a pro, never letting one break off, leaving his tea a crummy, soggy mess. I also know, thanks to my friend on the refreshments cart, that he often pays for a coffee for the person after him to "pass it on." He helps little old ladies carry their luggage off the train and makes sure they get to the gate safely. He often streams cartoons on his phone and gives it to tired and grumpy children to watch on their way home. I know his voice, his hands, his smile, his laugh.

And the final straw, the one that really sealed the deal and drew me in hook, line, and sinker: last month, when a little girl had tripped while getting on the train and skinned her knee, he performed magic to cheer her up. Actual, legit, honest-to-God, Harry Potter–esque magic. He made money, handkerchiefs, and playing cards disappear and reappear for almost an hour, much to the little girl's delight—and mine, of course.

That was the moment I knew—the moment *I just knew*—I was in love with him. This stranger on the train, my Man Crush Monday. Who can resist a super-hot dork who performs magic? Not this girl.

I sigh again, watching the back of his head as he slumps more comfortably in his seat, turning pages of his novel.

Maybe one day, I will talk to him, dazzle him with my sharp wit and sparkling personality. He'll have no choice but to fall madly in love with me and all my quirks, and we'll get a happily ever after worthy of any romance novel.

But today is not that day.

TWO

"Medium iced latte."

I grin happily and nod, stepping forward and taking the clear plastic cup as the barista, Ruby, sets it on the counter. "Thanks. See you tomorrow."

"Bye, Amy. Have a good day," she replies, already busy making the next person's drink.

"You too!" I wave with my coffee cup, grinning as I take the first pull on the straw, and head towards the door. It's my first coffee of the day, and it tastes like heaven. Iced coffee is my weakness; I can't resist it, so I usually make an early morning stop on my way to work to get one.

Just as I step out the door, I stop as someone's dog yips at my heels. He's been tied up outside while his owner gets their own caffeine fix.

I smile down at it, reaching down a hand to stroke its furry little head and scratch it behind the ear. "Well, aren't you a beautiful little fur baby!"

Okay, so maybe dogs are my weakness too. But in my defence, have you seen dogs?

I force myself to stand and leave the pup alone because I need to get to work. As soon as I'm back on my feet, something solid—or rather, *someone* solid walks smack into me at full force. I don't have time to react as my precious coffee cup slams against my chest, the lid popping off. I feel the shock of cold as the liquid bursts upwards; wet seeps into my white shirt and sloshes up my neck. Ice cubes skitter to the floor with a chink and a splash, and I blink in shock.

"Whoa! Oh shit!" a guy exclaims.

As the force of the collision propels me backwards, hands grip my upper arms, stopping me from crashing into the little metal table behind me. The cute little dog at my feet yelps and runs away a couple of steps, so he doesn't get trampled.

"Oh my God, I'm so sorry! Are you okay?" the guy asks, his hands still firmly gripping my arms.

I blink again, my mouth popping open in shock as I register the fact that over half a cup of liquid just exploded over me. I look down at the floor, seeing his phone lying in a puddle of coffee and that the dog is now back, lapping at the liquid with gusto.

I blow out a big breath, my shock now receding. "I'm okay," I mutter, stepping back and flicking droplets from my fingers.

"I was on my phone. I wasn't watching. This was totally my fault. I'm so sorry." His voice is apologetic.

I shrug, a smile now creeping up onto my lips as a chuckle bubbles in my throat.

Stuff like this happens to me all the time. Heather calls me her "liability mate"—the one who trips over the plugged-in phone charger or drops her ice cream and has to buy another, the one who gets lost on a night out or accidentally stalk-likes her ex's new girlfriend's photo on Facebook. Basically, I'm a liability.

"It's okay. At least it wasn't a hot one, so no third-degree burns," I joke, reaching up to brush the worst of the liquid from my shirt as I look up at him.

As my eyes land on his face, my heart squeezes and stops. Okay, that's an exaggeration; it doesn't stop, but I definitely get palpitations. It's *him*. My Man Crush Monday—but on a Tuesday, outside a coffee shop. I've never seen him outside of my work, and I feel myself begin to sweat as nerves and excitement swirl together in my stomach like a tornado.

He groans and reaches up to his breast pocket, pulling out the black pocket square and holding it out to me as he shakes his head in disbelief. "What a dick. I'm really sorry."

I swallow around my nerves. "It's fine, honestly. Thanks."

I slip off my handbag and set it and my half a coffee on the table next to us before taking the offered handkerchief; it's soft silk, and it feels expensive. I gulp and feel guilty, using it to try and blot the worst of the liquid from my shirt and dry off my neck. My eyes wander over him. Dark grey tailored suit today, crisp white shirt, and a black tie held in place with a silver pin. He looks incredible; it fits him flawlessly, showing off his athletic and toned body, his trousers stretching over his thighs like a wet dream waiting to happen.

"I'll pay for the dry cleaning."

I wrinkle my nose. "Dry cleaning? You're obviously under the impression that I work for somewhere reputable. This is tumble dry only," I joke.

When he laughs quietly, I award myself an internal high five.

"Do you have something to change into? You're on your way to work, I'm assuming?" he asks, cocking his head to the side as his eyes flit down to my jacket with the train company logo stitched into it.

I nod. "Actually, I do. I have a spare shirt in my locker for emergencies such as this. You might not believe me, but this happens to me a lot. Maybe not walking into someone at a coffee shop, but just general spillages. I'm that kind of person."

"I actually do believe you." One side of his mouth quirks up into a boyish smile, and it's so cute that my insides clench, and I grin back like a goon. He brushes off the couple of small droplets of coffee from his suit sleeves before bending to retrieve his phone from the puddle, shooing the dog away from the spill. "No more of that; you'll get the caffeine shakes."

I chuckle, watching as he gently tries to push the dog away again. "No one can resist an iced latte; one small sip, and you're hooked."

He grins up at me, that full-on devastating smile, and damn if I don't internally swoon.

"Is your phone okay?" I wince, watching as he gives up on trying to stop the dog and brushes the worst of the liquid off his sleek, expensive-looking smartphone before pressing a button to light up the screen.

"Yeah, all good," he replies, slipping it into his trouser pocket without really looking at it. His beautiful brown eyes travel down my body, assessing the damage as he stands and steps closer. "You have …" He reaches towards me but then seems to catch himself, and his hand stalls midair before he clears his throat and points at my chest.

I look down, too, to see a partially melted ice cube lodged between my shirt buttons and laugh before flicking it out. "Thanks."

I hand him back his now-ruined pocket square and pick up my bag and coffee cup.

He shuffles on his feet before nodding back into the shop. "If you won't let me pay to get your uniform cleaned, at least let me replace your drink." His eyes shine in apology as he reaches up and scratches the back of his neck almost shyly.

I press my lips together to try and hide my excitement that I get to talk to him for a few more minutes and nod. "Okay, that would be nice. Thanks."

He turns, grips the handle of the door, and pulls it open, gesturing for me to go through first. I toss my half-empty cup into the bin and step in.

We join the back of the queue and stand awkwardly, side by side. It's weird, standing next to him, doing something normal like this. I'm struck by how tall he is as he stands at my side; I only just come up past his shoulder. My guess at six foot was probably a little bit off; he's more like six two. We're the total opposites. He's all tall and lean and clean edges, professional-looking. I'm petite with thick thighs and a big bum, all soft curves. My coffee-stained shirt, polyester uniform, and ugly shoes are in direct comparison to his tailored expensiveness. He's a solid ten, and I'm maybe an average, albeit quirky, six. If it wasn't for his dorky side that I know he has (hello, he is level seventy-eight on Wizards Unite), I would say we were polar opposites. Yes, he's good-looking, but if it wasn't for me seeing his nerd side on our train journeys, I might not have looked twice at him. From the outside, we probably look out of place, standing next to each other like this, but I revel in it and raise my chin, soaking it all up and enjoying it while it lasts.

He clears his throat and turns to face me. "Do you maybe have time for a drink in rather than a takeaway?" he asks, and I almost choke on air.

My pulse races, and my insides jump for joy. *That sounds very much like a coffee date ... HELL YES!*

I start to smile and nod a yes, but then realisation brings me back down with a bump very quickly. I wince and look at my watch. "Oh, I don't actually. I'm already pushing it for time to get to work."

"Ah, okay. Never mind. I just thought you could dry off a bit better before heading out into the cold with a wet top on."

He shuffles forward as the queue moves, and I bite the inside of my cheek because he looks as nervous as I feel. It's adorable.

"Why don't you go try and dry off a bit while I order?" he offers, motioning to the toilets at the back of the café.

"Good thinking, Batman," I say and then immediately mentally face-palm myself when he chuckles.

"What would you like?" he asks as I shrug out of my damp jacket.

I tell him my order and smile gratefully as I prance to the back of the café and slip into the toilet. Once inside, I sink against the wall and sigh. Of all the scenarios I've played out of how I wanted our first real conversation to go, me looking like a drowned rat was not part of any of them.

"Get it together, Amy. Woman up." I mentally shake myself and push away from the wall.

Looking in the mirror, I groan. My shirt is beyond saving. Luckily for me, I do have a spare at work—that wasn't a lie. The jacket though … I look down at the soggy jacket and wince before wetting my hand and trying to wash off as much of the coffee as I can. Once it's as good as it'll get, I press the button for the hand dryer and hold it under for a couple of minutes with one hand while I look at myself in the mirror.

My reflection grimaces back at me, but if I'm honest, it could have been a lot worse. At least my make-up is still on point! I turn my head this way and that, carefully checking my reflection. My eyeliner is winged to perfection (I never leave the house without a sufficient wing, something I perfected at seventeen and never looked back from), and the coffee hasn't washed off too much of my foundation. My cheeks even have a subtle glow to them that I suspect is more from the pleasure of seeing him than the highlighter I applied an hour ago. And my hair, with its freshly applied rose-pink-pastel dye job from last night, is looking super cute, even if I do say so myself. As luck would have it, I even opted for a stylish plaited bun today and spent ages this morning teasing it into a pretty style I copied from a YouTube tutorial. Thank the Lord for small mercies!

Deciding to dry my shirt off a bit, I bend and, limbo-style, shove my chest under the dryer, giving it a quick blast of hot air too. When it's as good as I can get it, I shrug on my jacket, take a couple of deep, calming breaths, and tell myself to be cool and not to fuck it up. Then, I step out of the door. He's still in line, but his eyes are on the door of the bathroom, so as I step out, our gazes meet, and I can't help but grin as I send him a goofy wave.

Oh God, what happened to being cool, Amy?

He bites his bottom lip, his eyes narrowing slightly.

Oh dear God. That one look levels me and sends my hormones spiking. I clench my thighs because that little lip bite is so sexy that it almost knocks me sideways.

I make my way over to his side.

"That looks a bit better," he greets, his eyes flicking down to my top.

I gulp and nod, struck mute again.

He holds out his hand and smiles. "I'm Jared, by the way. Jared Stone."

Jared. Jared Stone. It's not what I expected. I figured a Mark or a Greg or something more generic, but Jared …

I like it. It's sexy, and it fits him perfectly.

"Amy Clarke."

As his warm, strong hand envelops mine and he gives it a little squeeze, pleasure washes over my whole body. His long fingers brush against the back of my hand in a move that sends a little shiver down my spine. My first feel of his skin, and it is addictive. I'm already imagining that hand on other parts of my body.

"Pleasure to meet you, Amy." His smile is a smirk, as if he can tell what fantasies the small skin-on-skin contact is creating in my brain.

He hasn't let go, and I don't want him to.

"Who's next?"

The voice at the till breaks into our bubble, and our joined hands finally release as he turns to the side. I take a moment to press my hand against my racing heart while he orders our drinks. Once he's paid, we move up to the collection area.

"So, what's it like, working on the trains?" he asks, nodding down at the company logo on my jacket.

The collection area is busy, so we settle off to one side, our bodies too close together for me to form coherent thoughts.

I shrug in reply. "It's okay. It has its perks." *Mondays are a perk for me …*

"Large black coffee and an iced latte?" When she places down our drinks, Ruby looks up at me, and her eyes widen as she catches sight of my coffee-stained shirt. "Amy! What happened to you, girl?"

I motion to Jared and shrug. "Hot guy got me wet." It's out of my mouth before I can stop it. My eyes widen in horror.

Next to me, Jared snort-laughs, and I feel the pressure of his arm pressing against mine as his body shakes.

I grin with relief. Another mental high five for me for making him laugh.

See, I can talk to guys. Piece of cake.

He picks up both of our drinks, the grin still on his face as he hands me mine. I wave over my shoulder at Ruby, knowing I'll be expected to give her all the gossip tomorrow morning. Her eyes slowly travel the length of Jared as he turns towards the door. I get it; he's very easy on the eye. I also notice a couple of other women glance in his direction—one of them even does a double-take and mouth-gape combo—as we walk out of the café.

Jealousy rears inside me like an angry cat.

Outside, we step around the milky puddle and smile sheepishly at each other as Jared kicks an ice cube under the table. "Guess the dog couldn't manage it all then," he jokes.

I motion to my bike that's been unceremoniously propped up against the wall outside. "So, this one's me."

His mouth drops open, and his eyebrows rise as he takes in all its glory. "This is your ride?" He leans forward, running a hand over the rust-coated handlebars before using one finger to ring the bell. A soft tinkle fills the air.

I place my drink cup into the front basket, adjusting the jumper I stuffed in there so it wedges the cup upright (this isn't my first rodeo), and pull the bike to standing. It takes a little effort, because the thing isn't exactly aerodynamic; it's sturdy, and it was built from metal a long time before they realised they should make bicycles lightweight.

"It gets me from A to B." I brush a bit of dirt from the seat before swinging my leg over, balancing it between my thighs.

Jared steps closer, placing a knee on either side of the front wheel and grinning down at it. "This is the saddest attempt at a bike I've ever seen."

I fake gasp. In all honesty, I know what my bike looks like; she's one of those old-fashioned heritage ones. I believe she used to be pale green, but nowadays, she's more rust than colour.

"Don't make fun of Bessy," I scold playfully.

He reaches out and squeezes one of my brakes, watching as the brake pad on the front wheel barely connects. One of his eyebrows rises. "Bessy," he says. "And where did you find Bessy? A rubbish dump perhaps?"

I feign shock and put my hand on my heart. "How very dare you, sir. I'll have you know, I paid just three pounds at a car boot sale for this excellent piece of engineering."

"Three whole pounds? You were robbed." He chuckles and shakes his head as he carefully wraps a hand over the handlebars and lifts the bike a couple of inches off the ground. "Damn, it weighs a ton."

I nod in acknowledgement. "Yep, but she's reliable. And cheap to run. Plus, I didn't get leg muscles like this from driving, you know; riding her is like a workout in itself. Who needs an expensive gym? Not this girl."

His eyes drop down to my thighs, lingering there for a second too long before flicking back up to meet mine. The appreciatory expression on his face makes my tummy clench. "You're right; cycling is definitely working for you."

I feel my face flush with pleasure.

He steps back and cocks his head to the side. "I should probably let you get to work before you're late."

Work. Damn, I forgot about it again! "Oh, right, yeah. Well, thank you for the coffee."

He frowns down at the ground and shuffles on his feet. "Maybe … maybe we could get together another time. Dinner? Tonight even, if you're free?"

I can't stop the dorky grin from stretching across my face. "Sure, I'd like that."

His gaze meets mine again. When he smiles, it's so big that his eyes crinkle around the edges, and it makes my whole body sing.

"Great. Here, put your number in, and I'll text you later to sort out times and stuff." He digs in his pocket and brings up his phone, waking up the screen and opening the keyboard.

I try not to do a little happy dance as I punch my number into his phone.

As soon as I hand it back to him, he presses a few buttons, and my own phone pings in my bag. "There. Now, you have mine too."

"Okay, well, I guess I'll see you later. Bye, Jared."

"Bye, Amy." He nods and steps back, giving me a wide berth to get past him, watching as I push away from the ground and put all my effort into making the heavy bike go.

When I turn to wave over my shoulder, the bike wobbles a little, and I quickly grasp the handlebars again to regain control.

I hear him chuckle behind me, and I can't contain my broad grin.

I did it. I finally talked to him, and all it took was a coffee in the face to get the conversation started. Why couldn't I have thought of that months ago?

THREE

Heather lounges on my bed, rifling through the outfits I laid there to get her opinion on. With her free hand, she shovels Frosties straight from the box and into her mouth and crunches loudly, uncaring of the crumbs that drop onto my duvet or into her bra.

"Nope. Nope. Nope," she says, casually discarding each one into a messy pile with a flick of her wrist. "Amy, come on; just try on some of the stuff I brought round."

I frown into my wardrobe, scanning everything that's left in there. I'll be honest; there isn't much. Almost everything I own is screwed up and has already been rejected by my best friend. I groan and let my head drop back, closing my eyes. "Hev, I can't go on a first date with the guy and not be me. The only thing he's seen me wear is a work uniform. I need to show him who I am and see if he runs away, screaming." I turn back and pick up my cute jean shorts, the ones with the Union Jack flag sewn into the rear to conceal my modesty, and a gold strappy top. "What about this? These are my lucky shorts."

Her nose wrinkles as I hold the clothes against my underwear-clad body and add a big fake smile to try and convince her. "Weren't you wearing that exact outfit when you pulled that Italian bloke who turned out to be a stalker?"

I frown down at them and realise, yep, they are. "Okay, not-so-lucky shorts." I toss them over my shoulder and reach for the next thing—a black dress with long sleeves. I hold it up and raise an eyebrow.

"You wore that to my aunt Lizzie's funeral."

I sigh and toss that too. Setting my hands on my hips, I groan in defeat. Heather and I do not have the same taste, like, at all. She's all girlie girl who likes figure-hugging bodycon dresses. I'm more dungarees and belly tops or retro T-shirts, but if I don't pick something soon, I'll be going out in the sexy black lacy underwear I'm currently sporting.

"Okay, fine. Show me what you've got."

She grins, clapping her hands and moving the cereal box to my sideboard where crumbs scatter over my alarm clock. I jump when I see the time glowing there. It's 7:42. Jared texted me at lunchtime to say he would pick me up at eight.

"Shit, I need to pick something now! He's going to be here in less than twenty minutes!" My hand shoots up to my neck, and I grip the pendant that's on my necklace, rubbing my thumb over it as I watch Heather pick up a black bin bag full of clothes and upend it onto my bed with all my stuff. As I thought, it's all slinky numbers and nothing like what I usually wear. I frown and push my hand through the pile. A red-and-black-chequered T-shirt dress catches my eye.

"I bought that by accident—impulse buy; it was on sale, and I left it too late to return it," she says, still looking through the pile for something more suitable.

I make a dive for it and hold it up against myself.

Short sleeves. Mid-thigh. Pockets. Win!

"Ooh, I like this!" I say, already unzipping it at the neck and widening the opening so I can fit it over my hair that I painstakingly teased into loose beach waves for the last half an hour. The dress skims my body perfectly, fitted at the top to emphasize the girls, cinching in at the waist to show off my curves. "I *really* like this." I turn back to the mirror, examining myself.

Heather comes up behind me, ripping off the tags and zipping me up. "Pair of black tights to make it more you and then ... fucking gorgeous." She grins at me in the mirror.

She's almost as excited about this date as I am. She's been listening to me talk about this guy for months now. She came straight over after work and has been helping me get ready for the last couple of hours. She is the best wingwoman a girl could ask for.

I pat her hand that rests on my shoulder and then slip away, over to my underwear drawer, where I pull out a pair of thick black tights. I sit on the chair to slide them up my legs, doing a little shimmy to sort the waist out.

In my wardrobe, I slide my eyes over my numerous pairs of Converse and then settle on the black-and-white ones.

"Oh no, come on. Trainers, really? How about a nice pair of heels instead?" Heather suggests as I slip my feet into them.

"No way. I'm already more dressed up than usual. I at least want to feel a little bit like myself. Heels will just make me more nervous too."

I bend and lace my Converse while she groans in defeat. When I stand and look back at my room, I grimace. It looks like the entire contents of a sewing factory threw up over it. There are clothes and jewellery everywhere, covering every inch of my bed, tumbling onto the floor. My eyes skim back to the clock—7:51.

"Shit! Hev, while I'm gone, can you ..." I wave my hand at the clothes and look at her in blind panic. "What if I want to bring him back here later? OMG." I grab a pile of shorts and unceremoniously dump them into the dresser, poking them and prodding them until I can get the drawer closed.

She makes a noise somewhere between a snort and a groan and shakes her head. "Oh no, you do not want to have sex with him tonight!"

"Uh, yeah, I do." I've been fantasising about it for months now.

Heather adamantly shakes her head and picks up three of my dresses that she said were too "out there" for a first date. (I'm not sure what *out there* means—doesn't everyone like *Space Jam*? And a *Space Jam* dress? Hello? Awesome!)

"No. No sex tonight. You want him to come back for more. Just give him a taste, chum the waters, bait the hook, and then—*bam*—reel him in," she says, hanging my clothes.

"Fishing metaphors? Seriously, stop watching that *Wicked Tuna* programme!" I roll my eyes.

She laughs but doesn't have time to answer because the doorbell rings.

My eyes widen when I notice he's early. "Bugger."

My body is suddenly a mess of nerves. My hands flutter to the hem of the dress, absentmindedly smoothing the skirt as I take a couple of deep breaths, trying to calm my racing heart.

What was I thinking? I can't do this! I can barely talk to the guy, let alone be alone on a date with him over dinner. This is sure to end in disaster.

"I want to see." Heather darts from the room.

I suddenly panic and run after her, racing her to the door, scared of what she'll say to him. She gets there first, but I press my hand against the door and shake my head. But she's not going for the handle; she's already squinting one eye at the peephole.

"Holy shit. He looks like Ryan Reynolds and Nick Jonas had a baby!"

"Right?" I chuckle and find my small black handbag, tucking my phone into it. "Christ, I'm nervous," I whisper.

She smiles, placing a hand on my shoulder. "You'll be fine. You look like a knockout. Just breathe, be calm, and don't order the spaghetti."

I frown. "Why can't I order the spaghetti?"

She knows it's my favourite, and Jared already suggested the Italian place not far from me when he messaged earlier.

One of her eyebrows rises, and her lips press into a thin line. I nod in understanding. No one looks sexy while eating spaghetti—well, maybe Shawn Mendes would, but that's just because he's an alien.

"No spaghetti—got it," I agree.

I place my hand on the lock as she steps behind the door, out of sight.

"Oh, and, Amy, don't mention anything about you crushing on him all this time. Just keep that to yourself. Pretend like you barely even remember him from the train. Better yet, don't even mention seeing him on the train unless he brings it up. And definitely don't tell him you fell in love with him while he was doing magic." She rolls her eyes and shakes her head. Heather does not agree with my opinion that dorks are sexy. "Be cool."

Be cool. Don't mention I'm crazy for him. No spaghetti. I got this.

I pull open the door, and when he smiles down at me, all sexy eyes and straight teeth, all thoughts of being cool are long gone.

"Fuck. Well, I just came," I blurt, and then my eyes widen in horror at what I just said.

"That was easy," he deadpans, cocking an eyebrow at me before we both burst out laughing.

Behind the door, I hear Heather groan and slap her palm against her forehead.

FOUR

I thought he looked hot in a suit, but this ... this is something else.

The casual look really works for him. Chunky black combat boots, loose and stylish; light-blue jeans covering long legs, just tight enough to make my thighs clench with a promise of what's underneath; a plain, soft-looking white T-shirt stretched over a broad chest. This is the first time I've seen him without a suit jacket, and his toned, tanned arms draw my attention. I imagine them wrapping around me, the feel of his skin against mine. I long to reach out and touch him. His smile is killer and will keep any girl up at night. And his laugh ... my God, I'm already done for the night, and we haven't even left the doorstep.

He's too hot to be standing in the dingy hallway with its peeling paint, questionable stain on the ceiling, and my worn welcome mat that Heather bought me as a housewarming gift that reads, *Did you bring margaritas?* He's in direct contrast with his surroundings. He's all beautiful and clean, and the communal stairwell that leads to my first-floor flat is ... anything but.

I wince and shake my head at myself. "What I meant to say was, hi."

One side of his mouth quirks up. "Hi."

As he holds out a bunch of pale pink roses, my insides thrum with pleasure.

"Got you these. They reminded me of you." His eyes flick to my hair and back down to my face.

I bite my bottom lip as I take them. "Thank you. They're lovely."

"You look amazing," he says.

When I look up from the flowers, I catch him in mid-examination, his eyes doing a slow sweep of my body, his jaw flexing with tension.

I hide my satisfied grin by burying my face in the flowers, inhaling their sweet perfume. "As do you, obviously. But I'm sure you got that from my earlier comment." I nod awkwardly and shift on my feet, looking anywhere but at him.

He laughs again, that deep, throaty chuckle that makes the hair on my arms stand up. Thankfully, he chooses not to embarrass me further. "Are you ready to go? I'm a little early. I can wait …" He trails off, but I shake my head.

"I'm ready. Let me just put these inside." I step back, the door bumping me as I shoulder it open and deliberately close it a little behind me, so he doesn't follow me in.

Heather rolls her eyes. "That was *not* being cool."

"Tell me about it!" I stage-whisper, handing her the flowers. "Vase in the kitchen. Thanks. Love you. I'll call you later … unless I'm too busy." I suggestively waggle my eyebrows.

She adamantly shakes her head. "No sex. Bait the hook, and keep him coming back."

I sigh in defeat but know she's right. If I have sex with him tonight, I'll likely never see him again. Well, until the next time on the train, and then that'll be uber awkward.

Picking up my handbag, I blow her a kiss. "Wish me luck."

She grins and crosses the fingers on her free hand, winking at me.

Jared is casually leaning against the wall outside my flat, one ankle crossed over the other, his long fingers tangled with each other. My eyes drink him in again—the flat stomach, the way the T-shirt fits across his pecs and falls looser to his waist. The material of it looks so soft that my fingers ache to reach out and touch it, to fist it up and yank his body closer to mine. I gulp, trying to douse my lust but it's hard, oh-so hard.

He straightens as I step out and moves to my side as we both head down the flight of stairs to the front door of my apartment block.

"Do you like Italian? You didn't say no, so I'm assuming you do, but we can go somewhere else if you prefer?" he asks as he leads me over to a sleek, expensive-looking black sports car.

"I love it." I beam with thanks as he opens the door for me, and I slide in.

As he walks around to his side, I settle into the soft leather seat and inhale. The car smells clean with a subtle undertone of his aftershave. I take my chance to look around, to learn some juicy gossip about him. But the car gives nothing away; there are no clues, no sweet wrappers or discarded bottles of drink or newspapers. Actually, there's nothing at all, and that is telling in itself. The inside of his car is spotlessly clean. If it wasn't for the bag of sugar-free strawberry boiled sweets tucked into the cupholder, I would assume this car was brand-new and unused.

He eases into the driver's seat, starting the engine with a sexy purr that sounds expensive. As he drives us to the restaurant, I squirm in my seat, my body hyperaware of how close his hand is to my thigh whenever he changes gear. My pulse is thumping in my ears, and I try to discreetly wipe my clammy palms on my skirt.

"So, how was your day? Did it get any better after some random bloke spilled coffee all over you?" he asks.

I shrug and turn a little in my seat, so I can watch him on the sly. "Nope. That was the highlight of my day actually."

"Pretty shitty day then." He purses his lips and nods solemnly.

"Pretty shitty," I agree, though truth be told, it was one of my better ones.

I'd been dreaming about speaking to him properly for months, and today, I spoke to him, and we are now out on a date. This is easily the highlight of my year.

The drive is only a couple of minutes, and he expertly glides into a parking space a little way away from the restaurant. I smile up at the red awning over the restaurant door as I exit the car. I've never actually eaten in here before but heard it is good. I've been in the cocktail bar upstairs once though; Heather and I were blind drunk, and I vomited into the bin. Hopefully, they won't recognise me.

His eyes meet mine as I wait for him to reach my side of the car. He's so close; his hands fiddle with the keys as we walk towards the restaurant. He reaches out and opens the door for me, motioning for me to go in first, and a little thrill runs through me at the gentlemanly gesture.

As we step in, it's like sensory overload. The smells coming from the place make my mouth water, the lighting is soft, and the music playing quietly in the background is subtle enough that you can talk. It's a very romantic place.

Jared steps to my side.

The greeter smiles over at us as Jared tells him he's booked a table for two.

"Follow me, please."

The greeter heads off into the restaurant, and as we follow, Jared sets a hand on the small of my back. It's such a small gesture, the tiniest touch, but I have to use all of my focus to keep myself walking in a straight line and to not turn and pounce on him. Screw food. All I want is to take him back to my apartment, strip him out of his clothes, and run my fingertips and tongue across every inch of him. My body is alight just from the barest touch. I can't even imagine how I'd cope if he touched me for real. I'd probably spontaneously combust.

When Jared pulls out a swanky leather chair for me, I sink into it and suck in a ragged breath. He slips into the seat opposite mine, our eyes meet and hold as his lips part, and somehow, I can tell he's feeling this too—this sexual tension that's consuming me and causing tummy flutters. And the room fades away. I could be anywhere, and I wouldn't care as long as those whiskey eyes never left mine.

The greeter sets down a menu in front of each of us, breaking the eye contact, and I'm back in the room again.

"Your waitress will be over in a few minutes to take your order. Can I get you some drinks, or would you like to look at the wine list?"

I clear my throat, hoping my voice won't come out as a ball of lust as I order a large glass of rosé. Jared orders a Diet Coke because he's driving.

Get a grip, Amy! Breathe.

I force myself to look down at the menu, trying to focus, but all I can think about is the warm spot on my lower back where his hand was. "Everything looks so good," I say, trying to quash the lustful feelings I'm still having.

Jared nods in agreement, and when the waitress comes over with our drinks, he leans back, not even noticing that her eyes linger on him for a split second too long. We order our food—tomato and basil pasta for me, chicken parmigiana and a green salad for Jared.

When we're finally alone again, I seize the opportunity to ask all the questions I've wanted to ask for the last five months.

"So, how old are you, Jared?" I pick up my glass and take a small sip, knowing I need to take it easy on the booze tonight. When I drink too much, I talk too much, and that really isn't going to help my *trying to keep it cool* image.

"I just recently turned twenty-eight. You?"

Perfect. I guessed he was around my age.

"Twenty-four." I smile. "You already know I work on the trains, but I don't know what you do."

I've always wondered this. He dresses impeccably for work, goes to London every other Monday, and always carries a briefcase. Now, I know he has an expensive, sleek car. I always assumed he's some sort of architect, designer, or something that involves being arty because I've seen him scribbling drawings into a notebook on occasion.

"I work for Jenkins and Banner. They're a PR company, and I'm chief advertising strategist. It's mostly finance, budgets, projections, calculating marketing trends and return on investment—that kind of thing."

Finance. So, he is math nerdy instead of art nerdy.

"Do you like it?"

He nods. "Yeah. I've only been there a year. It's a little different to what I thought it would be. There are a lot of changes I want to make, but it's hard to get anywhere when there's a board of directors shooting your proposals down without even looking at them. Plus, we're currently going through a huge company merger, so there are loads of negotiations and projections I've had to get involved in. Not really my job, but I've been drafted in to oversee things there."

He takes a swig of his drink, and I watch his throat bob. It's sexy. He's talking about board members and mergers, and what can I say? I like that shit. It's my sweet spot. Weird, I know.

"Sounds stressful. What do you like to do to unwind in your spare time?"

He reaches up and runs a hand through his hair. "I'll be honest; lately, I've barely had any spare time. Things are just a little crazy with work. When I do get spare time, I guess I spend it with friends and family or watch movies. I go watch Cambridge United occasionally. I also like to learn different languages."

Intrigued, my eyebrow rises at that. "Really?"

He nods, taking a sip of his drink. "Yeah. TV in the evening can be a bit naff sometimes, and I get bored easily, so I do online courses. Comes in handy with my job too, obviously."

"What languages can you speak?" My skin prickles with excitement as I wait.

"French, Spanish, Italian." He counts them off on his fingers. "This year, I've been learning Mandarin."

My stomach gives a little internal swoon, and my brain is instantly firing, wondering how I can get him to speak some French or Italian to me. I'm not sure I could think of anything sexier than that. He shrugs as if it's nothing, as if teaching himself foreign languages in his spare time is a normal thing. I don't think I've ever been more attracted to him.

"I also love live music, but I guess I don't really have any official hobbies. What about you?"

"I love live music too!" Just as I'm about to expand, the waitress comes over, carrying our food. The delicious scent of my tomato pasta wafts up, and my mouth waters, all other thoughts forgotten. I grin down at my plate like it's the winning lottery numbers.

"Parmesan?" the waitress offers, one of those twirly grater contraptions in her hand.

"One of my cardinal rules is to never say no to cheese," I joke, watching greedily as she grates it over my pasta.

After a few seconds, she raises one eyebrow, silently asking me if that's enough. I waggle my finger in a small circle, indicating she should continue. She continues and then, a few seconds later, clears her throat. Reluctantly, I tell her to stop when I can sense that I've gone beyond the socially acceptable amount even though I actually wanted the whole damn block on my plate.

When she leaves, I look over at Jared to see him watching me, his eyes twinkling with amusement in the dim restaurant lights.

"What? Cheese is life." I shrug casually, spearing a tube of pasta and thrusting it into my mouth. Flavours explode on my tongue, and I have a hard time containing my moan of pleasure.

Jared's gaze is fixated on my mouth, his eyes have gone dark, and his lips part. He clears his throat and shakes his head a little before looking down at his own food.

Continuing the conversation where we left off, Jared asks, "Favourite musician?"

"Of all time or current?" I shovel in more pasta as he starts on his chicken.

"Both."

I grin. Easy. "My all-time is Queen."

He purses his lips and nods, seeming impressed. "Nice choice. Like it."

"And current is James Arthur. His voice does funny things to my body."

One of his eyebrows rises. "Lucky voice."

I shrug, playing along. "Or lucky body." I take a couple of seconds to let that sink in. "Who are yours?"

It had the desired effect; he clears his throat as if coming out of a daze and answers, "Current, probably Post Malone. All-time, The Beatles."

I nod and grin. "It's official; we're compatible."

"Glad to hear it."

He grins too, and I notice those little crinkles around his eyes again. My fingers long to reach across the table to touch them.

The flirty banter continues back and forth as we order a slice of vanilla cheesecake to share. Well, the intention is to share, but when it comes, I dig in like a lioness devouring her prey, and he just has a couple of small bites before setting his spoon down. He doesn't seem bothered though; he just watches me with his eyes all dark and sexy.

Jared is a little quieter than I thought he would be; he's more of a listener than a talker. The picture I built of him over the last few months was a larger-than-life guy who chatted with everyone, a happy-go-lucky guy with smiles to spare. But tonight, he seems a little more reserved. It isn't a bad thing. I actually like the way he seems really into what I'm talking about, how he prompts explanations to some of my answers, delving deeper. Like he is actually interested. It's nice.

At the end of the night, after dessert and coffee, we ask for the bill, and I eat his mint chocolate as well as mine. It turns out, he's not got much of a sweet tooth. Oh well. More for me! He insists on paying. I glow in my seat as the waitress smiles down at him, but he barely notices as he taps his PIN into the machine and takes the offered receipt. He's all polite nods and words to her, no megawatt smile that I've already earned twice tonight.

Ha! Take that!

As we step out of the restaurant, it's pushing eleven o'clock, and the street is practically empty because it's a Tuesday night, not a weekend. Jared leads me to his car, and again, ever the gentleman, he opens the door for me.

Once he's in and started the car, my nerves spike. *Will he kiss me? Am I mere minutes away from our first kiss?* Now that I've thought about it, it's all that my brain can process. I fiddle with the air con, sending a stream of cool air over me to try and calm my jangled nerves. My skin feels hot, flushed, oversensitive.

When he pulls up outside my flat, I can barely breathe, and my legs feel a little weak. He cuts the engine and looks over at me, clicking the lock on his seat belt.

"I'll walk you up." He nods to my building and opens his door.

As he comes to my side, his hand brushes against mine, and I chew on my lip as a wave of desire washes over me. We're quiet as we ascend the stairs, my mind racing a mile a minute, trying to predict what will happen next. I can't help but steal little glances at his face.

He stops outside my door and steps closer to me. "I had a really great time."

He looks down at the floor, and it suddenly hits me that he's nervous. He's been thinking about this moment too. The kiss.

My stomach clenches in anticipation. "I did too."

I'm unable to contain myself anymore. I reach out and touch his T-shirt, rubbing it between my thumb and finger. I was right; it is smooth like butter. I want to pull him closer to me, press up against him, feel the warmth of him. His smell surrounds me, and it's the most intoxicating and bewitching smell ever. I'm already addicted. I want it all over me. I want to smother myself in it.

I blink up at him, fighting my desire to drag him into my flat and maul him to within an inch of his life.

He swallows, and his teeth sink into his bottom lip. He's definitely nervous. I like it.

"Would you like to go out again?" His voice is just above a whisper and comes out scratchy and husky.

I nod in answer, not having any words.

"Tomorrow night? We could catch a movie?" he offers.

"Sounds great."

His answering smile is dazzling as his hand comes up to my face. He catches a lock of my hair and gently tucks it behind my ear. His fingers give the tiniest brush against my hypersensitive skin, and it sends my body into the stratosphere. A heavy ache settles between my legs. I'm so turned on by that minuscule touch that I can barely stand still.

His eyes are latched firmly on my lips as he tilts his head a little and leans down slowly, so slowly that I think the wait might actually kill me. The anticipation builds, and everything else fades away as I go up onto my tiptoes, closing the distance, eager for it.

When his lips finally press against mine, it is everything I thought it would be and more. His lips are soft against mine, barely moving, controlled. His hands mould over my waist, holding me in place when I wobble on my weak knees. The kiss is all delicate lips, the barest of pressure. It's like a kiss from a movie. It's everything you'd want a first kiss to be. Beautiful and perfect for a first date. Memorable.

When he finally pulls away, I'm a jangled mess of desire. I can't even think straight. I want more. I *need* more. I feel like I'm in a daze as I settle back on my heels and look up at him through heavily lidded eyes and a fog of lust.

He swallows and looks like he's struggling for control. "I'll see you tomorrow then." He leans down and pecks my lips, just one more tiny, chaste kiss, and then he turns, heading for the stairs.

My eyes drop to his arse in his jeans, and my desire heightens to impossible levels.

I want him. I want everything.

The deviant part of my brain demands we go inside and get hot and sweaty.

No sex! In the back of my mind, Heather's words are rattling around. *Bait the hook, chum the waters. God, now, I'm doing fishing metaphors!*

But can I really let him leave? That kiss wasn't nearly enough to tide me over and take the edge off my lust.

My mouth says it before I can even stop myself, "Jared, wait."

He stops, turning to face me, one eyebrow raised in question. I move closer to him. He's only managed to descend one step, so as I step closer to him, we're eye to eye, mouth to mouth.

"I just need a little more than that, so I can replay it later when I'm alone." My eyes flick to his mouth, and I bite my lip in need.

He doesn't need asking twice. Almost instantly, his hand comes up to my neck, cupping my jaw, tilting my head a little further to give him access, and his mouth covers mine. I gasp against his lips as his other arm wraps securely around my waist, turning me so my back is against the wall as his hard body presses against me, pinning me there. His lips move against mine, and when his teeth scrape against my bottom lip, it's so sexy that I feel my lust ratchet up another level. I've never been so turned on by a kiss.

I whimper into his mouth and brace my hands against his chest as our tongues slide against each other. He tastes of coffee and the cheesecake we shared earlier. I've lost control of my hands now as they skim over his body, exploring the hard, warm skin hidden under his T-shirt. I can feel the bunched-up power of him, the muscles, the tension in his arms and shoulders as he kisses me like this is our last minute on Earth.

His fingers thread into the back of my hair, and he lets me come up for air. I suck in a ragged breath as his thumb teasingly strokes across my bottom lip before his mouth claims mine again. This kiss is so different from the first. The first was sweet and romantic; this one is more animalistic and out of control. I bloody love it.

He pulls away too soon. I'm breathless, and my skin is alive with sensation, my insides squirming with the need for more. His forehead presses against mine, and he breathes heavy. My mouth quirks with a smile as I realise he's just as turned on as I am. That knowledge gives me confidence. It's empowering.

"I should go," he finally says quietly, but he doesn't move away. Instead, his fingers press into my lower back, forcing us closer.

As our hips connect and I feel just how aroused he is by the kiss too, he makes a sound in the back of his throat that almost makes me lose my mind. His thumb strokes across my jawline as his eyes meet mine; his pupils are huge, dark, wanting.

"I should go," he says again, and it's more forceful this time. Unfortunately, he means it.

"Okay." Reluctantly, I release my grip on his shoulders and lick my lips, tasting him.

He gulps, his Adam's apple bobbing as he steps back and huffs out a big breath, reaching up to run a hand through his hair. A smile tugs at the corner of his mouth as he looks me over. I dread to think what I look like—a wanton, horny devil with smudged lipstick and wild, crazy eyes, I'd bet.

"I'll see you tomorrow at seven."

I nod, pushing myself away from the wall. "Okay. Sleep well. Try not to dream about me."

His eyes twinkle as he grins—the full-on, mesmerising grin—and it's almost too much to bear. "I'll try, but I can't promise anything."

He turns and heads for the stairs again, and this time, I let him go.

FIVE

I smile happily, and the girl in the full-length mirror smiles back at me, her face flushed, her eyes sparkling with excitement. A second date. I've been floating on a cloud ever since that kiss last night. Today at work, all my regular passengers kept asking if I'd won the lottery or something because I was in such a happy mood.

I smooth my hands down over my denim skirt and then straighten my favourite off-the-shoulder cream knit jumper. The straps of my black bra are visible, just teasing at what's underneath. The girl staring back at me looks confident and sassy. My hair is down again, like last night. It was a planned-out move. Last night, when he'd kissed me, Jared had threaded his hands into the back of my hair, and it was exquisite. I want that again tonight. I'm happy with my look. I feel cute.

I sigh happily and apply a last sweep of clear lip gloss across my lips, before looking at the clock—6:55. My excitement kicks up another notch. I can't wait to see him again.

When my phone beeps with a text, I practically skip over to my bedside unit and scoop it up. It's him.

> *I'm so sorry. I'm running late, and I haven't even left work yet. Meeting overran, and I couldn't leave. Sorry! Do you still want to go out? Totally understand if you want to blow me off. Though I hope you don't …*

Blow him off? Hell no!
I text him back.

> *It's no problem. I'll see you when you get here.*

I wait, staring down at my screen, seeing the blinking dots to show he's typing. I grin in anticipation.

> *Excellent. I'm now leaving. Will be there in 15. x*

When he finally arrives, he's in a navy-blue three-piece suit, paired with a maroon tie and matching pocket square. I quickly decide this is the best I have ever seen him look. It's so formal and smart, professional and just … edible. I'm wowed.

"Amy, I'm so sorry I'm late," he says, frowning, his eyes alight with sincerity.

I wave one hand and invite him into my flat. His eyes linger on me as I step to the side, his gaze appreciative, and I see a muscle in his jaw flex. I smile inwardly and feel my face flush with pleasure.

Jared thinks I look cute too.

Score.

"You're a little overdressed for the cinema," I observe, pursing my lips as I look him over again.

There's a subtle black check in the material of his suit that you can only see when you're this close. I silently wonder how many other people have been this close to him today to see it.

He groans and nods. "I know. But I didn't want to make myself any later by going home to change. I hope that's okay. I'll leave my jacket and waistcoat and stuff in the car."

He tugs on the knot of his tie and unfastens the top button of his white shirt with one hand. After, he works on the buttons of his waistcoat, leaving it hanging loose against his body. I watch, transfixed. Somehow, he looks even sexier now that he's a little dishevelled.

I swallow and nod, lost for words. *How is it that I get more attracted to the guy every time I see him? It's not fair.*

When his stomach rumbles loudly, he puts a hand on it and smiles awkwardly. "Sorry. I haven't had time to eat today. I was in back-to-back meetings all day. Last thing I ate was a protein bar on the way to a ten a.m. conference call."

I frown, not liking the idea of him not taking care of himself. "Do you want to go to dinner tonight instead?"

He shakes his head and slips off his tie, carefully folding it up and pushing it into his jacket pocket. "No, it's fine. I'll get popcorn." But his stomach rumbles again, louder this time.

My eyes scan over him. He looks exhausted and a little stressed. He's had a day.

"I have an idea. Why don't we order takeaway and watch a movie here instead? There's probably rubbish on at the cinema anyway."

I reach out and run a hand across the lapel of his jacket, feeling how smooth and silky it is. He likely paid a fortune for it.

His eyebrows shoot up. "Yeah? You don't mind?"

"I don't mind." I shrug.

His smile is so grateful that it makes my heart ache. I bite my lip and step closer to him, our chests almost touching, my eyes holding his as I slip my hands inside his jacket, gently easing it over his shoulders, tilting my mouth up towards his in invitation. His breath catches as he dips his head, his lips pressing against mine. I smile against his mouth. He's been eating the strawberry sweets from his car; I can taste them. The jacket slides down his arms, and he expertly catches it before it hits the floor.

I pull back a fraction and smile up at him. "Hi," I breathe.

He gulps. "If this is the greeting I get every time I'm late, I'm never going to be on time again."

I laugh and step back, bending down to unlace my Converse before toeing them off and kicking them into the disorganised pile of discarded shoes I always have next to my door.

"You can hang your stuff up there." I motion to the coat hooks mounted on the wall. "I'll grab my phone and see what we can get delivered. What do you fancy?" I call over my shoulder, heading into the lounge, wincing at how messy my place looks. I should have planned ahead and had a clean-up.

"Other than you in that skirt?" he playfully calls back.

My face fills with heat, and I grin at his compliment as I make a grab for discarded clothes and magazines, sweet wrappers, and empty drink cans. Scooping them up, I shove them into the sideboard, just managing to straighten up as he walks in. I gulp and pick up my phone, faking nonchalance.

"Pizza?" I offer, opening up the Just Eat app.

"Sounds good. Here, I'll order, so I can pay."

I shake my head. "You paid last night. My turn."

We settle on a meat-filled pizza, and I order while he looks around. His eyes skim my tiny studio flat, taking in my one room that works as a lounge, dining room, and kitchen. I flush and wince under his scrutiny of it; my place isn't exactly high class. As a rule of thumb, Cambridge is an expensive place to live, so every square foot increases the rent ... hence my tiny place filled with second-hand goodies. Jared's gaze settles on my ugly flesh-tone bra that

I wear for work; I abandoned it immediately as soon as I walked in the door tonight and dropped it onto the floor.

God, why am I such a slob?

I kick it under the sofa, and one side of his mouth quirks up into a smile.

While I order, he walks over to my windowsill and looks at the photographs I have there.

He picks up one and looks over his shoulder at me, one eyebrow raised in question. "Is this you?"

I nod. "Yep. And my bestie, Heather."

He ponders the photo. "You look so different with blonde hair."

I shrug and nod in agreement, looking down at the framed photo of me with a shoulder-length honey-blonde bob. "I know. My hair is naturally that colour, but …" I reach up and tousle my pink locks.

"So, blondes don't always have more fun?" he teases.

I shake my head. "Pink me does okay."

He purses his lips and looks from me to the photo, considering. "I like the pink better. It suits you and your personality. Pink Amy drives a kooky bike named Bessy and has no filter between her brain and her mouth; it's adorable." His eyes twinkle with amusement as he sets the frame back down.

Adorable. The word sends a shiver of happiness down my spine.

"So, you live here alone?" he asks.

I nod absentmindedly. "Yep, just me. I used to flatshare with Heather, but she went and got engaged and abandoned me about two years ago. I didn't want to share with a stranger but couldn't afford our two-bed place on my own, so I moved in here."

This place is a one-bedroom and barely big enough for me to swing a cat around in, let alone share with someone else.

I motion to the sofa and pick up the TV remote, turning it on and opening Netflix. "You sit down. I'll go see if I have anything in for us to drink." I hand him the remote. "You can choose something to watch."

"Ah, let's see what I can learn about you from your watch list."

He smiles, and I leave him flicking through while I head to the kitchen, thankful that I went shopping over the weekend and have loads of Dr Pepper and wine in the fridge. When I turn back, he's musing over some movies that I bookmarked.

"I don't have much choice, I'm afraid." I hold up the drink options, and he points to a can of Dr Pepper. I inwardly smile. "Good choice."

I slide the wine back into the fridge and head back, slipping into the seat next to him, conscious of how close we are and how he has little silver cufflinks personalised with his initials in his sleeves.

"So, what did you learn about me?" I joke, watching as he slides through categories.

He raises one eyebrow. "That you like true-crime documentaries and old-school slasher horror flicks as well as the occasional tearjerker. Not a bad choice in movies. I can work with it."

I smile as he gets to my Top Picks for Amy section. "I think Netflix knows me better than, like, ninety-nine percent of people," I joke, seeing all the recommendations.

He purses his lips. "So, what do you want to watch? I honestly don't mind. There are a few things on your watch list I haven't seen."

I shrug. "I don't mind. Just maybe not a series. I don't think we're ready for that kind of commitment."

He chuckles, and we settle on some action film that neither of us has seen. It surprises me that he didn't choose some sci-fi or fantasy-type film. Maybe he thinks I don't like nerdy stuff and is trying to keep me sweet by hiding that side of himself for a while.

The opening sequence has not long finished when the doorbell rings, and Jared pushes himself to his feet. "I'll get it."

"Great. I'll get some plates." I smile and watch his back as he walks to the door and collects the food while I choose a couple of plates from the cupboard, taking my time, trying to find two that match.

He's already eating a slice of pizza as he walks back to the sofa. An appreciative groan leaves his mouth that makes my stomach clench.

"Oh my God, carbs," he says.

And I fall in love with him a little bit more.

We eat, and I pretend to watch the movie, but I can't concentrate. Even though it's got Ben Affleck and Charlie Hunnam combined, it still isn't enough to take my attention from Jared. He's too close. This is like all my secret fantasies coming true. I can't contain my grin.

Halfway through the film, his hand closes over mine, pulling it into his lap, and he proceeds to rub small, gentle circles over my knuckles. I swallow. It's so erotic, but I don't know why. I feel my nipples pucker, and my sex clenches with a longing, burning need. I squirm in my seat, trying to relieve the ache but it's no use.

When he turns and catches my eye, the air in the room seems to shoot up a couple of degrees. My breath catches as his eyes flick to my lips, and I can't contain myself any longer. I lean in as he does, and our lips meet.

The kiss is sweet, just soft and tentative at first, but as his teeth nip at my bottom lip, I melt against him, and his hand tangles into the back of my hair, just like I wanted. My skin prickles with goosebumps as I press against him, our tongues sliding against each other. My arms wind around his neck as he pulls me closer.

The kiss gets hotter and hotter, and I feel the moment he loses his restraint. The kiss turns primal, almost animalistic, as his hands grip my hips and pull me onto his lap, so I'm straddling him. The new position takes my body to a whole other level of excited as I feel the hardness of his erection between my thighs.

I pull back and press my forehead to his. I'm so turned on that it's uncomfortable. His eyes are almost black with desire. His scent attacks me, making my mouth water. All I can think about is him and the need to be closer, to get hot, sweaty, and naked with him.

I gulp. *Are we really about to do this on a second date?* Somewhere in the back of my mind, I know I shouldn't.

He leans in again, his mouth pressing urgently against mine; his tongue massaging mine sets my stomach fluttering with something akin to desperation, and I just about lose my damn mind.

Yes, we're most certainly doing this.

SIX

I gasp as Jared gently tugs on my hair, tipping my head back so he can kiss my throat. A needy whimper slips from my mouth. I'm so overexcited that I'm like a rocket, waiting to go off. I've dreamed of this moment for months, and now that it's happening, it's better than anything I could have envisioned.

When I feel his fingers toying with the bottom of my jumper, I pull back and raise my arms as he pulls it over my head, tossing it to the floor. His hands tickle down my back as his head dips forward, kissing around my collarbone as he palms my thighs.

"God, you're perfect," he breathes, his eyes sweeping over me.

I secretly congratulate myself for choosing my sexiest, skimpiest underwear.

I kiss him again as my fingers work deftly, unbuttoning his shirt, tugging it from the waistband of his trousers. My greedy hands find hot skin and skim over tight muscles. When the kiss breaks, I look down, and my eyes widen.

"Holy shit. I didn't think people looked like this outside of movies and *Love Island*," I blurt.

Jared laughs and shakes his head. "I hate that show."

"What? You hate *Love Island*?" I fake gasp my outrage as he nods, his amused eyes meeting mine. "Maybe we're not compatible after all," I joke.

He chuckles. His fingers digging into my skin make my mouth dry with desire.

I gulp, my eyes drinking him in. His body is amazing—toned, tanned, perfect. He's not too muscly, more lean, like a swimmer's body. He has a six-pack, but it's sexily subtle. There's a small smattering of hair below his navel and that delicious V that I honestly have never seen in real life.

He. Is. Beautiful.

"You work out a lot, I'm guessing." My voice is a husky, lusty mess.

I trace my nose up the side of his, breathing him in.

The corner of his mouth quirks up into a smile that almost seems shy. "I run a bit, yeah."

I reach out and touch the little freckle under his left eye before leaning in and planting a soft kiss on it. "My idea of cardio is running out of fucks to give."

He laughs, and I kiss him, fisting my hand in the back of his hair, pressing my chest against his, skin on skin. It's delightful.

His hands stroke up my thighs, over my hips, and up the side of my ribs, his thumbs skimming the material at the bottom of my bra. It makes me shiver with pleasure and arch against him.

He groans into my mouth, and his arms tighten on me, turning and manoeuvring us so we're lying on the sofa. The weight of his body on mine is so delicious that it almost makes me giddy with desire. My nails dig into his shoulders as he kisses me again, his hand cupping my jaw as his tongue brushes expertly against mine, drawing out my excitement.

When he reaches out and tugs down the cup of my bra, bringing his face down and closing his mouth over my nipple, my whole body tightens in pleasure, and I moan his name.

My skirt is already bunched up around my hips, so when he grinds against me, I gasp and wrap one of my legs around him, pulling him closer. The friction is killing me. I need more. Much, much more.

The kiss deepens, and his hands explore my body as mine do his. My skin is alive with sensation, my core aching. His fingers brush over my underwear, and a bolt of pleasure pulses over me. My body spasms, and my hips press up, pushing harder against his hand. He raises one eyebrow, and I'm too far gone to feel ashamed of my loud moan that I accidentally let escape. I'm too overexcited; this is too much. I'm on the edge already, and we've barely even started.

As he pushes my underwear to the side and his fingers touch me for the first time, I pant and tug on his belt, fumbling but eventually getting it unbuckled, and then I push my hand down the front of his trousers. He groans against my neck as my hand closes around his length, stroking; my arousal is spiked higher at the feel of him in my hand. Steel under silk.

My body is on high alert, screaming for release as he pushes two fingers inside me, his thumb still rubbing my clit. I gasp, biting my lip as the pleasure builds to impossible heights. I'm on a cliff's edge, dangerously close to tipping over already.

"Oh shit, Jared. I'm gonna come any second," I moan.

His hand doesn't stop, but he pulls his head back, his eyes meeting mine. "I wanted to be inside you when I made you come for the first time."

His voice is almost a plea, and my hand tightens on his length, squeezing.

"Then, you either need to stop doing that," I pant, reaching between our bodies and pressing my hand over his, stilling him, "or get inside me real quick."

There's a moment of indecision on his face, but then his hand is withdrawn, and I let out a strangled whimper as he pushes himself up to his knees. He rummages in his pocket, pulling out his wallet and finding a foil packet.

While I catch my breath, I push up onto my elbows, watching the visible panel of muscles on his stomach move and contract. It's mesmerising, and my hand unconsciously reaches out, pushing his shirt off his shoulders a little more, tracing the lines on his stomach, my fingers dipping into his navel as I let out a content sigh. As I appreciate his body, his eyes linger on mine. I don't even feel self-conscious that I'm exposed to him like this; the look on his face is enough to give me confidence.

As he pushes his trousers and boxers down over his hips, releasing his erection, my breath catches, and desire pools between my legs.

Wow.

I watch, transfixed, while he rolls the condom down over his length, his fist gently stroking himself, the cufflinks on his sleeves glinting in the flickering light of the movie that plays unseen in the background. Jared's eyes are dark and hooded and firmly latched on me.

I smile eagerly and sink my teeth into my bottom lip as he leans over me again, one of his hands gripping my thigh, guiding my leg over his hip. I hold my breath, waiting for the delicious feel of him entering me, but instead, he just kisses me again, his mouth worshipping mine, whipping me into a frenzy before I feel him pull his hips back and line himself up at my entrance.

His eyes meet mine in silent question, but I don't answer; I can't. Words are long gone; all that's left is a carnal mass of desire and need. So, instead, I dig my nails into his back and raise my hips off the sofa, taking him inside me just a little. It's clearly enough to make him lose his mind, too, and his mouth crashes back against mine as he thrusts in one long movement. I moan against his lips as he fills me, burying himself to the hilt. It's intense and incredible and more than I ever dared to hope it would be.

"Oh shit," he groans, looking at me through heavily lidded eyes.

He kisses me once, twice, and then it begins. The most beautiful, erotic, and incredible sex I've ever had. It's sexy and sensual. Our clothes rustling with each movement are evidence that our desire couldn't wait another second. Our breaths tangle as the pleasure builds with each powerful stroke of his hips, and his lips, tongue, and teeth lavish attention on me.

The passion I feel for him is overwhelming. Flurries of sensations hit me over and over until my mind is a whirling mess of euphoria and rapture. When he reaches a hand between our bodies and circles it on the sensitive bundle of nerves, my orgasm hits me full force, an intense wave of pleasure and ecstasy. My body shatters, fracturing off into a million pieces. My hips buck up against his, and my teeth clamp down onto his shoulder as I moan his name. My internal muscles ripple around his cock, and that seems to send him over the edge, too, because he thrusts just a couple more times before he lets out a low groan and presses his face into the side of my neck. His whole body goes rigid before he sinks down on top of me.

We lie there like that for a couple of minutes, wrapped in each other as we catch our breaths. I can't temper my exhilaration. I'm still floating on a cloud of bliss.

Finally, he pulls back a little and smiles down at me. "That was my first legit *Netflix and chill* experience," he jokes, his fingers gently stroking the hair at my temple.

I laugh. "Mine too."

His sweaty body is slick against mine, and my hand unconsciously curls around his belt, holding him against me as he goes to pull away.

"No, don't get off yet," I whine, greedy for more of his touch. I don't want this connection to end yet—or ever. I want to live on this sofa with him, Netflix-and-chilling our life away.

He leans down and kisses me one more time before pushing himself up to his knees, my death grip on him having little to no effect. My body instantly misses the luxurious weight of him on top of me, and I frown and let out a sound like an angry cat.

"I have to go flush this," he explains, chuckling as he reaches down and tugs off the condom in one easy motion.

As he stands, he shoots me a smug smile that tells me he knows exactly how much I enjoyed myself. I sit up, now a little self-conscious of how exposed I am and push my skirt down my jelly-like thighs. When I reach for my discarded jumper, he bends and picks it up, passing it to me with a wink that sets my tummy fluttering all over again.

"Thanks. The bathroom is that one." I point to the door and right myself on the sofa, tugging my jumper over my head.

After a couple of minutes, he flushes the chain and comes out of the bathroom. He's fastened a couple of his shirt buttons, but it still hangs open enough to tease me with his tanned, toned skin and the V that leads down into his trousers, like an arrow pointing down to the good stuff. His eyes meet mine, and his head cocks to the side as he leans against the wall, watching me.

"So, I've got a breakfast meeting at six thirty tomorrow. I should probably get to bed," he says, reaching up and brushing a hand through his already-messy hair.

My mouth falls open, and my stomach drops as I realise what he means. He's leaving. He used me for sex. And now, he's leaving, and I'll likely never see him again.

The disappointment and sadness feel like a punch to the boob.

I school my features and force a smile when I see his eyes narrow and his eyebrows pull together in a little frown.

I stand and dismissively wave my hand, as if my heart isn't breaking inside. "Right. Yeah, of course." I can feel my eyes prickle with devastated tears, so I look away from him and grab the TV remote, turning off the end of the movie. "I'll just put these in the kitchen, and then I'll show you out." I pick up the used plates and empty pizza box and walk to the kitchen as quickly as I can, my eyes firmly on the carpet.

I hear him step up behind me as I push the empty box onto the counter and put the plates in the sink. I take a deep breath, trying to contain my emotions. I can't show him I'm hurting over this. I've been through this before—used and then discarded—but never by someone I cared about like this.

Embarrassed heat burns my cheeks and neck. *Why did I do that? Dammit, why didn't I listen to Heather's fishing metaphors?*

"Look, I never do that. I'm not a sex-on-the-second-date kind of girl." I scowl down at the counter, turning angry now, not at him—he's a guy, and that's what guys do—but at myself.

"I get that vibe from you, yeah."

I gulp and nod, but words don't come, so I push away from the counter and am about to walk past him when his arm stretches out, blocking the exit, forcing me to stop.

"Amy, I think you're misunderstanding what I said. When I said I should go to bed, I was hoping you'd ask me to stay the night. I didn't mean I wanted to leave."

My mouth pops open in shock, and I finally look up at his face to see his gorgeous brown eyes latched on to mine. He steps closer to me, his arm still trapping me against the counter.

"You … you want to stay the night?" My words trip over each other on the way out.

He steps even closer, his scent filling my nose as his eyes smoulder sexily down at me, one corner of his mouth twitching with a smile. "Yes, I want to stay the night. Because that, what just happened"—he nods over his shoulder towards the sofa—"wasn't even nearly all the things I want to do to you tonight." His voice is so husky and seductive that it sends a shiver down my spine. His body presses against mine as he reaches up and twirls a lock of my hair around one finger. "I want you naked. I want to feel you come on my tongue while your thighs shake around my head. I want to watch you lose control."

"Holy hell, Jared," I whisper. "Dirty talk? I like it." I'm panting now, my nipples pebbling against the lace of my bra.

He leans forward, his nose brushing down the side of mine before he plants a little kiss on the edge of my jaw. "Can I stay?" he whispers.

"Please. God, yes. Stay."

He chuckles, his hot breath tickling down my neck. My stomach clenches as my hands fist his shirt, pulling him closer to me. His mouth finds mine, and my insides explode with delight as I grin against his lips.

I step back, taking his hand and guiding him through my flat, turning off lights on the way. He checks the front door is locked as we pass it, and I smile at the thoughtfulness of him.

When we get to my bedroom, he stops in the doorway, watching as I head to the bed and fumble for the switch on the lamp, flicking it on to bathe us in a gentle yellow hue.

I hear a soft chuckle and look over to see he's grinning behind me.

"Not exactly the sexiest bedding I've ever seen, but we'll make it work."

I groan with realisation. "I didn't think you'd be staying over."

He saunters over to me, his fingers already working on his shirt buttons and cufflinks as we both look over at the *Game of Thrones Not Today* duvet set on my bed.

When our eyes meet again, his darken, his lids drooping sultrily. "Take off your jumper and skirt. I'll do the rest."

My eyes widen at the command.

Hot. Demanding. Masterful. Fuck.

I immediately comply, eagerly tugging off my clothes. I stand in my underwear as his eyes skim over me in such a way that it makes my mouth water.

"Amy, you look so perfectly fuckable." His voice is almost a growl, and I feel the thrill of his words from the top of my head to the tips of my toes.

Perfectly fuckable. That was probably the weirdest yet sexiest compliment I've ever had in my life.

From his trouser pocket, he takes out his phone and wallet, setting them on my bedside cabinet next to his cufflinks, before undressing himself. His eyes don't leave mine for more than a second as he removes his clothes, carefully folding them and setting them in a neat pile on my chair.

I greedily drink him in, my gaze ravaging every inch of exposed skin to the point of indecency, my insides squirming with desire. When he pulls off his boxer shorts—I notice he even folds those too—the sound that comes out of me is a cross between a grunt and a whimper. He is beautiful.

One side of his mouth kicks up into a knowing smile as he advances on me. I step back, my knees hitting the bed, because I'm not sure I'm ready for this. The heat I can see in his eyes promises something earth-shattering, and I need a couple of seconds to prepare myself for it.

My breathing hitches as he stops in front of me, hooking his finger under my chin, tilting my head up until my eyes meet his. The heat of his naked body against mine is so erotic that I feel a little shiver tickle down my spine.

With his eyes on mine, he reaches around me, expertly unclasping my bra, sliding it off my shoulders and down my arms so slowly that it causes my skin to break out in goosebumps. I gulp as air hits my nipples. This is too much.

His gaze glides down my body as his bottom lip rolls up into his mouth, his eyebrows pinching together, and a sexy little groan of appreciation rumbles from his throat. I gasp, and my eyes widen as his hands roam my body, brushing against my hypersensitive skin, catching the elastic of my underwear and sensuously sliding them down over my hips.

As they drop to the floor, he kisses me. I melt against him, my arms looping around his neck as he guides me back onto the bed and settles himself on top of me. I feel his thickening arousal pressing against my thigh, and my core gives a needy clench.

He moves, kissing down my neck and across my collarbone before his mouth closes over my nipple, his teeth scraping lightly.

"You're going to kill me," I whisper, squeezing my eyes closed.

He chuckles, his hot breath teasing my stomach as his tongue draws a line around my belly button before heading lower.

I try to prepare myself for it—I really do—but when his mouth gets to its desired destination, I let out a hissed curse, and my hips buck up. My hands fist into his hair as his arms wrap around my thighs, holding me in place as I start to wriggle, wanting to be away, wanting to be closer, just wanting.

Waves of pleasure roll over me as he expertly works his tongue, playing my body to perfection. I'm in heaven, and I writhe under him as it builds and builds. My back arches in ecstasy when he adds his fingers, pushing them inside me, adding to the tortuous, beautiful pleasure he's creating. When he curls his fingers, rubbing my inner walls,

MAN CRUSH MONDAY

I'm at the point where I'm about to lose my damn mind. My breath comes out in short, sharp pants. My moans grow obscene, but still, he doesn't let up. He pins me there, lavishing attention on my body until I come so hard that I feel my whole body tense and my thighs shake around his head—exactly as he wanted.

When he pulls back, he grins as he sucks on his fingers and then wipes his mouth. I can't speak. I'm done. I'm lost. He has officially killed me. My brain is mush.

When people don't see me for a couple of days, they'll be all, *Hey, where's that pink-haired chick who doesn't stop talking?* and then they'll come to my flat, investigate, and find me dead, sprawled on the bed, a look of sheer and utter satisfaction on my face. What a way to go.

He pulls himself back up the bed, hovering over me as his mouth claims mine in a kiss that's so hot that I feel the effects of it ripple through my spent body. The tangy taste of myself on his tongue as it strokes mine makes it even more erotic, and I moan into his mouth, clutching his body to mine, loving the heavy weight of him pinning me to the bed.

When he eases away and smirks down at me, obviously proud of himself, I feel my face flush. His eyes sparkle with both amusement and desire as he leans to the side and reaches for his wallet. I shake my head and raise one eyebrow. After what he just did to me, he deserves to lose his cool a bit too. I want to wipe that smug look from his face.

I wrap my arms around him and guide him onto his back, rolling on top of him and sitting up on his stomach, my hands on his chest. I can feel the hardness of him under me, and I can't resist a quick grind on top of it. His smile grows as he slips one arm under his head, the picture of ease as he watches me, his other hand gently kneading my still-quivering thigh.

I look down at him as my fingers follow the lines of muscle on his stomach and the V line at his hips, and my nails rake through the spattering of hair beneath his navel. He is so sexy; it should be illegal. When I replace my hands with my mouth, peppering little kisses across his chest and stomach as I shimmy down his body, I feel his cool demeanour begin to slip. His muscles bunch as I head lower.

When I get to his impressive length, I wrap my hand around it and revel in the grunt he lets out as I stroke him. I lick my lips, looking it over, my mouth watering. When I flick my eyes up to his face, I see he's watching me, his lips parted, his eyes tense, waiting to see what I'll do. I smile seductively before leaning over, teasing the tip with my tongue. The muscles in his lower abdomen tense, and I grin in triumph.

Ah, not so relaxed now, Jared Stone!

When I take him into my mouth and suck gently, he hisses through his teeth and groans my name. The way he breathes my name is like another wave of pleasure for me too. I love it. So, I take that as encouragement and go to town, sucking on his hard length, stroking and squeezing my hand around the base at the same time. I lose myself in the act, trying different things, different pressures, my hands exploring, my tongue lavishing attention on him.

He's propped himself up on his elbows, watching me, a look of sheer pleasure on his face. When he reaches down and scoops up my hair into a makeshift ponytail, holding it in his fist so he can get a better view, I push down as far as I can, gagging as he hits the back of my throat and closing my eyes, which just makes him groan louder.

"Oh shit. You should stop. I'm not going to last five minutes with your mouth on me like that," he growls, reaching for my hand.

But I don't stop. I want to see him lose control too, as he made me. So, I push his hand away and suck harder, hollowing out my cheeks, pushing down deeper each time. His head drops back onto his shoulders, and his breathing quickens as I take him to the edge of the cliff. I feel so powerful at that moment, so desired. It's incredibly hot.

After a few minutes, one of his hands goes to the back of my neck, his fingers tangling in my hair, and he looks down at me through heavily lidded eyes. "Amy ... I'm gonna ..."

He tries to ease me away, but I don't allow him to. Instead, I push down and close my eyes, gagging and repeating until he finally comes. I force myself to swallow and finally pull back, gasping for breath, my heart racing in my chest, my whole face tingling and flushed.

I push myself up to sitting and wipe my watery eyes as I look over at him.

He's flopped back against the pillows, watching me in a state of shocked euphoria.

"Fucking hell. Best blow job I've ever had. Christ." He's breathing heavy, and his voice comes out as a ragged rasp that makes the hair on the back of my neck prickle.

He's looking at me in awe, and I grin proudly.

"Honestly, I'm not kidding. I think my soul left my body there for a few seconds."

I burst out laughing and crawl up his body, settling myself against him. His arm slips around me, his thumb drawing lazy patterns on my back as he cuddles me. He smells amazing, raw, sexual, and I press my face into his neck, snuggling into him as he pulls the sheets up around us.

I'm so relaxed and satiated that my brain is already turning off.

"So, what are you like then? What kind of sleeper are you?" he asks, turning his head and planting a soft kiss on my forehead.

"Stage five clinger," I joke.

He laughs, a deep rumble that I feel against my body. He stretches one arm over the side of the bed, and I think he's about to turn off the light, but instead, he picks up his phone.

I watch as he goes into his Clock app and sets an alarm for five thirty.

"So early," I grumble. "Who schedules meetings for six thirty?"

"My days are long sometimes. It's chaos at the moment with this merger. I promise I'll try not to wake you when I get up."

He turns his head and kisses me. I sigh contentedly when I pull away and nuzzle into his neck, my eyes fluttering closed.

Seconds later, I hear the click of a camera. I groan and try to cover my face, but he's already got what he wanted. He shows me the screen, and I simper when I look at the photo he took. It's him, grinning up at the camera and me snuggled into his neck. You can't really make out my face, but you can see a small, satisfied smile on my mouth. It's tasteful, and it doesn't show anything inappropriate other than my naked back and his naked chest. It's so intimate that I feel my face flush.

"New screen saver. That'll get me through some long workdays."

He pushes his phone onto the bedside table and switches off the light before turning towards me, pulling my body closer to his as he tangles our legs. It's so comfortable that I already know I'll hate sleeping alone from now on. His naked skin on mine is all I can think about as I descend into sleep, wrapped securely in his arms.

SEVEN

I wake before the alarm even has a chance to go off. Somehow, I know I'm alone. I roll onto my back, stretching so hard that my legs shake. A satiated grin slips onto my face. My muscles ache in a delightful way they haven't in a long, long time. I can smell him on the bedclothes and on me. I smile wider.

Best. Night's. Sleep. Ever.

Rolling, I check the time to see it's still ten minutes before my alarm is due. A piece of folded paper next to my lamp catches my eye. It has my name written on the front.

I reach for it and sit up, clutching the sheets against my naked chest. Jared's handwriting is a small, neat print.

> *Amy,*
>
> *I didn't want to wake you.*
>
> *Call me when you get up.*
>
> *Jared x*

I grin and flop back against the pillow, letting out a little squeal of delight as my teeth sink into my bottom lip. Last night was everything I'd dreamed it would be and more.

I clutch the note to my chest as events from last night play out in my head—his taste, his touch, his smell. Excitement bubbles in my tummy at the thought of speaking to him. Swinging my legs out of the bed, I grab my dressing gown from the chair and pull it on, knowing I need to start my morning routine before I call. As usual, I have just over an hour to get ready before I have to leave for work, and after last night, my hair is sure to be a wild sex knot at the back of my head, so I need to allow extra time for that.

After a quick stop in the bathroom to pee, I head to the kitchen and pick up the kettle, filling it and turning it on.

I can't wait any longer. I need to speak to him.

I dial his number and lean against the counter, chewing on my lip, hoping he'll suggest another date because if he blows me off after last night, I'm going to be devastated.

He answers on the second ring. There's a heated discussion going on in the background as he says, "Good morning, Amy. Would you hold one moment, please?"

His voice is professional and curt, and I don't know why, but it turns me on even more. I feel a shiver tickle down my spine as I remember that voice purring dirty things to me last night.

"Sure."

"Gentlemen, would you excuse me, please? I have to step out and take this," Jared says off the phone.

I wince when I realise he's still in his morning meeting he mentioned. *Awkward.*

There are muffled voices and murmurs of agreement and then sounds of a door closing.

Then, he's back on the line. "Hi. Sorry about that."

"You're still in your meeting? Sorry. I should have texted instead of calling. I got your note, so …"

"No problem. I was waiting for your call anyway. Did I wake you when I did my walk of shame this morning?"

I chuckle. "No, I sleep like the dead."

"That's good. I tried to be as quiet as I could. Though, I must admit, I was kind of hoping you would wake up. Do you have any idea how hard that was for me, leaving you naked and unravaged in the bed like that?"

I close my eyes at his seductive tone and grin. "How hard?" I flirt.

"Rock hard." He blows out a big breath that crackles on the line. "I had a great time last night." His voice drops an octave, and I can tell he's thinking back to our naughty exploits.

I swallow and feel the blush heat my cheeks. "Me too," I admit, reaching up to grab a mug as the kettle starts to boil.

As I pluck out a mug, I notice the plates in my kitchen cupboard have been reorganised, stacked neatly according to size—smallest to largest. I frown and then notice that my kitchen looks different from how I left it last night. The plates and glasses we used for dinner are gone from the sink. My gaze flicks back to the cupboard, and there they are—washed, dried, and put away in an orderly little stack. Even the empty pizza box is missing from the side.

"Jared, did you tidy my kitchen?" I glance around, seeing he even wiped the sides and folded my tea towel, hanging it from one of the drawer handles.

He clears his throat. "Uh, yeah. I just washed up the stuff we used last night. I didn't want you to have to wake up to it."

I blanch, my scalp prickling from the sweetness of that gesture. My hand tightens on the handle of the kettle as I pour hot water over my tea bag. "That's super cute," I gush, grinning.

He just laughs, and I can imagine the twinkle of his eye and shrug of his shoulders.

"How's your meeting going?" I ask.

He groans. "Not good. I think we'll be here a while."

"Ah, hopefully not a day like yesterday where you don't have time to eat," I reply, straining the tea bag on the side of my mug and stepping on the pedal of the bin.

As the lid lifts and I'm half a second from dropping my tea bag, I notice there's no bag inside the bin. My heart clenches. He even emptied my bin and took it and the used pizza box out for me.

Sweet!

"So, can I see you tonight?" he asks just as I'm about to gush some more about how adorable he is.

My heart is instantly screaming, *YES*, but my brain—the more rational part of me—lets me down with a bump.

"I can't," I sigh. "Heather is coming over tonight for some girl time. Thursdays are always BFF days."

"Every Thursday?"

I nod. "Yep, Tequila Thursday. It's a tradition Heather and I have. It started when we first moved out together. We were totally skint, and our local pub used to do a happy hour on a Thursday—two shots of tequila for the price of one. We've been doing Tequila Thursday for years, though it's evolved a bit now."

"Evolved?"

"Yeah. Did you know the main ingredient of a margarita is tequila?"

He chuckles. "Right, got ya."

"Sorry. Rules are, you can't cancel a Tequila Thursday unless you're out of the country or dead. Since I'm neither, I'm afraid I'm busy tonight."

He laughs, and I head to my bedroom, carrying my cup of tea. I set it on my dressing table before heading to the bathroom and turning on the shower to warm up.

"I'm free Friday night though," I add. Even I can hear the hopeful tone to my voice.

Jared groans. "I can't on Friday. We have these extremely important clients over this week from Japan. I've been roped into taking them out on Friday for dinner and drinks on the company," he explains. "What about

Saturday? We could meet for lunch and spend the afternoon together, go bowling or something? Maybe you'll invite me to stay over again; you never know," he flirts.

I blush from my neck to my hairline as my skin tingles with excitement. "Whoa, you're jumping the gun a bit there, Jared Stone. I'd need to see your bowling skills before I can decide if you're worthy of third-date sex," I joke. And it is definitely a joke. He is *so* being invited to stay the night!

"Amy, I don't think I was worthy of second-date sex, so I'm just taking each day as it comes," he replies.

"Literally," I joke.

He laughs, and the sound makes my tummy flutter. "Yeah, literally," he confirms.

"Saturday then," I agree.

"Great. I should really go back in my meeting and see if I need to break up any fights," he sighs.

"Okay. Well, I hope your day improves."

"My day started on a high. Can't get better than waking up in bed with a gorgeous girl, so it was always only ever going to go downhill from there."

I grin. "Well played."

"Thanks. See you Saturday then."

"Bye." When he hangs up, I grin at my phone and bounce on the balls of my feet.

Saturday seems so far away. I am addicted.

That night, I'm more than ready for girls' night. I already showered the day's crappiness from my skin and changed into my loungewear and have taken off my bra. Now, all I need is my bestie to show her face, so I can start on the huge blender of frozen margaritas I just finished making.

My mouth waters as I set the jug and our two glasses—salted edges and all—down on the coffee table, ready. I pick up the bowl of crisps and start munching, frowning when my doorbell rings. Heather usually just lets herself in.

I push myself up from the sofa and head over, yanking it open, expecting my best friend. But it's not Heather standing on the other side; it's a guy barely out of his teens, chewing gum with his mouth open and wearing a black vest with *Hugh's Hampers* stitched on it.

"Delivery," he announces, barely looking at me as he thrusts a brown box towards me.

I frown and take the box. It's slightly heavy, and I hear something shift noisily inside. "I haven't ordered anything," I mutter. "Are you sure it's for me?" My eyes search out the address label as he looks at the little plastic gadget in his hand.

"Amy Clarke?" he asks, looking at the number 5A on my door.

I nod.

"It's for you." He shrugs and holds out the contraption for me to sign for it.

I use my finger to scribble something that doesn't resemble my signature in the slightest.

The guy barely waits for me to withdraw my hand before he turns and starts for the stairs. I frown down at the package as I head back inside, pushing the door closed with my bum. The label emblazoned on the top of the package also says *Hugh's Hampers*.

I frown. I've never heard of it, so it's definitely a mistake.

Curiously, I head back into the kitchenette, grabbing a knife and carefully sliding it along the tape.

As I lift the lid, I see a card on the top—white with black printed type.

MAN CRUSH MONDAY

Dear Miss Cheese Is Life,

I thought you'd enjoy this more than chocolate or some other lame romantic gesture. A little something for you and the BFF to enjoy during Tequila Thursday.

Jared x

My mouth pops open in shock. He bought me a present? And his note mentions Tequila Thursday. I only told him about it this morning, so he had to have ordered this hamper today. Same-day delivery probably cost him a fortune.

I reach out and remove the layer of tissue paper, eager to see what it is. In the box are several types of cheeses, two packs of crackers, some tiny jars of chutney and preserves, all nestled in paper shredding. I take each item out, inspecting it with a massive grin on my face. Underneath all the produce are a wooden cheeseboard and a cheese knife.

"Holy shit."

A moronic grin slips onto my face as I carry it all over to the coffee table and lay it out. I set the typed note next to it, so I can show Heather. This is the most thoughtful thing any guy has ever bought for me. I would have been ecstatic with chocolates or "some other lame romantic gesture," but this is perfection. *He* is perfection.

As I'm gushing over the present and reading the card for the third time, Heather lets herself in my flat. "I've arrived! Make mine a large one. I need to pee," she calls to me as she drops her coat and bag and heads straight for the bathroom.

I grin and pour two drinks.

"Wow, you've gone all out," Heather says a couple of minutes later as she motions to the cheeseboard and plops down onto the sofa next to me. "How come?"

I laugh and nod. It is decidedly more extravagant than my usual spread of stale peanuts and whatever they had in the reduced section of my local supermarket on the way home from work. She leans forward and picks up the knife, slicing off a chunk of Stilton and adding it to a cracker, hungrily stuffing it in her mouth.

"Jared sent me it."

She raises one eyebrow, chewing quickly. "Seriously?"

"Seriously." I pass her the card, watching as she reads it. "I said, 'Cheese is life,' on our first date when we went for dinner," I explain, nibbling on my bottom lip as a warm feeling spreads across my tummy.

"Wow." Her eyebrows rise into her hairline. "That's seriously thoughtful. Not only did he actually listen to you, but he also then sent you a corresponding gift? I have no choice but to stan." She sighs deeply. "I wish Tim still did stuff like that. His idea of a thoughtful gesture nowadays is brushing his teeth before he comes to bed if he's been eating cheese and onion crisps."

I laugh at her exasperated expression. "Poor Tim. Don't hate on my boy!"

I always defend Tim. He and Heather met not long after we moved to Cambridge together. He was studying nursing and now helps sick kids for a living. What could be better than that? They've been together for years now. He is one of my best friends and a genuinely lovely bloke. I adore him like a brother.

She rolls her eyes and shoves in another huge bite of cheese before reaching into her bag, pulling out two pots of face mask. "I snagged these from work."

Heather is a beauty therapist. It works out fantastic for me. I get free beauty treatments on tap and get to sample new products that they send to her salon.

"Gold leaf or tee tree?" she asks.

I point to the gold one and grin.

We spend the next ten minutes chatting about our days and catching up while we smooth face mask on each other, eat cheese, and start on our second glasses of margarita.

"This is so good," I moan, cutting off more Brie, greedily licking my fingers.

"So, how was the date last night? Pretty good I'm assuming if he same-day delivered you a damn cheese hamper." She wiggles her eyebrows as much as her green muddy face mask will allow.

"Amazing," I reply honestly. "He was tired and hungry when he arrived, so I suggested staying here and watching a movie with a pizza instead of going to the cinema."

"Oh, really?" She turns in her seat, tucking her feet under her butt. Her eyes twinkle with excitement. "So, tell all. Did you let him past first base?"

I grin and run my fingernail around the edge of my glass, collecting the salt from the rim and sucking it from my finger. "He hit a home run."

Heather chokes on her drink as she takes a sip. "What!"

I nod proudly. "And he did a victory lap."

"What the hell? I've been here for almost half an hour, and I'm only learning this now? Details. I need details, woman!"

So, I tell her every single detail because I've learned from previous experience that Heather will not stop probing until she has every juicy fact.

By the time I've finished running through my sexcapades, she's staring at me with wide eyes. "Damn, I don't even smoke, and I feel like I need a cigarette after that," she says. We both burst out laughing, and she picks up her glass. "To your crush not being a total letdown in bed."

I chink my glass against hers and nod. "To Jared being a total stud."

She looks back at the cheeseboard and smiles knowingly. "Now, I know why he sent you a cheeseboard.

BJ on the first night? Bet he thinks his ship has come home."

Heather leans over and picks up the blender, tipping the dregs into my glass. Both of us look at the empty jug. My eyes widen.

"Not it!" we both shout at the same time, but I'm a split second faster.

I shoot her a smug smile and settle back onto the sofa as she groans in defeat and pushes herself up, heading to my kitchenette to make us a second batch.

EIGHT

An annoying, angry tune drags me from my slumber so quickly that it makes me gasp. I groan and grope around on my bedside cabinet, slapping blindly for my phone. My eyes blink at the alarm clock—2:39 a.m.—but my foggy, sleep-filled brain can't make sense of it. I get the phone to my ear and croak a hello even though I'm pretty sure I still have no idea what planet I'm on.

"Amy, I'm so sorry I woke you."

"Who is this?" I rasp, my voice full of sleep.

"It's Jared."

"Jared?" For about three seconds, the name means absolutely nothing to me, and then thoughts of him flood my brain all at once. "Is everything okay?"

He clears his throat. "Yeah. It's just ... in the interest of full disclosure, I wanted to tell you that I'm at a strip club."

I reach up and rub my stinging eyes. "What?"

"Look, I've seen too many movies where the guy does shady shit and doesn't tell the girl. Then, she finds out, and it all goes pear-shaped. So, I just wanted to tell you now, so it doesn't come back and bite me in the arse. I'm at a strip club right now, but I don't want to be." He blows out a big breath. "Amy, I like you. I like where we're at right now, and I don't want this coming out sometime in the future and ruining anything."

I chuckle at his exasperated tone. In his garbled rant, the only thing that was important enough for my tired, disorientated brain to latch on to was the fact that he'd just said he liked me. Jared Stone likes me.

"Why are you there if you don't want to be?" I snuggle down in the bed, pulling the covers up to my chin.

He sighs. "The Japanese clients I told you about. We went out for dinner and then drinks, but now, they're drunk off their faces, causing all sorts of trouble and commotion. They wanted a 'titty bar' … their exact words, not mine … so here we are. But I don't want this to ruin anything between you and me, so I figured I'd just full disclosure the shit out of it and hope it doesn't ruin my chances with you."

"I'll let you off," I muse. Sleep is already calling me as I close my eyes.

Jared lets out what I assume is a sigh of relief and chuckles. "I've called in reinforcements. Someone from the office is here now to take over for me because these guys are nowhere near done drinking, and I'm dead on my feet. I've been at work since eight, and babysitting drunken, grown-arse men isn't my idea of a good night out. I was thinking, instead of me going home, could I come to yours?"

Come to mine? "I'm sleeping," I mumble.

"I know, and I'm sorry. I just really want to see you. It's been a crappy day, and I wanted to end it with a high."

"Jared, I'm really tired. I'll be honest, I'll likely be back to sleep as soon as you hang up the phone, so there's no point in you coming here. I'm too tired to get frisky with you." Though the thought of getting naked and hot with him is waking up certain parts of me.

"I don't care. I just want to sleep there with you. No frisky business. Please?" When I don't answer, he continues, "I'll make you breakfast in bed."

I smile at that, my interest piqued. "Well, what sort of breakfast are we talking? Like toast and cereal or something good?"

"Something good," he answers.

"You cook?"

"Yes, I cook," he confirms.

I smile, more than a little impressed.

"Please? I don't want to do anything. I'd just much rather wake up in bed with you than on my own. Please?"

"I already took my make-up off," I warn.

He chuckles. "So did I."

I smile and force my tired body up to sitting, rubbing at my eyes as I swing my legs out of bed and stumble in the dark towards my bedroom door. "Fine. Come then. But I'm going back to sleep, so I'm gonna put a key under the mat, and you can let yourself in without waking me again." When I reach the front door, I pluck my spare key from the hook and open the door, wincing as the light from the communal hallway burns my eyes. After checking the coast is clear, I lift the mat and put the key under it before letting it drop back down again. "Just so you know for the future and in the interest of full disclosure from my end, I like my sleep. I'm not one of those girls you can wake up anytime, who are all cheerful and cute; that'll never be me. I'm more of a *wake me at your peril* kind of girl. I will fight you."

"Duly noted." He sounds amused. "See you soon."

After hanging up, I close the door and smile to myself as I pad back to my bedroom, slipping back in my warm bed, falling back to sleep almost as soon as my head hits the pillow.

When I wake again, luxurious heat is seeping into my back. I'm on my side, and a pair of strong arms is wrapped around me while someone breathes heavily down my neck. I grin, snuggling closer as I dip my head and press my face into the crook of his arm. He smells divine. I let out a little happy sigh. On his wrist, there's a chunky, expensive-looking watch, and I crane my neck to check the time. It's only just past eight in the morning, so I know he won't want to wake yet.

I lie there for a few seconds, listening to his steady breathing, fighting the urge to roll over so I'm facing him. I want to see his face, I want to watch him sleep, I want to snuggle in his arms forever. I ponder my options. Do I roll over, so I can see him, like I desperately want to do, or do I do what my brain is screaming at me to do and get up to go see what my face looks like? My brain wins. I love waking up with him, but it is a little too early in our relationship for me to feel comfortable with him seeing me *au naturel*.

Wincing, I ease myself out of his arms and scoot over to the edge, quietly pushing myself up. When he doesn't wake, I turn and look down at him sleeping peacefully in my bed. His chest is bare, and his face is relaxed and angelic. My heart squeezes as my teeth sink into my bottom lip. I'm so in love with this man that it's not even funny. Today will only be our third official date, but I was in love with him way before that coffee shop incident.

My eyes follow the planes of his chest, drifting lower, and I have the insane urge to reach out and lift the quilt to see if he's completely naked. My mouth waters at the thought alone, and my breathing hitches. I shake my head and force myself to move because I'm dangerously close to pouncing on him and ravaging his body. I turn and head towards the bathroom. As I pass the chair in the corner of the room, I notice he folded up his clothes again into a precise little pile. It's so cute; I can't help but beam a smile. Everything about Jared is neat and organised; even the way he comes to bed is structured and methodical. It's the total opposite of my *leave it where it lands*, more chaotic mentality as I undress.

I head to the bathroom, peeing quickly and then leaning over the sink to wash my face and wipe away my eye boogers before swilling some mouthwash. Grabbing my make-up bag, I apply a thin layer of foundation and a quick sweep of mascara. It's subtle, so hopefully, he won't notice.

After running a brush through my hair and redoing my braid, I head back to the bedroom and slip back in bed with him, happier now that I'm a little more presentable. In his sleep, he rolls to his side, his arms instantly encasing me, pulling me against his hard chest. My nose presses against his collarbone, and I inhale, my eyes drifting closed at the scent of him. He smells edible. I wriggle closer, my body brushing against his, and I'm almost disappointed when I feel the material of his boxer shorts graze against my tummy, so I now know he's not naked.

We lie like that for a long time; I'm deliriously happy.

When he finally begins to stir, I close my eyes and pretend I'm sleeping and that I always wake up, looking this fresh-faced and perfect. Little lies never hurt anyone. He yawns, pulling back a little before he leans in and plants a soft kiss on my forehead. I blink a couple of times for effect and tilt my head to look at him. He smiles down at me.

"See, much better than waking on my own," he says, dipping his head and pressing his lips to mine. "Good morning." His voice is all croaky and filled with sleep, and it has never sounded sexier.

"Hi."

I smile against his mouth as his hand traces down my back, across my hip, and down my thigh. When it gets to my knee, he wraps his long fingers around it and pulls, hitching my leg over his hip. I gasp as his morning glory intimately rubs against me, and he takes the opportunity to deepen the kiss, his tongue lavishing attention on mine. He rolls, so he's on top of me, and my arms loop around his neck.

He pulls back and smiles, hovering above me. "I'll go make you breakfast in bed, as I promised."

My needy eyes widen, and I groan in frustration, digging my fingers into his back as I tilt my hips up to meet his, eliciting a throaty growl of pleasure from him. "After," I beg, pulling his mouth to mine.

He shakes his head and pulls back again. "Amy, once we start, I'm not going to want to stop, so let me feed you first." He laughs as he leans in and softly kisses my forehead before pushing himself off me.

A little thrill passes through my body, and I decide I can wait. Maybe I'll need the energy, if the promise in his voice is anything to go by. "Fine. Do you need any help?"

He shakes his head. "Nope."

I watch his tight arse as he struts confidently from my bedroom in just a pair of boxer shorts, looking all kinds of glorious.

I flop back in the bed and let out a happy sigh, listening to sounds of him clunking around in the kitchen for a while before he comes back in, carrying a tray with two plates and two cups of coffee.

He sets the tray on my lap, and my eyes widen.

"I had the ingredients to make all this?" I ask doubtfully. The smell from the cinnamon and syrup wafts up towards me, and my mouth waters as I look longingly at the stack of French toast piled on the plate.

"I might have stopped on the way here to get a few things." He shrugs, taking both coffees and putting them on my bedside cabinet before reaching out to take one of the plates.

I swallow my squeal of delight and lean over, pressing my mouth to his. He kisses me back, and even though I have French toast and syrup in front of me, food is the last thing on my mind.

He playfully winks at me as he pulls back and picks up his knife and fork, cutting off a huge piece of his breakfast and shovelling it in his mouth.

I follow suit, starting on mine. As the sweetness hits my tongue, I groan and close my eyes in pleasure. It's heaven. "I can't believe you can cook too," I mumble, hacking at my breakfast and greedily chomping on it.

"I'm a man of many talents," he replies, shrugging.

I nod in agreement and get to work on devouring my breakfast. I'm not exactly a good cook, so things like this are only ever eaten in restaurants. "It was a great idea, you coming over here last night."

He smiles and watches as I take the last few bites of my food before reaching over to take the tray from my lap, setting it on the floor with his plate. I suck my teeth with my tongue, my eyes raking over the muscles in his back as he leans over.

When he turns back to me, I crawl over to him.

"Jared, you look like a Greek god, screw like a porn star, and cook like Gordon Ramsay. So, here's the million-pound question. … how come you're still single?" I raise one eyebrow, waiting for his answer.

He laughs loudly, and I throw my leg over his, sitting on his lap, straddling him. His hands immediately grip my hips as his eyes meet mine. I rest my hands on his shoulders, waiting for the answer. It was a genuine question. Why on earth has this guy not been snapped up already? How has he made it to twenty-eight without someone "accidentally" getting pregnant, so he would be forced to marry them?

When he realises I'm waiting for an answer, he sighs and shrugs one shoulder. "I don't know. I don't really have the time to date. For the last few years, I've just been focussing on my career. Plus, I guess I've just never met the right person. My last girlfriend, if you can even call her that"—his eyebrows pull together in a frown—"we were together about six months. Let's just say, I'm pretty sure she liked spending the money I earned more than she liked spending time with me," he explains.

I scowl at that. She was clearly an idiot.

"What about you? How come a girl like you is still single?" His nose brushes up the side of mine as his arms wrap around me, and he lies back, pulling me down with him. My stomach tightens in anticipation of the promised naked time. "You've never met the right person either?"

"Oh, I met the right person," I reply as Jared rolls, so he's on top. "He was marriage material. We talked about a future with a little house on the river. Kids. We promised to love each other forever."

He stops the exquisite kisses he was peppering against my throat. "Who is he? I'm gonna fuck him up."

I burst out laughing at the growl in his voice. He pulls back, and his eyes become suddenly curious as they meet mine.

"What happened?" He looks concerned now. A frown lines his forehead as if he's waiting for some sad, grim ending.

I sigh dramatically. "His dad landed a job in America. His whole family just upped and left one day. He didn't even write to me. I was six when I experienced my first heartbreak." I dramatically shake my head.

A smile twitches at the corner of his mouth, and I swear his shoulders loosen at my joke. "That's rough. Poor little six-year-old Amy."

I grip my hand around the back of his head and arch into him. "Enough talking now."

He makes a little groan in the back of his throat as his mouth claims mine in a kiss that's hot enough to scorch the sheets.

NINE

I climb out of Jared's car and look up at his building. I know it's expensive because of the design. The building is curved, glass-fronted, and sleek. It screams high-end.

"This is where you live?" I ask, looking around with wide eyes.

His hand closes over mine, and he nods. "Yeah, I've been here about a year. I used to live alone here, but six months ago, my brother asked to stay for a few nights and never left." He playfully rolls his eyes.

I let him lead me into the building, and we stop outside the lift, Jared nodding a greeting to the concierge as we pass him. This building is in glaring contrast to mine; you could fit my whole flat in the communal entrance alone. As we step into the lift, he turns and kisses me. Even though we not long ago got dressed and we'd had sex twice already this morning (including a particularly hot shower scene that I am sure to mentally revisit every time I step in there now), I feel my body melt against his. I can't get enough of him.

The door pings open, and he breaks the kiss, looking down at me with a smile on his face as he brushes my hair behind my ear. "Come on then. I'll be as quick as I can, and then we can go out and do something fun."

I nod and follow him to his front door.

As we step into his apartment (because in no way can this be called a flat), I gasp at the sheer luxury of it. I've never seen anything more stylish in real life. It's slick, elegant, shiny, and sophisticated. This place is Jared all over. Although I knew it would be classy and well designed, I didn't expect the lounge to be quite so modern. It's open plan, like mine, but instead of mismatched, cheap clutter, his is filled with comfy-looking sofas and polished hardwood floor. His kitchen is sleek white gloss and marble tops, but the best thing about his apartment by a clear mile is the wall of curved glass and wraparound palladium-style balcony outside that looks out onto the communal gardens.

"Damn. Nice," I grunt, my eyes fixed on the view outside.

Jared laughs quietly. "Yeah, it's pretty nice," he replies, curiously looking around. "Doesn't look like my brother's home. He usually dumps his keys and wallet here." He motions towards the empty sideboard in the small hallway. "Theo, you home?" he calls. When there's no reply, he turns to me and shrugs.

I gulp, unblinking. "If you have this place, why are we staying at my poky little flat tonight? We could get drunk on your balcony, under the stars." I point to it, my mouth open in awe. I would kill for a balcony.

We already agreed that Jared would stay over at mine again tonight, so we could go out together.

He snorts and shakes his head. "You wouldn't want to hang out here tonight. My brother will be here; we'd get no privacy at all."

"Oh. I definitely like the privacy," I agree.

He laughs and leans down, planting a soft kiss on my lips. "Make yourself at home. I'll just quickly change and pack some fresh clothes for the morning, and then we can leave." He shrugs out of the suit jacket that he wore to work Friday and then his clients' night out last night.

MAN CRUSH MONDAY

I nod, and as Jared disappears through a door, I take my chance to nose around. I head to the bookshelf first, seeing lots of the titles I've seen him read on the train. I run my finger down the spines before my eyes flick over the ornaments and knickknacks set on the sides. I grin when I get to his nerd shelf. There're all kinds of statues there—collectable, expensive ones by the look of them—ranging in size. Most of them are Marvel, and I look wide-eyed over them. They're amazing. There's everything from Ghost Rider through to Iron Man doing the snap. I want them all.

I force myself to keep looking. I want to take as much opportunity to learn about Jared as I can. On the wall in the lounge, there are two large movie posters in frames hanging from the wall. They're instantly recognisable, and I grin at the nerdiness of them. One is *Back to the Future*, and the other is an original *Star Wars* poster. As I step closer, I notice that they're signed by Michael J. Fox and Mark Hamill and Harrison Ford respectively.

My mouth drops open. "Wow." I'm totally geeking out.

Swallowing the awe, I turn and cast my eyes around. His apartment is a typical boy fashion—all designed for practicality. There are no fluffy cushions on the sofa, no photos of his friends or family, no unnecessary trinkets that they just "had to have" on a visit to IKEA or Dunelm. There are no personal touches at all other than the few collectable statues and the posters.

Frowning, I head to the coffee table. A sketchpad lies open with a handful of pencils on top of it. I look back behind me and cock my head—he's still in his bedroom—so I pick it up and peruse through. The sketches are fabulous, all different types of things varying from comic book characters, animals, trees, right through to a rough sketch of Tower Bridge and The London Eye. I flick through in awe of his talent. I've seen him scribbling in this notebook before but never really had the opportunity to look through it. I revel in it.

When I hear him coming, I set the sketchbook down and head to the window, looking out over the view. He likely wouldn't want me to have looked through that, as drawings are sometimes personal. I feel the smallest pang of guilt for looking, but in my defence, he shouldn't have left it out for me to see if he didn't want me to.

He comes back in, carrying a black sports bag. His body is covered in worn jeans and a white T-shirt. He throws a stylish brown jacket over the top. "Come on then, gorgeous. Let's blow this joint," he says, holding out his free hand.

"Your place is amazing," I gush, threading my fingers through his.

I secretly hope I get invited to stay here one day. I'm intrigued by what his bedroom might look like. My mouth waters as I imagine the scent of his bed, and I get a pang of longing to sink down and get tangled with him in his sheets.

He smiles and heads for the door, tugging me alongside him. "It's a nice day. Instead of bowling, how about we do something outside?"

"What do you have in mind?" I ask, happy just to do anything where I spend time with him.

He smiles down at me. "I have an idea."

I sigh at how romantic this is. I've lived in Cambridge for the last five years and sampled many of its attractions ... but I've never been on a punt before. When Jared hops down into the small wooden boat and turns to hold his hand out for me, I grin from ear to ear.

"This was a *great* idea," I congratulate, slipping my hand into his as I cautiously step down into the boat.

I laugh as I stumble, and Jared has to catch my waist to hold me steady.

We settle on the padded green seats, his arm around my shoulders, my hand on his knee, as the driver guy steps onto the back and pushes us off from the side, using what looks like a huge wooden pole.

The slow, lazy float on the river is breathtaking, and I've never really appreciated how pretty my city is until now, seeing it from the boat. Jared sits at my side, and we chat about the buildings, the trees, the stunning views. When some swans and ducks glide over and poke their heads over the side of the boat, Jared is ready with the purchased seed and hands it to me. It's then that I decide this is the best date I have ever been on.

After the chilled boat ride, we agree on a picnic and find a secluded spot by the river in the shade of a willow tree. He was right; it is a nice day. Although it's nearly the end of September now and we're in the very last dregs of summer, it's still warm. The sun is bright, and there's not a cloud in the sky. Perfect picnic weather.

"So, what else are you planning on doing with your two weeks off work other than visiting your family?" he asks, forking in a mouthful of his chicken salad.

I shrug noncommittally. "I don't know. Sleeping in mostly. Maybe a bit of decorating. Binge-watching Netflix. Nothing specific. I just haven't taken any time off all year and had to book some, or I'd end up leaving it too late and losing my holiday entitlement."

He nods, chewing on his food, his eyes thoughtful. "Sounds nice. I can't remember the last time I lay in and didn't have any plans."

"You should pull a couple of sickies and come binge some Netflix with me," I joke.

One side of his mouth quirks up into a smile. "Maybe I should."

I swallow my squeal of delight. I would love that. The eye contact holds for longer than necessary, and I feel my insides thrum with happiness. The air around us is thick with the sexual tension, and he looks away just as I'm about to unceremoniously toss my sandwich and jump him on the bank of the river with all the ducks and swans watching.

"My job has been hectic lately. I'm definitely owed some lieu time after last night," he says, rolling his eyes.

"Have the Japanese clients gone home now or …" I ask. When he nods in answer, I tilt my head to the side, intrigued. "What is it you actually do that you had clients come over from Japan to meet with you?"

He blows out a big breath and scrunches up his nose. "It's pretty boring."

I shrug, moving until I'm sitting cross-legged and facing him so I can give him my undivided attention. "I don't care. I want to know."

A smile tugs at the corner of his lips. "Okay, so say you're a company and you have a million pounds you want to sink into advertising to grow your business."

I raise an eyebrow at the figure, but he doesn't bat an eyelid, as if he's used to working with sums that large on a daily basis.

"So, you'd come to me as the advertising strategist and tell me about your business and what you hope to achieve through advertising. I then take that information and go away, researching your business and businesses similar to yours. I'll check market trends, see what's working and what's not. I'll see where investment ads of your product type are making the most impact for the lowest price—that's called return on investment. I then combine all that information and create a recommended portfolio of where I think your money will be best spent and who to target based on their likelihood to buy the product. After you agree on the portfolio, I then liaise with our marketing and art departments to create the graphics and materials, slogans, copy—everything we need. Then, my team and I implement the ads and serve them, checking progress in real time, tweaking and amending to make sure they're fulfilling the proposed potential. It's tough but rewarding. I love it."

Throughout his whole speech, I watch him, more than a little impressed and proud of him. His job sounds incredible and hard!

I playfully purse my lips. "So, you're responsible for those ads I see on Facebook and Instagram?"

He lets out a laugh that makes my insides flutter. "Guilty as charged. But I don't just do ads on socials though; sometimes, it's TV adverts or radio, event sponsorships, supermarket end caps, billboards, bus stops or the underground. Depends on the product and target audience. And budget, of course."

"Impressive. And the Japanese clients?"

"They're trying to break into the UK market with some of their technological gadgets." He skirts around, giving no details.

"And you're not allowed to talk about it," I guess.

He chuckles. "And I'm not allowed to talk about it," he confirms. "What about you? Are you living your dream job on the trains, or is there something else you'd rather be doing?"

"It's hardly a dream job, but it gets me out of the house and pays for my Dr Pepper addiction," I joke. "When I was younger, I actually wanted to be a continuity editor. I even got a media studies A level in preparation."

He raises one eyebrow. "And a continuity editor is …"

I pick a blade of grass with my free hand and roll it into a little ball between my fingers. "You know when you're watching a movie and the camera changes angles, you suddenly notice someone's drink that was half-full is now full again?"

He's watching me, interest clear on his face as he nods in understanding.

"That's what a continuity editor's job is. Basically, I thought I would just get to watch movies all day and point out the mistakes. Imagine my disappointment when it turned out that there was more to it than that. Dream crushed. There wasn't anything else I was ever interested in, so I just started applying for full-time jobs. I bounced around from job to job for a while, but I quite like this one. I get to chat with people all day, so there's that. It's a bit boring and repetitive though."

He laughs and reaches for my hand. "Oh, well, at least you have a couple of weeks off you can enjoy before you have to go back. So, tell me about your mum and dad. What are they like?"

"Just my mum. My dad isn't around. Mum lives with my nanna." I chuckle and drop my eyes to my sandwich, picking at the lettuce inside and throwing it on the grass behind me. *How do I describe my mum to someone who has never met her?* "Mum's ... a character."

One of his eyebrows rises, and his head cocks to the side. "Uh-oh, what does that mean?"

I laugh and press my lips together. "She's into some out-there stuff."

"Like?" he prompts.

I wince a smile. My mum is like Marmite; you either love her weirdness or hate it. I happen to adore her very soul. "Like astrology, tarot cards, palm reading—all that kind of stuff. That's what she does for a job actually—a fortune-teller."

"Like one of those gypsies with the crystal ball?"

I almost choke on air and playfully elbow him. "Don't ever let her hear you call her that. And no, no crystal ball. She's very good. People come from all over to get a reading from her. I've seen her predict loads that have come true."

He seems a little lost for words as he looks at me curiously, and I get the impression he's checking to see if I'm making it up.

"Seriously?"

I laugh and nod. "Yes, seriously."

"Does she talk to ghosts and stuff?"

Jared looks slightly disbelieving, but I don't mind. I've had my whole life with people giving me that look when I talk about my mum.

"No, she's not a spiritual medium. More like reading the signs and general feelings. She senses things about people. My nan used to do it too, but she said she was sick of seeing into the future and wanted to retire to live in the now."

He laughs at that. "So, it runs in families?"

I shrug. "Supposedly, but I don't have the gift. I got all the dorky weirdness without the talent."

I smile awkwardly down at my sandwich and wonder if I've just scared him off. A lot of people find this kind of stuff weird and hard to accept. I've lost boyfriends before who thought I came from a crazy farm. But to me, this is my normal.

His lips press together in a thin line as he thinks about something. Finally, he says, "And what would your fortune-telling mum think about me, do you think?" He scoots closer to me, his arm casually slipping around my shoulders as he tips his head back and closes his eyes, basking in the sun.

I grin because he's clearly not fazed. "Well, what star sign are you?"

My mum would check out compatibility and make her judgment from that.

"I don't know."

"When's your birthday? Did you say it was recent?"

"Yeah—24th September."

My eyes widen as everything drops into place and makes sense. "You're a Libra."

"Is that good?"

I shrug and nod, aiming for nonchalance, but I'm secretly thrilled with this little sliver of information. I'm an

Aquarius, and while the two star signs are not a total match, it is known that Aquarians can fall in love with Librans immediately. That was literally me with Jared on the train. I fell for him before I even knew him. The two work well together and balance each other out. My mum will love to hear this and analyse every bit of it.

"Your star sign means you're a balanced person, a thinker, someone who doesn't rush into anything, decisions especially. You like facts and figures; you're a problem solver and someone to come to when something needs to be done."

He opens one eye and looks at me, seeming a little shocked at my analogy. "That's …"

I smile smugly. "Accurate, am I right?"

He nods, reaching up to rake a hand through his hair. "Yeah, pretty accurate. But you know, even though you just nailed me, I don't believe in any of that stuff. I'm a grounded person. I believe in only what I can see in front of me—science, facts, numbers. Astrology and psychics and stuff"—he shrugs almost apologetically—"I just don't believe in it."

"But you believe in magic; that's not science or facts," I counter, thinking back to him doing tricks on the train for the little girl.

He shakes his head. "Nope." When I frown in confusion, he continues, "I believe in tricks and sleight of hand. With enough practice, anyone could learn to do 'magic.'" He uses his fingers to put air quotes around the word *magic* for emphasis.

"Oh." I must admit, I'm kind of disappointed by his answer. I was hoping for a real-life *rabbit from a hat* kind of magician believer.

"Sorry." He winces. "But we can agree to disagree, right?" His eyes meet mine, and one of his eyebrows rises in question as he reaches out and brushes a strand of my hair away from my cheek.

My heart stutters, and my skin flushes where he touched me. "Yeah, we can."

He doesn't answer, just leans in and presses his lips to mine, rendering words unnecessary.

TEN

By the time I arrive at my mum's house, after a one-hour train journey and enduring a taxicab that smelled like stale Saturday-night-out puke, it's after three in the afternoon. After paying the driver and watching him speed off up the quiet street, I look over at the three-bedroom semi-detached bungalow I grew up in. The smile slips onto my face as I let out a happy sigh. Home. I love it here; it's my safe place.

I don't bother knocking on the front door. I know they won't answer. Instead, I head down the little alley that leads to the back garden. I can already hear Mum's dog sniffing and snorting at the gate as I approach.

As I let myself in, Puzzle, the overweight pug, skitters around my feet, yapping happily as he announces my arrival to the world. I grin and bend down, picking him up and giving him a stroke and a scratch behind the ear. His big black eyes meet mine, and his tongue flicks enthusiastically, trying to lick my face.

"Hey, Puz. You a good boy?"

"Amy, don't let him lick you! He's been eating his own shit again," Nanna calls.

I groan and feel my stomach roll as I pull him away from me and set him back down on his feet, disgusted. "What? Why? Why would you do that, Puzzle? Why?" I groan, gently pushing him away from me when he tries to jump back up at me again.

I look up just in time to see Nanna laughing into her teacup. She's sitting at their little, round garden table with a big, floppy straw hat on her head and a pretty, flowery dress hanging off her scrawny frame. Her azure-blue eyes, the exact shade of mine, lock on to me, and a big smile stretches across her wrinkle-lined mouth.

I drop my overnight bag and march over, planting a noisy kiss on her cheek as she wraps her arms around me and gives me a big squeeze.

"Oh, Amy baby, I've missed you, sweetheart."

I hug her back, feeling guilt bubble inside me. I've missed them too. It's been a few weeks since I've made the trip back home for a visit. "You too, Nanna." I pull back, and my eyes flick around the garden. I'm shocked not to see my mother bent over a flower bed with a trowel. "Where's Mum?"

"I'm up here!"

I squint in the direction the voice came from, seeing the bottom of a ladder propped up against a tree. A huge branch drops to the ground with a crunch of leaves, and I jump, shocked as I run for the ladder, holding it steady as my mum descends awkwardly, holding a savage-looking saw in her hand, wobbling precariously.

"Mum, that's not safe!" I scold, frowning and carefully taking the saw from her as she climbs down the last couple of rungs.

Sometimes, I think my mother forgets that she's sixty-four years old. She was late to motherhood, almost forty when she got pregnant with me, and I swear she still thinks she's a teenager sometimes.

"Oh, stop. Trees don't prune themselves you know. Someone has to do it." She rolls her eyes and wipes the sweat from her brow as I drop the saw into her tool bag that she left at the base of the tree.

I grin over at her.

My mother is beautiful, inside and out. I got my eyes from my nan, but I got my thick, wavy blonde hair and my bust from my mother. Today, her hair is pulled back into a stylish bun; she's wearing cream capri pants with a white shirt tucked into it, open at the throat, with a navy ascot scarf tied at her neck. Elegant ladies-who-lunch attire—while gardening. That's my mother all over.

"Now, let me look at you."

Her eyes make a long, slow sweep of my body, and I purse my lips to fight my smile, tilting my head to the side, wanting to see if she will guess correctly. I wasn't lying when I told Jared that she was good at reading people.

"There's something different," she says, tapping her finger on her lips, thinking. Suddenly, her eyes widen. "You've been on a date!"

I laugh and wrap my arms around her, crushing her against me. "I have," I confirm happily.

"What? What date? Don't stand over there, yapping where I can't hear. Come and give me the gossip too!" Nanna calls, dramatically waving her hands to the empty chairs at the table.

Mum wraps her arm around my waist, and we make our way over to the table where Nanna is happily pouring more tea from the teapot into her posh bone china cup. She's abandoned her book now, and I look over at the front cover and wrinkle my nose. My nanna's choice of reading material is decidedly racier than mine. Don't get me wrong; I love Fifty Shades as much as the next girl, but Nanna's choices are decidedly more ... *risqué* than mine. Now that she's in her eighties, her hunger for erotica novels hasn't diminished. It's awkward, especially when she reads them so unashamedly in public.

"So, who is he?" Mum asks excitedly, pulling off her dirty gardening gloves and setting them on top of the book when she catches me staring at it.

MAN CRUSH MONDAY

"More importantly," Nanna chimes in, "does he give your vagina a heartbeat when he walks into the room? Because if not, then he's not the one."

"Nanna!" I burst out laughing, my face burning. I don't tell her that yes, yes, he does.

"What? A good physical connection will see you through a lot of bad points and make up for them lacking in other areas, like when he farts at the dinner table. Sometimes, you have to put up with things if you're getting physically satisfied," she explains, dismissively waving her hand. "Your granddad—"

But thankfully, my mum cuts her off, "I don't want to hear about your bedroom antics with my father, thank you very much."

"Wasn't limited to just the bedroom," Nanna mumbles under her breath.

I fake gag, and we all laugh. Puzzle comes wandering over, so I bend and pick him up, settling him on my lap—facing away from me, of course. I decide then that I definitely do not want to smell his breath for the next couple of days that I'm here for.

"Wait there. Let me go make a fresh pot and get some cake, and you can tell us all about the new man," Mum says, sending me a wink, standing quickly, and taking the teapot with her as she marches inside.

Nanna and I talk about the dog eating his own faeces and how he now has a farting problem that my mother refuses to admit. When my mum comes back with a tray laden with tea and an assortment of shop-bought Mr Kipling cakes (none of us are particularly skilled in the kitchen!), she looks at me expectantly.

I can't contain my grin. "Okay, so remember the guy I told you about? My crush from my train?"

They both nod in unison, Nanna looking at me with wide eyes. "The guy you're hopelessly smitten with?"

I shrug one shoulder. "Yes, him. Well, on Tuesday morning, I bumped into him—*literally*—at a coffee shop.

We got to talking, and he asked me out!" I squeak with delight and hunch my shoulders before letting out a dreamy sigh. "His name is Jared Stone. He's twenty-eight. I've seen him several times this week already. He's smart and funny, and he sent me a cheeseboard."

"A cheeseboard?" Nanna queries.

I nod.

She purses her lips and narrows her eyes. "You should marry him."

I chuckle and pick up a Battenberg slice. "If I get the chance, I will."

"And how's it going, love? Is he everything you thought he would be?" Mum questions, leaning forward, watching my reactions.

I nod, swallowing a bite of cake. "It's going great," I admit. "Jared's absolutely adorable. He's smart and a real, proper gentleman, so he pulls my chair out and stuff, which makes me swoon. He's a good listener, and he has these wicked one-liners that make me crack up. He's gorgeous, and he smells divine. Also... he's killer in bed." I sip my hot tea, grinning from ear to ear. I know my face is flushed from thinking about Jared, but I hope they won't notice in the slowly darkening afternoon light.

"He sounds lovely. When do we get to meet him?" Nanna asks.

I wince at the thought and take a large swig of my tea. "Never."

Mum nods sadly. "It's true. You should keep him away from your nanna; she'd frighten him away for sure. Let him fall in love with you too. Shouldn't take too long," Mum replies, smiling smugly. "How could he resist you? Look at you! You're marvellous!"

"Ah, but you have to think that; I'm your kid. Mothers have to think their kids are the best thing since sliced bread; it's the law."

Nanna snorts. "Not true. I don't think that about my kid."

But then she winks at my mum, and we all crack up laughing.

We hang out, chatting and laughing. It feels easy and wonderful, catching up with these ladies who mean the world to me, and it's just like I never moved out five years ago. We talk about the garden, mum's job, and the elderly neighbour who threatened to call the police on Nanna when she wouldn't stop sunbathing in her garden—topless.

As day turns to night, we're still in the garden. Mum pulls out fluffy blankets and turns on the outside light and gas patio heater, and we switch from tea to wine. Nights like this remind me of home. It's all I've ever known, hanging in the garden with these two ladies.

"Let me grab my cards, and I'll give you a reading, Amy. We've not done one for ages," Mum says, standing and walking off before I can even protest.

She's back in record time, a pack of well-worn tarot cards in her hand. Nanna reaches out and moves the glasses out of the way as my mum shuffles the cards.

I roll my eyes. My mum can't resist. I tend to steer away from a reading as much as I can. I mean, it's like seeing spoilers for a book.

"Just a small one, three cards at most. Just give me the highlights. I don't want a proper reading."

A frown lines Mum's forehead, but she doesn't protest as she hands me the pack and asks me to cut them. Nanna leans in, watching eagerly. She loves this stuff too. As much as she says she had enough of it and wanted to retire, she can't just turn it off, as she hoped.

Mum dishes out the three cards, arranging them on the table in her usual pattern. I look down at them, hoping that they'll make sense but they never do. I tried to learn once, but I just don't have the talent for it. They're just pictures, and I might as well be playing cards for all I know.

Mum purses her lips. "Okay, interesting. I can see you're content at the moment, both in your work life and personal. But this one"—she points one finger to a card—"it's change. There's something coming, some sort of decision you're going to have to make. You're at a crossroads, two distinct paths, and you have to navigate between them."

I sit back in my chair. "At work or in my personal life?"

She looks over the cards again. "Personal life, definitely." She points to another card. "I see you struggling with the decision. But your well of luck is full at the moment, so just know that neither path is the wrong answer; you just have to work out which way you want to go."

I scrunch my nose and shrug my shoulders. "Well, that was helpful."

Mum laughs and shrugs too. "I just tell it as I see it, love. Maybe I should do a full reading? Get more clarity on it?" she offers, picking up the cards and adding them to the deck again, shuffling them.

I hold up a hand to stop her. "No, thanks. I like surprises. I'll deal with my crossroads choice when I get to it." I roll my eyes and pick up my wineglass. "To surprises and paths yet undecided."

They both pick up their glasses and chink them against mine, and I gasp as Puzzle lets out a huge fart and then runs away from himself.

Nanna tsks her tongue. "Well, that ruined the moment."

ELEVEN

I spend four amazing days with two of the most important ladies in my life before I make the trip back home again. I'm sad to be back. I had a nice break, but it is always hard to leave my mum and nan. My flat—after staying in a crazy, busy, loud household for four days—feels small, empty, and a little depressing. It's times like this that I miss Heather being my flatmate.

However, I couldn't have stayed there any longer. Tequila Thursday is a must, and a girl cannot break tradition, so I had to come home yesterday morning to spend time with the other most important lady in my life that night.

I've missed Jared to the point of ridiculousness while I was away. We've been texting back and forth—and I love it—but nothing beats seeing him in the flesh, feeling the warmth of his skin on mine, the taste of his lips, or how I feel when I fall asleep in his arms. Because of all of that, we arranged for him to come straight over after work tonight, a Friday, and spend the weekend with me.

So, picture me now, sitting on the sofa, knees bouncing in anticipation, trying to control my breathing and kerb my excitement all because he just texted me and told me he was now leaving work and would be here in fifteen minutes.

When he knocks on the door, I squeal in delight and run for it. As I fling the door open, grinning from ear to ear, he raises one eyebrow, and a small smile tugs at the corner of his mouth.

"Did somebody order a booty call?" he jokes.

Impossibly, my smile widens, and I reach out and grip his tie, pulling him inside. He drops his overnight bag, and his arms slip around my waist—one hand heading up to tangle in my hair, the other warming the small of my back. I sigh in contentment as his delicious scent surrounds me. When his head dips and his mouth presses against mine, my body slackens, and I'm secretly glad he's holding me so tightly.

God, I missed this.

Jared bends his knees, tightens his arms around my waist, and stands back up, lifting me with ease. My feet dangle around his shins, and I beam as he steps further into my flat, kicking the door closed behind him in one swift, sexy movement.

"Hi." His breath blows across my face, and my mouth waters at the scent of strawberry sweets he must have eaten on the way over.

"Hi." My voice comes out a husky, needy mess, which makes him smile.

When he makes no move to put me down, I wrap my legs around his waist and clamp myself to him like a baby monkey. This is now officially my most favourite place in the world.

He smells incredible, and I lean in and press my face into the crook of his neck, inhaling before letting out a little groan of appreciation.

"Jeez. I forgot how good you smell." I want to rub myself over him like a cat, cover myself in that scent until I'm drowning in it.

He chuckles, and I pull back to look at him, my arms tightening on his neck. His eyes flick over my face, and a little sigh leaves his lips, which makes the hair on my arms tingle.

"That seemed like a long few days," he admits, pressing his lips to mine again.

I nod in agreement as he walks over to the sofa, carefully sitting down with me still attached to him like a limpet. I can't help but smile smugly as I feel how excited he is to see me again. Just the fact that Jared fancies me so much makes me feel incredibly desired and beautiful.

After a long make-out session, his hands stroke my back as we talk about his day and mine and my margarita-drinking session last night with Heather. The whole time, he is so interested in what I have to say, listens so intently, that it makes me feel like the most important person in the world. With Jared's full attention on me, I feel a hundred feet tall. I revel in it, greedily soaking it all up.

"Have you eaten?" he asks after he's been here almost an hour, and I haven't even moved an inch off his lap. When I shake my head, he smiles. "I brought some food with me. Figured I'd cook for you."

My mouth drops open. "You're going to cook for me? You want me to blow you again tonight, don't you?" I joke, raising a teasing eyebrow.

A muscle in his jaw tightens as his eyes darken. "Well, I hadn't even thought about that, but now that you've mentioned it, yes, yes, I do."

His fingers dig into my hips almost painfully as his tongue traces his bottom lip. I can sense the desire rolling off him in waves.

I shoot him a coy smile, loving how tense his body now is. "Go cook for me; I'll see how good it is first." Winking, I ease off his lap and settle myself on the sofa.

He groans, and his head drops back as he closes his eyes in defeat. "Damn, I don't think I'm going to survive tonight. If it's as good as last time, I might meet Jesus."

Laughing, I chew on my thumbnail as I watch his pained expression, and his gaze turns to me. I love the power I have over him right now; I've honestly never felt so sexy or desired as his eyes wander my face and settle on my mouth. He's two seconds from begging me—I can sense it—so I playfully push his thigh with my foot.

"Go cook for me."

With a sigh, he pushes himself up, and I try—unsuccessfully—to keep my eyes away from the straining zipper in his suit trousers. I watch as he heads first to his overnight bag, pulling out a carrier bag of groceries, and then to my little kitchenette.

"Is there anything you don't eat?" he calls, unpacking vegetables, oil, and herbs onto the cluttered worktop.

"Only beetroot." I shudder at the thought.

"Okay, you're safe then." He smiles and turns back to his bag, searching through the cupboards and drawers until he finds my chopping board and the one sharp knife I own.

It's strange, watching him in there. He's almost too big for the place. My kitchen is comprised of only six base cupboards with drawers, four top cupboards, a sink, a fridge, and an oven that's on its last legs. Compared to his sleek, shiny gloss kitchen, mine is like one from *The Hobbit*, but he doesn't seem too fazed as he pulls more ingredients from the bag and sets them on the side before washing his hands.

Twisting my seat so I can see him and resting my chin on my hand, I watch, transfixed, as Jared sets about making dinner. He's a competent chef; I can tell that by how confident and methodical he is as he chops vegetables. It's surprisingly sexy to watch him cook. He's taken off his cufflinks and tie and rolled his shirtsleeves up to his elbows, so I can see his tanned forearms.

He tidies up after himself as he goes, washing up things he used and wiping over the sides. It's almost OCD tidy. I bite my lip and smile, my eyes drifting over his back and pert little behind, watching the muscles in his shoulders and arms as he fries what smells like onions and garlic, chops salad, and cracks eggs. He really came prepared!

Jared is most definitely not my usual type. My usual type is silly, goofy, happy-go-lucky, and a fly-by-the-seat-of-his-pants guy, who, I'll admit, is likely to still live at home with his mum. Jared is none of that. He's dependable, organised, and someone you call when you need an adult. It's different but extremely nice.

Half an hour later, he comes back to me, carrying a plate of something that smells so good that my mouth waters. He sets a can of Dr Pepper—which I know I didn't have any of, so he must have brought those over too—on the coffee table and passes me a plate containing a wedge of something he made and an artfully arranged side salad. It's probably the healthiest thing I've eaten in weeks. I'm more of a microwave meal or frozen pizza kind of girl.

He smiles almost shyly as I look over at him.

"This looks so good!" I gush. "What is it?" I pick up my knife and fork, cutting into it, my eyes widening as I spot a big slab of cheese on the top.

"Halloumi, red onion, and spinach frittata."

"You had me at halloumi." I nod appreciatively.

"Yeah, I figured that would be a hit with my cheese lover."

I've never eaten a frittata before. It sounds like something you'd order off a menu. He stands there, watching, seeming almost worried as I eagerly cut into it and blow on it before taking a tentative bite. I can't help but moan in appreciation as the flavours hit my tongue. It's incredible.

"Oh my God," I mumble, my mouth full. "This is like an orgasm on the tongue. I think we should get married." It's only a joke but not really.

"Wow, what a proposal," he replies, grinning so big that he gets those little lines around his eyes again. He winks at me and heads to the kitchen to get his drink and plate. Then, he comes back and plops down onto the sofa next to me.

"Do you eat like this all the time?" I ask, greedily shovelling in my food.

He shrugs. "Yeah, I like to cook. It's relaxing. My mum taught me. She's a chef, so I picked up a few things before I went off to university."

"Lucky. All my mum taught me about food was how to open jars and how long to microwave bacon for." I wince at the admission. Cooking is not one of my family's skill sets. "Also, no wonder you look like that"—I wave my fork at his chest and stomach—"if you eat this healthy kind of stuff every day."

He shrugs. "I told you, I run a bit too. At lunchtimes and sometimes before work if I have time. I keep in shape because, twice a year, I run a half-marathon to raise money for a dementia charity."

I raise a suitably impressed eyebrow at the revelation. "Really? A half-marathon?"

He nods. "Yeah, my grandmother had dementia, so I do what I can."

"I'm sorry." I reach out and squeeze his arm.

He shrugs and shakes his head, smiling sadly. "It's okay. She died a while ago, but I like to give back and do what I can. I enjoy running, so it's not such a hardship," he replies, finishing his food.

He watches as I devour the last couple of bites of my food, even forcing in the salad to try and impress him. I put my empty plate next to his on the coffee table and resist the urge to lick it clean.

"So ... do I get points for effort?" He raises his eyebrows, and I know what he's asking.

I press my lips into a thin line to suppress my smile as I pretend to consider, secretly knowing I'd do whatever he wanted tonight even if he hadn't just cooked the best damn meal I'd eaten in forever. "That depends ... did you bring any dessert?"

He nods smugly. "French macaroons."

My eyes widen. "Seriously?"

"Seriously."

"Oh, well then, you definitely get points for effort," I reply, laughing as he drops his head back, closes his eyes, and pumps the air with one fist in celebration.

"So, I've got something I want to talk to you about," he says, kissing the skin below my belly button, his teeth scraping against my oversensitive skin.

It's now Sunday morning, and we've spent a blissful weekend together, just hanging out and lazing around.

I close my eyes and softly brush my fingertips across his shoulders, enjoying the sensation. "Hmm?" I've not long ago woken up, and I'm so relaxed that I'm almost serene.

"I was wondering," he says, "if you wanted to be exclusive with me."

My whole body jerks in shock, and I accidentally knee him in the stomach. He grunts in surprise, and I gasp.

"Oh my God, sorry. Are you okay? I … I …" I wince, sitting up and looking down at him apologetically as I hold the sheet against my naked body.

He laughs and pulls himself up to sitting, too, rubbing at his stomach as he rolls his eyes. "Was it *that* unexpected?"

Unexpected? Hells yes! Never in my wildest dreams did I expect those words to come from his mouth this early on—okay, so, in my wildest dreams, yes, but not in real life.

"You want to be exclusive?" I ask quietly, my voice barely working.

A smile tugs at the corner of his mouth. "Well, I'm not interested in seeing anyone else. Are you?"

I shake my head. I haven't been interested in anyone else for months. Only him. "No."

He reaches out and takes my hand, interlacing our fingers, and I pray my palm isn't sweating from nerves. He shuffles closer to me, our bodies only a hair's breadth away from each other.

"Amy, I really like you. You're amazing, we get on great, I'm really interested to see where this will go between us, and I can't think of anyone else I want to be naked with. That pretty much all leads to exclusivity in my book. I don't want you seeing other guys. The thought of it …" He huffs out a breath and shakes his head as his eyebrows pull together in a frown. "No, I don't like the thought of that *at all*."

My eyes have widened during his speech, and my joy is consuming me. "I'm really interested to see where this goes too."

"That's settled then?"

I nod in agreement, my teeth sinking into my bottom lip so I don't ruin the moment with one of my word-vomit outbursts. He nods, too, his eyes twinkling as he smiles that heart-stopping smile and leans in, pressing his lips to mine.

Just as the kiss is beginning to get hot and my skin is starting to come alive with sensation and need, he pulls back. "There's something else," he says, cupping my neck with one hand, his thumb tracing the line of my jaw.

"Something else? What else is there?" I raise one eyebrow in prompt.

"Now that we're exclusive, I think we're ready to take the next step in our relationship."

"Oh?" I cock my head to the side, not having a clue as to what he is talking about.

His mouth opens and closes, and he gulps before saying, "I think we're ready to commit to a Netflix series."

He presses his lips into a thin line and waits for my reaction.

I burst out laughing at his randomness and roll my eyes. Pushing myself up, I climb onto his lap, straddling him, wrapping my arms around him. I revel in the skin-on-skin contact as every inch of me presses against every inch of him so intimately that it makes me almost purr in contentment. "That's a big step, Jared," I joke.

He nods. "I know, but I think we're ready."

He leans in and kisses me, his tongue exploring mine, and my whole body tightens with excitement. We are absolutely ready.

He pulls back after a couple of seconds. "We need to have a rule though: no skipping ahead and watching extra episodes without the other person being there. We only watch together. Do we have a deal?"

I sit back on my heels and bite my lip as I bring my right hand up between our bodies, little finger extended. "I pinkie swear."

Jared laughs as he looks down at it, but then he copies me, wrapping his little finger around mine as he shakes it. "Pinkie swear," he confirms. "This constitutes a binding contract. You know that, right?"

"I don't take pinkie swears lightly."

He laughs, and when I go to pounce on him, he pulls back, and his eyebrows knit together in a frown.

"That wasn't what I was actually going to ask you. I just chickened out at the last second," he confesses, seeming a little awkward and nervous.

"Okay?" I'm intrigued now.

He takes a deep breath and seems to steel himself as he strokes his thumb across my cheek. "Next month, on Bonfire Night, there's a party for my dad's birthday at my parents' house. Do you want to come?"

My mouth drops open in shock, and I almost choke on fresh air. "To meet your family?"

He nods, his eyes searching mine. "I understand if you think it's too soon for all the *meet the family* stuff, but I'd just like you to be there. You can say no if you want to; I'll understand. It's a big thing to meet the family, especially all the family in one go. Talk about being thrown in at the deep end." He laughs and rakes a hand through his hair.

I gulp. Both nervousness and exhilaration hit me at full force. *He wants me to meet his family. He is that serious about me?* This information thrills me. Bonfire Night is almost four weeks away.

"You think we'll still be together then?" I tease, trying not to let my happiness show.

"Yes." He recoils a little, his eyebrows shooting up in shock. "Don't you?"

I like his shock. It is almost like he hasn't even considered we wouldn't be.

"Yeah I do," I confirm. "At least, I know I'll still want to be with you," I admit sheepishly. I'll still want to be with him when we're ghosts, so next month is nothing. "I'd like to come with you."

He relaxes then, his shoulders losing some of the tension as he smiles. "My family is going to go crazy for you," he says, tickling his fingers down the sensitive skin over my ribs.

I grin and throw myself at him, ending the conversation as my need for him becomes unbearable. With Jared, enough is never enough.

TWELVE

"So, you met this guy in a coffee shop?" Tim, Heather's fiancé, asks, taking a large gulp of his beer.

Heather and I exchange a glance and nod in unison. Tim is adorable and has a heart of gold, but he can't lie or keep a secret to save his life once he has more than two pints of beer inside him, and I don't want him drunkenly blurting out that I've been in love with Jared since before he even knew I existed. I love the guy like a brother, so I don't want to have to junk-punch him.

"Yep," I lie.

The bar we're in is rapidly filling up. It's always busy on a Friday night here, and tonight will be even busier because there is a band playing. We haven't seen them play before, but their poster looked intriguing enough for us to arrange this little double date where I'll get to show Jared off for the first time. We're seated off to one side on a tall table, and my feet dangle precariously at least a foot off the ground. I can barely even reach the footrest. These stools were not designed with short people in mind.

"Oh, did I tell you I almost died today?" I announce dramatically, shaking back the sleeve of my shirt to reveal scratches up my forearm in example.

Tim and Heather both look at me quizzically.

"Funny story, but don't repeat this to Jared when he gets here. I don't want him feeling guilty about it." I give them a pointed look.

Tim scrunches up his nose. "Is this gonna be some weird sex thing? Because if it is, I don't want to hear it."

Heather grins. "Ooh, I definitely want to hear it!"

I chuckle and shake my head. "Nothing like that. So, a couple of days ago, Jared announced that he wanted to fix Bessy. He turned up with tools and everything. Apparently, he'd noticed my brakes needed tightening or something when we met at that coffee shop, and he'd been thinking about it ever since."

"Aww, cute," Heather cuts in.

I nod and grin. "So, he fixed up my bike, right? Bloody thing works like a dream now; the wheel doesn't squeak or anything. I was riding her home from the shop, bags full of food dangling from my handlebars"—I mime holding handlebars—"and I was minding my own business when I spot the cutest dog, like, a hundred yards up, right? So, I pulled the brakes to start to slow down—because Bessy takes that long to stop, so you have to have a bit of forethought when riding her. And the bike just stopped. Just like that." I click my fingers. "I wasn't prepared. My feet didn't move off the pedals because, mentally, I was coming to a slow stop a hundred yards up, next to the pup. I literally just wobbled and fell off. The bike fell on top of me, my bags split, and my food went everywhere. There was a tin of spaghetti and sausages I didn't even manage to find after, so I don't know where that went. Also, I was slowly being crushed to death by Bessy, too, because she is heavy! Luckily, some old lady saw me and yanked me out. My arse hurts something rotten. And the worst part? I didn't even get to stroke the dog!"

Heather laughs. "Mate, you are a liability!"

Tim rolls his eyes and picks up the jug full of frothy, murky orange liquid and refills my glass. "Here, you earned this for the longest, most ridiculous story of the day."

I grin and pick up my drink, tipping my glass in silent cheers. "I'll drink to that!"

"So, what have you been doing for your two weeks off?" Tim asks.

"I can't believe my holiday is almost finished," I groan. "But it's been fun, and I feel so relaxed. I went to see my mum and nan for a few days last week, and then this week, I've just been hanging with Jared a lot. We painted my bathroom the other day and went bowling. Other than that, we've just been chilling. Oh, but we have been watching *Stranger Things*."

Tim's eyes grow excited at that. "Have you finished the new season? Did you cry?"

"Whoa, spoilers!" I hold my hand up and *shh* him loudly. "No! Turns out, Jared hadn't seen any of them. Can you believe it? I told him we had to watch it. We went back to the beginning and started over, so he could catch up, and then we'll watch the new episodes together when we get there. I'll admit, it's slow-going though. We've been watching almost a week now and still haven't made it through season one."

Tim frowns in confusion. "How come? It's only, like, eight episodes. You can do that in a couple of days, easy."

My eyes drop to the table, and I fight a smile. "We get distracted a lot."

He scoffs, and Heather giggles.

Where I'm sitting, facing the door, I see Jared step in, and my heart stutters in my chest. "Ooh, there he is!" I squeal excitedly and stand, balancing precariously on the footrest of my stool, wobbling uncertainly as I wave to get his attention.

He takes a couple of seconds but finally sees me waving like a loon over the crowd and raises a hand in acknowledgement.

"That's him?" Tim asks, staring at Jared as he strides confidently towards us, struggling because the room has really filled in the hour we've already been here.

I nod proudly and notice Tim's frowning—scowling in fact.

"What the hell, Amy? Why is he good-looking? You normally drag home geeky, nerdy guys with crap haircuts, who look like they got dressed in the dark. They usually make me feel good about myself." He turns back to me and looks a little affronted about it. "I'm always the good-looking male when we double date."

"Really?" Heather says, faking disbelief before sending him a playful wink.

"Ha-ha," he scoffs and looks back at Jared, who's still working his way through the crowd. "Jesus, he looks like he should be in an aftershave advert. He's every girl's wet dream. Ugh, I should have put on a shirt." He looks down at his jeans and T-shirt he's wearing. He looks smart-casual, like he always does.

"He's come straight from work; that's why he's dressed up." I let my eyes wander Jared's exquisite form in his black suit trousers and white shirt with the sleeves he's rolled up to his elbows.

He definitely looks like a wet dream.

Heather leans in and pinches Tim's cheek. "Looks like you'll have to up your game if you want to try and compete for best-looking male in the group now."

He groans and shakes his head. "I'll have to settle for being the funny one."

As Jared steps to the side of our table, I smile reassuringly, sensing his unease as his eyes flick from me to Heather and Tim. He nods a greeting and starts to say hi, but I throw my arms around his shoulders, pulling him closer to me.

"Me first," I grumble, raising one eyebrow.

Where I'm still standing on the footrest, we're the same height, our eyes meet, and his hands reach for my waist, steadying me as I wobble.

When he presses his lips to mine, I melt against him and sag in contentment. It was yesterday morning that I last saw him—he made me coffee in bed just before he left for work—but it feels like forever. I am quickly becoming addicted to him. We've been exclusive for five whole days, and in that time, we've spent more time together than apart. He's stayed at my place every day this week—apart from last night. Hello, Tequila Thursday!

He breaks the kiss, his eyes remaining locked on mine as if we are the only ones in the room. "Hi, beautiful. God, you taste good."

I glow with pleasure at his compliment. "It's the cocktail. Between the Sheets, it's called."

He raises one eyebrow. "Oh, really? And is it good, Between the Sheets?" His hand slides down to my bum, squeezing gently.

I grin at his double entendre. "I have no complaints."

Tim clears his throat, and Heather says sarcastically, "Oh, you two just carry on. We'll wait."

I giggle, and Jared pulls back but leaves his arm around me.

"Hey, sorry. I'm dating a pathological attention seeker. What you gonna do?" He playfully rolls his eyes and shrugs. "I'm Jared. It's nice to meet you."

As I sit down on my stool and pick up my drink, Jared holds out his hand, and Tim shakes it, smiling warmly.

"This is Heather"—he quirks a thumb at her—"and thanks to you, I'm now the DUFF, Tim."

We all burst out laughing, and I almost choke on my drink at the movie reference, but Jared misses the context of the Designated Ugly Fat Friend joke, so he smiles politely but doesn't seem to get it.

Instead of sitting, Jared nods at the almost-empty drink jugs in the middle of the table. "I'm not late, am I?" He frowns and checks his watch, the muscle in his jaw tensing. Jared abhors lateness.

I smile, slipping my hand into his. He's right on time. "You're not late. We got here an hour ago, so we could get a good table."

He seems a little relieved and nods in understanding. "Ah, good. Well, shall I get a round in?"

Tim grins. "I like you already."

"I love it when a plan comes together," Jared replies, and I can tell the retro A-Team reference wins Tim over that little bit more. "What are we drinking?"

Tim laughs and reels off the drink order. I send Jared a wink as he heads to the bar, and then I look back at my friends and raise an eyebrow.

"Well, he certainly raises our group's average hotness score a couple of points. But I'll reserve my character judgement until a little bit later," Heather says, nodding.

I chew on my lip, hoping tonight goes well. Things are going great with Jared, and these two sitting opposite me are as good as family to me. It's important that they all get along. I'm not sure what I'll do if they don't like each other. It doesn't bear thinking about.

It takes a while for him to get served, but when he finally comes back with a fresh jug of orange-coloured cocktail and another one full of beer, I smile over at him and pat the seat next to me. He pulls another glass from his pocket, followed by two packs of plain crisps, which he sets in the middle and sends me a knowing smile. He sits, pouring himself a drink, while I reach for the crisps, tearing open the packet so we can all share them. I grin, happily munching away. He already knows me so well.

"Amy's told me a lot about you. It's so nice you're so close after all this time. You and she went to secondary school together?" he asks Heather.

She nods in reply, giving a noisy pull on her straw, sucking up the last dregs from her glass. "We did. She's the Rachel to my Monica."

One of Jared's hands softly strokes my back as he reaches for the cocktail jug with the other and refills Heather's glass, like the perfect, attentive gentleman that he is. "And you and Tim have been together how long?"

"Four years," Tim answers. "Four wonderful, *long* years." He widens his eyes in exaggerated horror on the word *long*, which earns him a slap to the chest from his fiancée.

Jared nods, looking thoughtful. "So, you're probably the best people to come to for advice on how to deal with this one then." He motions to me and smiles as he fiddles with a lock of my hair. "Do you have any advice for me, any pearls of wisdom that'll help me navigate the awesome craziness that is Amy Clarke?"

Tim laughs, his eyes sparkling with amusement. "Amy's like a gremlin."

My mouth drops open in outrage, and I fold my arms across my chest. "Oh, gee, thanks."

He holds up a hand and raises one eyebrow. "Just calm your tits there, Gizmo. Hear me out."

Jared takes a sip of his beer, his eyes firmly latched on Tim, waiting to see where this is going.

"Gremlins are great if you treat them right. They're loving, cute, happy, affectionate, and they make great pets. All you have to do is keep them warm, safe, loved, and most importantly, fed." Tim sits back with a shit-eating, smug grin on his face, clearly pleased with himself for the ridiculous analogy.

Jared purses his lips, thoughtful, and then replies, "I already noticed the food thing. I've never seen her happier than when she's eating. She hums when she eats."

I gasp and look at him. "I do not!"

One of his eyebrows rises in challenge, so I look at Heather for help, but she just nods in agreement. My mouth snaps closed, and I feel my cheeks burn with embarrassed heat.

Hmm, you learn something about yourself every day.

Tim picks up the jug of beer, refilling his own glass and Jared's. "Just a heads-up though. Gremlins are simple creatures, and they might look cute and cuddly, but don't mistreat them; otherwise, they'll fuck you up. And watch out; they run in packs." He subtly motions his head towards Heather. "Hurt one, and feel the wrath of the group."

Heather must kick him under the table because Tim jerks, groans, and spills some of his beer in his lap as he frowns at her.

I chuckle and turn to Jared, plucking another crisp from the packet. "But of course, you can feed me after midnight. That's all good."

The bar is filling up even more now, and people crowd around our table as the band starts to set up on the stage. When a drunken guy, who looks barely legal to drink, walks past and smiles at me, Jared frowns and reaches down, gripping the leg of the stool I'm perched on and pulling it closer to his. I squeal and giggle, setting my hand on his thigh and leaning in to him. When he plants his foot on the rung of my stool, I feel my tummy flutter. It's a possessive gesture, distinctly alpha male marking his territory. I actually love it.

He doesn't mention the move at all, just turns to Tim to continue the conversation as if nothing happened. "Amy says you're a nurse at the hospital?"

"Yep, I work in paediatrics. It's tough going some days but rewarding. I love it," Tim replies. "What about you? What do you do?"

I lean forward excitedly. "Ooh, ooh, I can answer that!"

Jared looks at me quizzically but waves a hand in a go-ahead gesture.

I clear my throat and lean in to make sure I'm heard over the crowd. "Okay, so you know when you're chatting on the phone one day, and you casually mention that you really fancy a soft-boiled egg. And then the next day, you're scrolling Facebook, and *bam*, you see adverts for a boiled egg machine."

Heather bursts out laughing. "A boiled egg machine?"

"No wonder you live off ready meals and cereal," Jared jokes, leaning in and planting a soft kiss on my forehead.

I shoot him a warning glare and turn back to Tim and Heather, who are still laughing. "Do you want to hear this story or not?" When they nod, I roll my eyes and continue, "So, yeah, the boiled egg machine comes up in your news feed. That's Jared. He uses the wiretap information to learn about you, so he can sell you shit through advertising." I turn to Jared and raise an eyebrow in question. "Is that about right?"

His eyes sparkle with amusement. "Nailed it."

Tim is grinning. "And how many boiled egg machines do you sell, Jared?"

"Surprisingly few," Jared answers, deadpan.

"I'll cheers to that," Tim says, raising his glass.

We all laugh and chink our glasses as the band starts up behind us, rendering conversation impossible for the rest of the night.

When Heather looks up and catches my eye, she sends me a discreet thumbs-up gesture. My insides fizz with pleasure. Jared gets the BFF stamp of approval.

THIRTEEN

My time off goes by in what feels like a blink of the eye, and before I know it, I'm back in my old routine of early mornings and swaying in rhythm on the train.

I've been back at work a full week now already, too, and my holiday seems like a lifetime ago. Today marks another momentous occasion that excites me to my very core. Today is what I used to call Man Crush Monday. But it's the first time I'm going to see Jared on the train since our very first accidental meeting at the coffee shop four glorious weeks ago. The whole dynamic of our relationship is different this time; we're no longer strangers who don't speak. I've seen him naked and smelled his morning breath; he's touched every part of me, seen me with no make-up and unbrushed hair, wearing tracksuit bottoms and a T-shirt that I dropped pasta sauce down after a disastrous attempt to cook for him one night. I no longer feel nervous around him. He makes me feel at ease, confident, wanted, even when I am at my worst.

I can barely wait to see him this morning. It is sure to be the highlight of my day. What is going to make this experience even better is that I haven't seen Jared for two days because I went home to my mum's house for the weekend and only got home late last night.

I'm standing on the platform, outside the door at the front of the train, eagerly waiting for him to arrive, when one of my daily regulars walks up to me and stops at my side, folding up her newspaper and tucking it under one arm as she sips her coffee.

"Good morning, Amy."

"Hi, Angela. How are you today? Good weekend?"

She nods but scrunches her nose up at the same time. "Same old, same old. Back to the grindstone now though!" she huffs, rolling her eyes. When I beam a smile in reply, she narrows her eyes at me. "What's got you so chipper this morning? No one should be this happy on a workday." She waves a hand in the direction of my face and my wide smile.

I shrug nonchalantly. "Just love Mondays; that's all."

"Ugh, you're the only one, I'm afraid. I'd rather still be in bed." Angela takes another swig of her coffee and steps on board the train, sending me a little wave as she heads in to find a seat in the already-packed train.

I smile at her, and then my eyes wander down the platform, searching him out. It's five minutes until departure, and Jared hasn't made his appearance yet. It is definitely his week to travel to London—I keep a little secret code on my calendar of when his weeks are. I had two weeks off work, and then he wasn't due last week, but this week, he is. I'll admit, I didn't mention anything to him about those train rides and how I fell desperately in love with him and his dorky ways before he even noticed my existence. Heather and I agreed it was best to just pretend it never happened unless he brought it up first; she said I'd look less like a crazy stalker then.

When he still doesn't make an appearance, I frown and wonder if I've gotten my days muddled. I saw it on my calendar this morning though; I am sure of it. The little MCM scribbled in the corner of the box with today's date next to it. I went through the whole rest of the year one drunken night, not long after the little girl and the magic show, and marked all of his weeks onto it, so I could count down to seeing him again.

Suddenly, with one minute to spare before departure, I see him. He's speed-walking towards the last carriage of the train, sidestepping around a slow walker. My eyes rake over him. He looks a little less put together today, a little less neat than the usual pristine guy I'm accustomed to. His jacket is undone and hanging loose, there are no crisp edges to his shirt, and his tie is a little off to one side and not the perfect, neat Windsor knot I've seen him fuss with in the mirror for ages until it is just right. Whatever this meeting is for in London every other week is obviously, decidedly more casual than his usual day-to-day job. He looks smart still, just not the impeccable, professional man I'm used to seeing.

He climbs aboard the carriage at the opposite end of the long train to me, just as my walkie-talkie announces it's time to make last-moment checks before the doors close.

I do my checks and then signal that we are ready to leave and step onto the train, locking the doors. When we're safely moving, I head out of the room at the end and start my ticket collection duties. As predicted in my morning briefing, the train is unusually busy today, crammed full of people who spill out of the carriages and into the corridors. We've been forewarned that there is some sort of huge convention in London today, so we expect extra passengers, but my bosses didn't predict it to be this rammed; otherwise, there would have been another conductor assigned to help me.

I work my way through the train, collecting money, punching tickets, and dodging people who sway dangerously in the aisles. It takes me so long to work my way down the train that we are almost at London by the time I get to the last carriage. A few people have gotten on and off along the way, the crowd thinning a little, but mostly, the train is still packed.

I can see Jared; he's in the corridor right at the end, near the toilets. He's leaning against the wall, knees slightly bent, briefcase settled on the floor between his feet, one hand stuffed into his trouser pocket, the other holding his phone as he scrolls through something with his thumb. My legs are trying to force me to abandon my job and go to him, but I hold my ground and perform my duties.

As I get closer, my excitement builds. He doesn't look up as I serve the last few people, and I silently reflect on how nervous I would usually be at this time. Approaching Jared (or my crush, as I called him back when I didn't know his name) is always the highlight of my fortnight but also the most nerve-racking too. It is an oxymoron how I'd be so excited yet so scared of the moment when I approached him.

Now though, as I serve the last person and step into the corridor with him, pressing the button to close the door behind me so we're on our own in the cramped little space, he looks up and smiles. My heart melts.

"Morning," he greets cheerfully, reaching into his pocket and pulling out his prepurchased ticket.

I step forward, my eyes latched firmly on his face as I gently push the ticket out of the way and press myself against him, feeling every inch of his hard body against mine, not even caring that people could see us if they craned their necks and looked through the glass on the partition door. Jared's body stiffens as his eyes meet mine, and he sucks in a ragged breath through his teeth.

"You look so perfectly fuckable." My words echo the ones he growled at me that very first night.

His lips part, and I see his eyes widen fractionally before I quickly lean in and kiss him hard. He doesn't react immediately; instead, he seems a little taken aback as his hands find my waist and hold me still. My hand goes up to the back of his head as I kiss him again, moaning in the back of my throat.

When I pull back, one of his eyebrows rises, and his whole posture screams shock. I grin. He probably didn't expect me to be so forceful at my workplace; Jared is extremely professional like that.

"Whoa," he mumbles, his eyes flicking down to my lips again before coming back up to my eyes.

His tongue traces his bottom lip, and I feel like I'm going to lose my mind.

When my walkie-talkie crackles to life, announcing that there are two minutes until the final stop, I tilt my head towards his, my lips brushing his teasingly as I speak, "I've only got two minutes. You'd better make them count."

This time, when I kiss him, he responds, immediately kissing me back, pulling me closer to him as his teeth nip at my bottom lip. When his tongue strokes mine, I taste coffee and toothpaste. I moan into his mouth as his hand slides down my back and settles on my rear, squeezing gently as I step between his legs. My thighs brush against his in a delightful way that reminds me of how he holds me at night—one leg thrown over me, trapping me against him in a warm, delectable Jared sandwich. Things are getting hot as my skin flushes with pleasure, and my hands slide up his chest and inside his jacket, feeling the warmth of him through his shirt.

"Amy?"

"Amy, are you there?"

"Amy!"

I blink, the spell broken as I pull back from the kiss and open my eyes, coming back to reality as I realise my walkie-talkie is screaming at me. I gasp, noticing the train is literally coming to a stop at its final destination. My eyes widen in horror.

"Shit!" I gasp, wrenching myself from Jared's arms. "I have to go."

I turn and jab at the button on the carriage door, seeing people are out of their seats already, bundled around the exit doors, fingers poised over the Open Door button—unknowing that they won't open because I'm at the wrong end of the train, making out with my boyfriend, instead of being where I should be, ready to press the Lock Release button.

"Wait!" Jared calls behind me.

I wave dismissively over my shoulder, already rushing through the carriage. "I'll speak to you later!" I call back, fighting to get through the crowds.

I apologise over and over as people struggle to allow space to let me pass. I groan inwardly and continue to fight my way through the sea of people who are now complaining that the doors won't open.

When I finally make it to the other end of the train, my fingers fumble on the keypad, struggling to input the code to gain access to the staff area because my fingers are trembling a little. When I finally fall into the room, I slam my hand down on the release and breathe a sigh of relief as a little cheer goes up behind me, and people stream out of the train in their droves.

"Amy?" my walkie summons again.

I pluck it from my belt and raise it to my still-tingling lips. "Bert, I'm here, sorry. I got pinned at the wrong end of the train. It's so busy."

I feel a little bad for lying. Bert, the train driver, is lovely. He's an older man, nearing his retirement, and he has always treated me as if I were one of his four daughters he dotes on. If he knew I was at the back of the train, snogging my boyfriend like a lovesick teenager, I could only imagine the disapproving scowl he would subject me to.

"Oh, okay, love. I thought there was a problem or something. You had me worried about you for a second there," he replies.

"No, sorry about that." I lean against the wall and put a hand to my heart, feeling it stutter against my palm as I smile to myself. *Best workday ever.*

FOURTEEN

Later that night, when I open the door to Jared and he jokingly announces, "Honey, I'm home!" I can't help my squeal of happiness as I launch myself at him, barely giving him enough time to drop what he's holding and catch me before we crash against the wall with a loud thump that's sure to make the neighbours think someone has just been murdered.

His mouth claims mine in a scorching hot kiss that I feel all the way down to my toes.

"God, I've missed you," I mumble against his mouth. "I've been thinking about you all day!"

That is the damn truth. Every spare second, and even seconds that weren't spare where I should have been concentrating on something else, I thought about him today. That little occurrence on the train this morning had kick-started my hormones and left me on edge all day. It has been a long few hours, made worse by the fact that Jared usually doesn't come round until about seven in the evenings because he likes to go home after work to shower and change and pick up his overnight bag and a fresh set of clothes for work the following day. We've wasted precious make-out hours.

"Oh, yeah?" Jared replies, kissing at my neck as my hands tangle into the back of his hair.

"Just shut up and get your kit off already," I order.

"Easy there, sex pest. I've got something for you first."

He chuckles darkly at my growled protest, and instead of doing what I suggested, he holds me tightly against him with one arm and crouches, picking up his overnight bag from the floor before walking us both into the lounge. He sets his bag down on the messy coffee table and unzips it with one hand. I pull back, unwrapping myself from around him and wobbling awkwardly as he sets me back on my feet. When he finally works the items from his bag and I see what he's brought, my heart stutters in my chest.

"Happy almost anniversary," he says, offering me the bunch of pink roses and a small package wrapped in purple tissue paper. "I thought it was okay to give you these now. I know, technically, it's not our four-week dateversary until tomorrow, but seeing as I'll be leaving before you wake up and I am working late tomorrow night, I figured I'd give it to you now."

I press my lips together as a wave of emotion washes over me. Jared Stone is the sweetest thing ever. So thoughtful and adorable. I am one lucky, punching-above-my-weight, spoiled girl. I let out a content, happy sigh as my eyes meet his. My heart is fit to bursting, my stomach fluttering. He holds out the items, and I take the flowers, my finger brushing over the soft petals of one of the roses as I chew on my lip, fighting tears.

Four weeks. Four perfect weeks since our first date. I am more in love with him now than ever.

"Thank you," I croak around the lump in my throat. "I didn't think you'd remember."

That isn't usually a guy thing, remembering stuff like when a first date was.

He raises one eyebrow and cups one hand around the back of my head, pulling me closer so I'm forced to go onto my tiptoes as his mouth covers mine. My body softens against his as I smile against his lips.

When he pulls back, he holds out the small package, and I eagerly tear it open, seeing a bottle of my favourite perfume.

My mouth drops open. "How did you know?"

He shrugs, flopping back onto the sofa, raising one arm in clear invitation for me to sit with him. "Noticed you were running low and took a photo of the bottle, so I could find the right one."

"Bloody adorable," I congratulate. And instead of sitting with him in the offered spot, I shake my head. "I have something for you too. One sec."

Before he can say anything, I rush to my bedroom and go to the bottom of my wardrobe, pulling out the striped maroon-and-blue tie I purchased for him that I knew would go perfectly with his three-piece blue suit I loved. Then, an idea hits me, and instead of giving it to him in the gift-wrapped bag I bought, I decide to re-enact the scene from *Pretty Woman*. I strip out of my clothes, knot it around my neck, and walk back out to him, butt naked.

As his eyes widen in shock and then narrow in appreciation, turning dark and predatory, I can tell he likes his gift.

"Here you go." I set a cup of tea down on the table in front of him.

Jared flashes me a grateful smile. "Thanks. Though after that, maybe I should have a sports drink to rehydrate and replenish my electrolytes," he jokes, gripping hold of my waist and pulling me down onto his lap, kissing me as he toys with the edge of his T-shirt I'm wearing, his fingers teasing at my thigh.

Wrapping my arm around his neck, I wriggle to get myself more comfortable as I reach for the TV remote.

"I'll buy you some next time I go shopping." Opening Netflix, I select the next episode of *Stranger Things*.

"Wait, before you put that on," he says, "I wanted to talk to you but got distracted by all the skin and tie sexiness." He smirks at me, and I feel a blush creep onto my cheeks. "I was wondering if—not this Friday, but next Friday—would you accompany me to a work function?"

"A work function?"

He nods. "Yeah, I told them I wasn't going originally, but I found out today that some smart-arse in the higher management has now decided to make the function mandatory for my department, good for morale and team bonding apparently." He rolls his eyes. "I don't want to go, but I don't have a choice now. It's going to be incredibly awkward and boring."

"Incredibly awkward and boring. You're really selling it to me," I joke, eliciting a chuckle from him. "Won't all your work friends be there? Can't you hang out with them?"

He scrunches his nose and snorts. "Amy, I'm the boss. My team all hates me. When I was brought over from another company last year, I made a lot of changes, got rid of some people who were useless at their jobs, and changed a lot of the outdated practices they were used to. None of that made me very popular there. They think I don't know that they all call me Iceman and Stone Heart behind my back, but I do. It comes with the territory. No one likes being told what to do by a 'jumped-up know-it-all,' or so I've heard." He does air quotes around the jumped-up bit and shrugs casually. He doesn't seem too bothered by their opinions.

I raise one eyebrow, my hackles rising as my instinct is to find these people and junk-punch them. "They call you Iceman?" I inquire. He nods, and I purse my lips, trying to make the best of it. "You know, maybe that's not a bad thing. Iceman from *Top Gun* was pretty damn cool and super hot."

He laughs and shakes his head. "No. More like, I'm cold as hell and hard as ice. Or they play on my surname and say I have a stone where my heart should be."

He clearly isn't bothered, but I am.

"Oh." I shoot him a sad smile and clutch him closer to me. Jared isn't like that at all though. How could anyone hate him? "And are you cold as ice and just as hard when you're at work? What kind of boss are you?"

He shrugs, settling himself at my side, propping himself up on one elbow. "I don't think I am. I'm a bit particular, I suppose. I like things done in a certain way, and I like things done right the first time. And if I have to ask for something twice, then you've not done a good job in my opinion."

I smile as realisation dawns on me. Jared—the perfectionist, OCD, tailored suit–wearing professional—is a hard-arse boss.

"Oh!" I raise one eyebrow.

He grins and rolls his eyes as he realises what he just said. "Okay, yeah, maybe I am a little hard to please."

I bite my lip and chuckle.

He raises one eyebrow in question. "So ... you'll come with me? It's a dinner dance at a posh hotel." He sticks out his bottom lip and pouts pleadingly.

Posh. I don't like that word. I wince. "Posh meaning like cocktail dresses and black tie? I don't think I even have anything to wear." My mind flicks to my wardrobe, considering my options. I definitely don't have anything suitable.

Jared pulls me closer; his body pressing against mine is almost too distracting for me to stay on track, but I force myself to. "Please? I'll buy you something if you don't. Please? I hate going to these things. It will make it almost bearable if you come with me. I can't think of anything worse than socialising with my subordinates."

I burst out laughing. "If you call them subordinates, I'm not surprised they hate you."

He laughs too, dipping his head, kissing me lightly. "Come with me, please? Save me from the boring night where I'm forced to make polite small talk with people who hate my guts. Please, baby?" he whispers against my lips, his hot breath tickling my skin, and I'm done for.

He could ask me for the moon, and I'd give it to him if I could.

"Okay." I nod in agreement. When he grins in response, I reach up and press my palm against his cheek. "I really like it when you smile this big. You get these little crinkles at the corners of your eyes. They're sexy as hell." I rub my thumb over the creases and let out a little dreamy sigh.

He snorts a laugh, his eyes twinkling as he leans over me, just staring down at my face. "Amy, at the risk of scaring you away, I just want to say that I'm well on my way to falling in love with you. You know that, right?" A muscle in his jaw tightens as he watches for my reaction.

I grin sheepishly, my insides glowing with pleasure at his words. *He is falling in love with me?* I didn't know that. I *hoped* he was feeling this connection growing between us like I was, but I didn't *know*. I'm secretly thrilled at this revelation.

I want to scream and whoop in celebration, but instead, I force myself to remain calm and collected as I reply, "Well, that's very nice to hear, but I'm not going to say it back. If I do, it'll just sound like I'm copying you."

His shoulders lose some of their tenseness as he turns his head and plants a little kiss on my palm. "I don't mind you copying me."

He eagerly looks up at me, but I shake my head.

"I'm not going to; I like to be original. So, instead, I'll just say … I love your eye crinkles."

He bursts out laughing; it's loud and free, and it makes my tummy flutter with pleasure. "You're so wonderfully weird."

I smile and chew on my lip. "I'm taking that as a compliment."

My insides are simmering with excitement, his words playing over and over in my head.

"I'm well on my way to falling in love with you."

"As it was intended," he replies, leaning in and kissing me before effortlessly manoeuvring my body so he's spooning me from behind, his arm under my head, his other wrapped securely around me, his fingers drawing a little pattern on my bare stomach, causing goosebumps to rise on my skin.

As he reaches for the remote and presses play on the next episode, I snuggle back against him, blissfully happy. My hand catches his, and our fingers interlace as I pull his hand up to my mouth and kiss his knuckles.

As the opening sequence music plays, I smile and decide to throw him a bone. "Just so you know, I'm well on my way to falling in love with you too," I admit. That doesn't even come close to how I feel though.

I feel him grin against the back of my neck, and his hold on me tightens, pulling me closer to him as he throws his leg over mine, cloaking me in a warm Jared sandwich of luscious skin. He doesn't say anything, and I don't need him to. How firmly he's holding me says it all.

FIFTEEN

"I'm still not convinced this is a good idea," I mutter. My stomach aches from nerves, and I look up at my childhood home, my brain whirling through all the things that could go wrong.

Jared laughs and advances on me, his eyes locked on mine as his hands come up to cup my neck, tilting my head back, forcing me to look up at him. "Of course it's a good idea; it was mine," he rebuts playfully as his head dips and his mouth captures mine in a soft kiss that makes my heart sing.

My arms instinctively grip his waist as he gently eases me against the side of his car, leaning into me, his hard body pressed against the length of mine.

I groan and close my eyes. "My nanna is going to eat you alive."

"You underestimate me," he replies.

I shake my head. "You underestimate her."

Jared came up with this not-so-brilliant plan during the week. As next weekend is both his work dinner dance and his dad's birthday party, I will be meeting everyone who is important in his life over the space of two days. Because of that, he thinks it is only fair that he meet my mum and nan. I tried to talk him out of it—I definitely want to put that off as long as possible—but he has been adamant and worked on me all week until I agreed.

He shrugs, playing with a lock of my hair, twirling it around his finger this way and that. His eyes are latched on mine. They're dizzying, but then I realise it's because I've forgotten to breathe again. He does this to me a lot. One day, I'll die from it, just randomly keel over because he's mesmerised me so much that my body has completely forgotten basic survival function.

"It'll be fine. I met Heather and did all right there; she was probably the one I was most worried about meeting."

My hand strokes against his coat, toying with one of the buttons. He did better than all right with them. They love him. Tim and Jared even exchanged numbers at the end of the night and are planning on going to watch a football match together in a couple of weeks, as they both support Cambridge United.

"It's not that I don't think you'll do all right; I know you'll do great. They'll love you; who wouldn't?" My stomach gives another nervous twist. "It's just … my family is a bit …" I search for the correct word to describe them, but nothing comes to mind, so I groan and drop my head onto his chest, letting his smell fill my lungs. "I just don't want you taking one look at them and thinking, *Oh, so that's what Amy will be like in thirty or fifty years*, and run screaming for the hills."

He chuckles, and it rumbles through his chest. "I won't run, trust me."

And for some reason, I do. "You're so cluelessly cute."

He smiles, and my heart races in my chest.

Jeez, that smile. I can't contain my happy sigh.

With one finger, he traces the line of my cheek, leaving behind a burning trail. "Amy, I don't think you realise how utterly crazy I am about you," he whispers, leaning in, brushing his nose up the side of mine. "You're amazing, charming, beautiful, funny, captivating." He punctuates each compliment with a soft kiss, trailing them from my lips to my ear.

When he gets there, he nips at my earlobe, and I giggle, unable to mask my happiness.

He pulls back and smiles down at me, his eyes showing me the truth of his words. He really is crazy about me; I can see it hidden in the depths of his deep amber-coloured pools.

"I'm crazy about you too," I admit, gripping fistfuls of his jacket, holding him against me.

He nods confidently. "I know." A cocky smirk slips onto his face as he pulls back, taking my hand and nodding towards the house. "Come on then. Let's go meet the parents."

I groan and lead him up the path, towards the back gate. I just have to get through the next couple of hours intact, and then everything will be fine. I just pray they don't say anything to scare him away; both my mum and nanna can be a bit hard to handle, but together, they are overwhelming.

Luckily, I had the forethought to make this a short visit. Usually, I stay the night when I come home, just because; otherwise, it seems a long way to come just for a couple of hours. But because Jared is accompanying me this time, I already called ahead and told them we would arrive after lunch and leave in the early evening. Three or four hours are more than enough for a first meeting. Both my nan and mum promised to be on their absolute best behaviour.

As we make it to the gate, I give his hand a squeeze and reach for the handle. "Okay?" I ask, giving him one last chance to back out.

We could just go home to my place. I could call with some cholera or explosive diarrhoea excuse and put this off for another week. I must admit, I'm kind of hoping he backs out.

He huffs out a breath and reaches up, fixing his hair. He fusses with his coat a bit before nodding. The tightness to his jaw and straightness of his back, mixed with the fact that his hand has mine in a death grip, show me he's nervous.

"I'm okay. Let's go."

A rush of affection warms my blood as I think about him being nervous. It's endearing, and it shows he cares. I like that their opinions matter to him. He can do it though; I am sure of it. Jared Stone is not one to back down from a strong, feisty woman. Trouble is, three of them in one go … I feel a little sorry for him.

As we step through the gate, Puzzle bounds out of the plants, barking so loud that it hurts my ears as he runs for us, his legs moving so fast that his body can barely keep up.

Jared stops, obviously thinking he's about to get mauled by the fat, greying, half-blind pug. "Er …"

"He's friendly," I insist, quickly closing the gate behind us.

As he nears, Puzzle's bark turns into an excited yap as he starts dancing around our feet. He sniffs and snuffles at Jared's leg. My eyes widen, as I know what's coming but I'm too slow to stop it. He immediately wraps his front paws around Jared's leg, proceeding to hump it.

Jared looks down at the dog and then at me, his face set in stony resignation. "Well, this is awkward," he deadpans.

I chuckle wickedly and bend, shooing Puzzle down before scooping him into my arms. I shoot Jared a grin. "To be fair, I get that excited around you too."

He laughs and reaches over to stroke the dog, who is going loopy in my arms, trying to lick the gorgeous stranger to death.

My mum and nanna are both chuckling by the time we cross the garden to where they're sitting. Nanna waves, and I see her eyes assessing every move Jared makes.

Mum stands and beams over at us. "Excuse the dog. He has no manners."

"He could have at least bought me a drink first," Jared replies, shrugging.

There's silence for a few beats, and then we all burst into laughter. I see the tension leave Jared's shoulders as a smile blooms on his mouth.

I grip his hand, proudly looking up at him, my free hand wrapping around his forearm as I snuggle against his side. "Guys, this is Jared. This is Mum, Anne. And Nanna, Peggy." I point to each lady in turn and give his hand a little reassuring squeeze.

He shoots them a charming, self-assured smile. "Ladies, it's lovely to meet you. Amy's told me a lot about you both." His tone is the professional, polite one he uses whenever I call him at work.

Nanna's eyes light up, and she sends him a mischievous smile. "You're even better-looking than I pictured. And I have a *very* vivid imagination." Her tone is flirty, and I roll my eyes.

"And so it begins," I groan.

Jared laughs awkwardly. "Uh, thanks."

I chuckle and shoot him an *I told you so* look. "Just so you remember, this was your idea to come …"

SIXTEEN

We've been here four hours already, and surprisingly, both Mum and Nanna are actually staying on their best behaviour.

Jared is doing amazing. He's holding his own and managing to keep up with the fast stream of conversation, he doesn't flinch or mention it when Puzzle passes gas, he politely has his palm read by my nanna even though I can see he doesn't believe a word of what she said. He drinks all the tea they've plied him with, and he even has a tour of the garden. He's just generally being the all-round supercute, polite, adorable guy I've gotten to know over the last five weeks. He's charmed them completely, and I couldn't be prouder. He makes my heart melt.

"We should probably make a move, miss the traffic?" I suggest, looking over at him now.

He's currently in the middle of a game of gin rummy with my nanna and losing badly because he has no idea that she's cheating whenever he looks away.

"Hmm?" he grunts, chewing on his lip and frowning in concentration at his cards.

"Leave? We should probably go once you've finished that hand," I reason.

MAN CRUSH MONDAY

Mum leans forward. "Oh, can't you stay the night? I have some burgers in the freezer. I'm sure Jared could drag the barbeque from the shed and get it going?"

I scrunch my nose in apology. "We can't, Mum."

"Ha! Rummy!" Nanna shouts, slapping her cards down on the table and smugly pointing at Jared. "Loser!"

He laughs and shakes his head. "How did you beat me five times in a row?" He looks at her cards and frowns, moving them around to see what she had. "And how did you get four aces again? Did you shuffle them properly from last time?" His forehead creases with a frown, and I can tell the suspicion is starting to dawn on him now.

Nanna's eyes sparkle with mischief as she shrugs in answer, puckering her wrinkled lips and reaching down to stroke the dog who's fast asleep on her bony lap.

Mum cocks her head to the side. "Jared, what do you think?"

He drags his gaze away from the cards and looks from Mum to me and back again, his expression blank. "Sorry, Anne, what did I miss?"

Mum smiles. "Amy said you have to leave now. But I've just suggested you two should stay the night. I'll make us some dinner. You could just go home tomorrow. Saves you from rushing off tonight in the dark."

"Mum, we can't." I butt in. "Jared has stuff he needs to do tomorrow morning for work. That's why we said we would just come for the day," I lie quickly. It is something I prepared for this exact occasion. We planned on a short visit, and I knew she would ask us to stay, but I don't want to push my luck too far.

"Oh"—Jared looks at me—"I don't mind."

I raise one eyebrow incredulously because he's going off-script. "But what about your work stuff?"

A smile twitches at the corner of his mouth. "I can just do it in the afternoon."

"Well, we didn't bring a change of clothes or anything." I try a different tactic.

I would be okay. I have spare stuff here for emergencies, but Jared literally only has what he is wearing. *Surely, he doesn't really want to spend the night?*

"I'll just wear this stuff again tomorrow," he replies casually.

I glance back at my mum, seeing her joyful smile, and decide to try and give him one last opportunity to say so if he doesn't want to stay. "I only have a single bed here."

His eyes glimmer with amusement at my list of excuses. "Then, I guess we'll be sleeping pretty close."

He raises one eyebrow, and I feel the smug twitch of his lips like a jolt between my thighs.

Mum claps her hands and stands with a triumphant smile. "That settles it then! Jared, can you be a dear and go into the shed and pull out the barbeque?"

A confused frown creases his forehead. "Barbeque? It's the end of October," he says incredulously, as if the time of year makes any difference.

Like I said before, we're outdoor garden people. Even in the rain, my mum and nanna will sit out, just under their gazebo.

Mum scoffs, "What difference does that make?"

Jared doesn't answer, just stands up and nods. "Shed is that way?" he asks, pointing at the end of the garden as if it were the most natural thing in the world.

"I'll go sort the burgers," Mum says, heading off towards the house, calling Puzzle to go with her.

Nanna gathers up the playing cards, her beady eyes flicking to me. "Is he a Gemini?"

I shake my head. "Nope, Libra," I confirm.

She purses her lips in thought and then shrugs. "A Libra, really? Hmm, interesting." Then, she leans in and grins at me. "He looks at you like you're his dinner. It gives me chills."

"I know, right?" Laughing, I sit back and watch across the garden as he struggles to haul the large gas barbeque through the small shed door. I love the way Jared looks at me; it gives me chills too. "I'd better go help him." I push myself up from the table and walk to his side, pulling open the door wider and helping him line up the machine so it has millimetres of space to clear the door.

When we finally get it outside, he smiles over at me and then nods back towards the table as he takes my hand and pulls me flush against his body. "How am I doing with them?" he whispers, his eyes tight with worry.

I smile reassuringly. "You're killing it."

A wide grin spreads across his face as he steps closer to me and plants a noisy kiss on my lips before proceeding to drag the barbeque a safe distance from the shed, so he can light it.

While he's busy connecting the gas bottle up, I head inside to help Mum. She's slicing burger buns in half on a chopping board, a couple of boxes of supermarket burgers ready on the counter.

Mum smiles at me as I walk to her side. "He's wonderful."

A dreamy sigh drops from my lips as I lean a hip against the counter. "Isn't he?"

She clears her throat. "But …"

I flinch, looking over at her, shocked. "There's seriously a but?"

There are no *buts* where Jared is concerned.

Mum nods, her mouth pressed into a thin line as she holds her finger and thumb a sliver apart. "Just a really little one. It's just … he's so different to your usual guys. He's lovely and polite and extremely good-looking. But you usually go for the life and soul of the party, the one you have to compete with for attention. You're an extrovert through and through; he's more of an introvert. I'm not saying you're not suited because I can see you get on like a house on fire, and you clearly adore each other. But from what you've always told us about him, I was expecting someone distinctly quirkier."

I nod in understanding and shrug. Jared isn't the waste of space, idiotic man-child I'd normally bring home; she's right. "I suppose he's a little different to my usual picks, yes."

She purses her lips and looks at me. I can tell she's reading my mood to gauge my feelings. She always does this. She doesn't even really need to ask how I'm feeling; it's probably written clear as day on my face for her.

"But you're happy. He makes you happy." It's a statement, not a question.

A content sigh leaves my lips. "He makes me really happy. I'm so in love with him." It's all I can think of to say, and it's the truth. I fell in love with him on that train, and it's only grown stronger as time has passed.

Her eyes shine with emotion as she steps forward and cups my cheek. "And that is all a mother ever wants to hear. Like I said, he's wonderful. Forget I even said a *but*." She picks up the boxes and motions to the door. "Come on then. Let's go eat."

A couple of hours later, Nanna excuses herself off to bed, and Mum stands and starts stacking up the empty plates and glasses we didn't bother to clear away from dinner earlier in the evening.

"It's getting a bit chilly and damp in the air now. I'm going to go to bed. You two should move inside," Mum says.

I nod. I'm ready for bed now too. I'm always up for that when Jared is around. "I think we'll probably just go to bed too."

I pick up the two empty wine bottles we managed to polish off tonight. Well, I say *we*, but it was mostly my mum and nanna. Jared and I only had a glass and a half each.

Jared reaches out, closing his hand over my mother's wrist when she goes to lift the stack of plates. "I'll take that, Anne. You get yourself off to bed. Amy and I will wash up."

I raise one eyebrow at him. "That's a bit of an assumption to make about me."

He grins. "Sorry. Correction: I'll wash up, and Amy will supervise while watching my butt, like she usually does."

I nod, giggling because I didn't know I'd ever been caught looking at his bum when he washed up. "Better."

Mum yawns. "Are you sure?"

"Positive." Jared stands and picks up the dirty dishes, striding confidently to the house without another word.

"He's a keeper, that one," Mum says when we're alone, winking at me before leaning in and planting a kiss on my cheek.

I glow with warmth despite the chilly air and follow her inside. In the kitchen, I watch as she goes on tiptoes and grips Jared's shoulders, pulling him down so she can kiss his cheek too.

He's got soapsuds up to his elbows, and he is in the middle of scrubbing a plate, but I see him swell with pride as he grins at her.

I pick up a tea towel and dry the stuff as he passes it to me, putting it away in a bid to get to bed quicker. When we're finally finished, I smile seductively, and we make an escape for my bedroom.

His warm, soft hands are on my waist, under my jumper, and his mouth is nuzzling at my neck, making my tummy flutter in anticipation of some naked snuggling with him as we stumble across the lounge towards the back hallway where the bedrooms are located. As we round the corner, Mum is just stepping out of the only bathroom down the hall. She's already in her silk pyjamas.

One of her eyebrows rises, and she holds up a hand to halt us.

"I obviously don't mind you two staying the night together, and what you do in the privacy of your own homes is none of my business. But under my roof, I don't want to hear any sex," she states. She turns to Jared and points at his crotch. "If I do, I'll put a curse on your penis, and it'll shrivel and drop off. And don't think I can't do it."

Jared laughs, his hand gently stroking my back. "Understood."

"G'night, Mum." I roll my eyes and tug on his hand, pulling him into my small box room. There's barely any space for furniture in here, just a bed, wardrobe, and a shelf that I use as a dressing table.

His eyes roam around, settling on my single bed, and a small smile tugs at the corner of his lips. "You weren't kidding about the bed."

Reaching for the bottom of my jumper, I tug it off over my head and drop it on the floor. His eyes darken immediately and drop to my breasts covered only in a pink lacy bra. My teeth sink into my bottom lip as I reach for him, but surprisingly, he steps back, accidentally bumping against the door because the space is so tight.

He shakes his head. "Oh no, I'm not risking a shrivelled dick."

Ignoring his protest, I begin to open the fly on my jeans, my fingers lingering teasingly across my tummy and hips. I can see the pained, wanting expression on his face. "She only said she didn't want to hear it. We'll be quiet."

He scoffs, shooting me a smug smile, "Baby, you can't be quiet." Before I can push my jeans down over my hips, he steps forward, wrapping his arms around me. "Don't. For Christ's sake, don't. I can't handle it." He closes his eyes and holds me against him.

I chuckle at the needy quiver in his voice. "Seriously? She was only joking around."

MAN CRUSH MONDAY

He nods, kissing the top of my head. "Yes, seriously. Not tonight. Come on; I'm doing so well. Let me at least respect her rules. If you take off those jeans, I'm going to fuck you, and she'll hear it—believe me. The whole damn street will hear it and know my name."

The promise and sexy growl in his voice, coupled with his thickening arousal I can feel against my tummy, forces a needy whimper from my lips. I groan, looking up at him to check that he's serious. Unfortunately, he is.

I pull back and sigh heavily, my disappointment crushing. "Fine, but you're making it up to me tomorrow."

"Without a doubt." He swats my behind, and I flush with pleasure.

I awkwardly step around him in the tight space and pull open a drawer in my wardrobe, finding the spare pyjamas I keep here. "I'll go get changed in the bathroom. I need to take my make-up off anyway."

I don't wait for an answer as I slip from the room, pulling my top on over my head as I go. In the bathroom, I change and do my business. By the time I get back to my bedroom, Jared is in bed and has turned off the light. I stop in the doorway, looking through the gloom at this huge beast of a man stretched out on my childhood bed. His feet protrude from the end, and he takes up three-quarters of the space. It's surprisingly sexy.

Sighing, I close the door and traipse over to the bed. "I take it, I'm against the wall?" I guess, reaching out in the dark to feel he's lying at the edge of the bed.

"You want me to? I don't mind; it's just that you usually sleep on my left side," he replies, shifting to the side.

I put my hand on his bare chest and halt his movements, secretly loving that I have a usual side. "It's fine."

I lift a leg, accidentally kicking him as I manoeuvre over the top of him, both of us laughing and me pretending not to notice how turned on he is still. As I settle down at his side, trapped between his hot, hard body and the wall, his arms wrap around me, pulling me against him as his leg tangles with mine.

When he kisses me, I smile against his lips. "Don't start something you can't finish."

He chuckles and pulls back.

Light creeps in from under the door and through the crack in the curtains, so I can just about make out his face in the murky darkness as he strokes a hand through my hair.

I close my eyes, sleep calling me already as I snuggle against him, loving the feel of his body against mine. He smells divine. I want to crawl inside his skin and live there.

Suddenly, he lets out a heavy sigh.

I blink up at him. "Are you okay?"

He dips his head, pressing a soft kiss against my forehead. "Yeah. I was just lying here, thinking."

"Did you hurt yourself?" I joke, running my hands down his back, stopping just before I get to the waistband of his boxer shorts, trying to respect his boundaries tonight.

He huffs a laugh, his hold on me tightening. "Amy, I know we've only been together for five weeks, and that's not very long really. But I just gotta tell you … being with you is like falling down a rabbit hole. It's disorientating and scary but exhilarating. I have no idea how deep that hole is—maybe I'll just keep falling forever—but I really can't wait to find out."

I gulp at his sweet words, emotion hitting me and making my eyes prickle with tears. "Jared …" I breathe.

"I love you," he adds.

The three words from his mouth hit me like a punch directly to the heart. He loves me. My mouth pops open in shock, and my fingers dig into his back. I wasn't prepared. I had no idea how incredible those three simple words could sound until that moment.

He leans in, kissing my lips while I'm still reeling from the shock of it. I feel a tear slide down my cheek as his hand traces up my back to tangle in my hair. The kiss is so full of emotion and affection that I feel it in every nerve ending. My whole body prickles with pleasure and happiness.

When he pulls back, kissing my lips, my nose, my forehead, I whimper and close my eyes. I've never felt happier than at that moment, lying in the dark with him.

"I love you too, you know," I whisper against his throat.

I feel him smile against the top of my head. "I do now."

I grin up at him in the darkness, hyperaware of where his body is in relation to mine. "Jared, shut up and kiss me."

And so he does.

When I wake in the morning, the bed beside me is cold. I squint against the shadows, reaching out my hand for Jared … but he's not there.

I frown and sit up, rubbing at my eyes and stretching like a cat as my body shakes off some of the tiredness. Morning snuggles with Jared are my favourite, so I'm a little bit miffed to wake on my own.

Swinging my legs over the side of the bed, I throw off the quilt and pad across the room, yawning. As I step out of my bedroom, the delicious smell of bacon and eggs greets me, and I follow the scent down the hallway and across the lounge to the kitchen. It's there that I'm greeted by Jared's naked back and my nanna's wide grin. He's sitting at the table, shirtless and sockless, just in a pair of low-hanging jeans. In front of him is an almost-empty plate with the remnants of some scrambled eggs. He's chewing on toast and chatting with my nanna like it's the most natural thing in the world for him to be doing. My mum is in her velvet dressing gown, hair in rollers, washing up pots and pans at the sink.

I smile and head over to him, trailing my hand across the tops of his shoulders, savouring the feel of his skin under my fingertips. He looks over and offers me a warm smile as his arm slips around my waist.

"Good morning, gorgeous," he says against my lips as I bend to kiss him.

"Hey. I wondered where you'd gone."

He smiles apologetically. "Sorry. I got up to go to the bathroom and got collared by this one," he jokes, hooking a thumb towards my nan.

My nanna beams over at me and pushes a clean teacup in my direction. "There's some in the pot, love. Sorry I stole your man for a little while. Jared has been helping move some boxes that were too heavy for your frail, old nan."

Jared smiles affectionately at her, and I narrow my eyes, wondering what she's up to.

Frail, old nan, my arse. There is nothing frail about my nan in the slightest; she is the toughest old bird I know.

"It's not a problem. And the breakfast more than made up for it." Jared pats his tummy. "Thank you, Anne."

"You're very welcome," my mum replies.

I plop myself down on Jared's lap and take the piece of toast from his hand, taking a bite. "Do I smell bacon?" I smile expectantly over at my mum.

Mum shrugs, shooting me an apologetic smile. "Sorry, love. That was the last of it and the eggs. There's cereal, if you're hungry?" She pushes a box of cornflakes towards me.

I gasp, faking outrage. "Oh, that's nice, huh."

Jared chuckles, his body shaking under mine as he wraps his arms around my waist.

My mum shrugs unapologetically, an amused smile twitching at the corner of her mouth. "Jared's the favourite now. You'll just have to deal with it."

I sigh and look over my shoulder at him. The twinkle in his eye makes my heart clench as I think about him saying those words to me in the dark last night. Everything has changed today. Those three words, just eight letters, have solidified our relationship and altered it forever.

I nod and rub my hand over the back of his neck, pressing myself closer to him. "Yeah, he's my favourite too," I admit and am rewarded with the eye-crinkled grin that I just love to death.

Nanna pushes herself up to standing, putting her hands on her lower back and wincing obviously. "Jared dear, if you're all done here, I have something else you could help me with, if you're sure you don't mind?"

"Of course, Peggy. Whatever you need." Jared immediately pats my thighs, signalling for me to move.

Raising one eyebrow, I vacate his lap and watch as he jumps up like an eager-to-please puppy, following my hobbling nan from the room.

"What's wrong with Nanna's back?" I ask worriedly.

Mum shakes her head. "Absolutely nothing."

I frown in confusion and reach for the teapot, pouring myself a cup. When I hear them in the hallway, I head to the door and lean on the frame, crossing one ankle over the other. The loft hatch is open, and Jared is stretching, reaching for the ladder. My gaze drops to his naked back, watching the muscles move and contract. It's hypnotising. As he bends over to pick up a box, I suddenly realise what my "frail, old nan" is up to. My suspicions are confirmed almost immediately. As he climbs the ladder, Jared's bum gets level with Nanna's face. Her eyes narrow, and her hand goes to her mouth as she sighs in appreciation. She's looking at him like he's a snack.

My mouth drops open in shock before I'm overcome with a fit of giggles.

Mum steps to my side, leaning on the wall next to me, sipping on her tea. "She's playing the fragile, old lady card to perfection, and she's had him lugging boxes and moving furniture around for the last hour. Poor lad has no idea," Mum says, her eyes fixed on my hot boyfriend too.

"She's a damn pervert." I chuckle.

She nods. "In her defence, I've enjoyed the spectacle too. Very well done, sweetheart." She winks at me before patting me on the shoulder and heading back to her washing up.

SEVENTEEN

"**W**ow. You look absolutely amazing." Jared's eyes do a slow, sweeping appraisal of my body as his bottom lip rolls up into his mouth.

Tonight is his work function, and I've been painstakingly getting ready for the last two hours. Based on his expression, my preparations were worth it.

I proudly raise my chin and beam at the lust I can see clear as day on his face. Reaching down, I smooth the skirt of my sparkly, slinky, fitted black evening gown I shimmied my way into. The dress hugs my curves in all the right places without being too over the top, there's a beautiful illusion neckline that makes my cleavage look killer, and I'm even wearing heels. Granted, they're only one and a half inches, but they're heels!

Jared steps into my flat and tosses his car keys onto the sideboard. He puts down his overnight bag before reaching out, touching the material of the dress as his eyebrows pull together, and he lets out a strangled sigh. When his eyes meet mine again, they're black like a shark's, and I can see a muscle twitching in his jaw. From that one look alone, I feel incredibly sexy. I'm not the most beautiful girl in any room, but with Jared looking at me like I'm a glass of water and he's been lost in the desert for a month, I feel like I am.

"You look simply stunning. I can't wait to take you out of this dress later." His voice is hoarse and thick with arousal.

I swallow my lust and sigh. "You might have some trouble. I'm wearing the biggest, tightest pair of hold-me-in knickers known to man. I don't even know how I'll get them off. I might have to live in these things now."

My Spanx go from just under my boobs to mid-thigh, and putting them on was one of the hardest things I'd ever tried to do. I am dreading attempting to go to the toilet later without Heather there to help crowbar me back into them.

"I'll get them off you; don't worry." His eyes glitter with amusement as he raises my hand to his lips and plants a soft kiss on the back of it, sending my pulse skyrocketing.

Nodding behind me, I pull him forward a few steps, so we're in front of my full-length mirror that's mounted on the wall in the hallway. Standing next to Jared, who's decked out in a black three-piece suit and tie, white shirt, and shiny black shoes, I can't help but grin at our reflection. We look great together.

"Damn, we look so hot, even I hate us," I joke as his arm slips around my waist.

He laughs, and his phone beeps with a message. Pulling it out, he checks his text. "The Uber's here. Are you ready to go?"

I nod quickly. "Yep. Let me just grab my bag." I pick up my clutch purse, shoving in my lipstick, phone, and powder compact, and some cash before taking Jared's hand and letting him lead me out of the building and down the stairs.

My stomach rumbles in the taxi, and Jared smiles.

"Don't worry, baby. There'll be food there."

"Is it a buffet? If so, I'm gonna show it who's boss," I joke.

"Lady in the streets, freak at the buffet," he replies, winking at me.

When we pull up outside the hotel, I let out an appreciative whistle. It's on the outskirts of the city and huge; it's quite secluded and set in beautiful grounds with trees and sweet-smelling blooms that hit you as soon as you step out of the taxi. The gravel driveway to the hotel is lined with sculpted conifer trees that are lit from the base, casting a beautiful glow. It's magnificent.

"Wow, this is gorgeous," I whisper, looping my arm through Jared's when he holds it out in offering.

As we step inside, I gasp and look around. The reception is beautiful, all stone floors and shiny surfaces. A concierge steps up to us and smiles; he's carrying a silver tray laden with flutes of bubbling champagne.

"Good evening. Are you with Jenkins and Banner?" he asks.

Jared nods, and the concierge smiles, offering us the tray. I raise my eyebrows and watch as Jared takes two glasses. Suddenly, I feel out of my depth. Unless I'm at a wedding, posh dresses, beautiful hotels, and free champagne are not really things I come across in my life.

"Um, I don't actually like champagne." I wince apologetically, and Jared nods in understanding, setting one glass back on the tray.

"No problem. I'll get you something else." He turns to the concierge. "Is there a bar?"

"Yes, sir. Inside the ballroom where your function is being held, there is a fully stocked bar." He points to a huge set of oak doors at the end of the hallway where another waiter is poised to open the door for us.

My feet are rooted to the spot, and I take a couple of deep breaths. I look up at Jared for reassurance, and he smiles down at me, setting his hand on the small of my back, guiding me forward.

As the ballroom door opens, I gasp in delight. There's a live brass band playing music off to one side near an empty dance floor. A few people are already standing around, chatting in little groups. The scent of something delicious fills the air, and my mouth waters. The room itself is massive with a high ceiling, polished marble floor, and gilded gold edging, and several sparkling chandeliers hang from the ceilings. There are about fifteen large round tables, all laid out with gleaming cutlery and side plates and beautiful, understated flower arrangements in the centre. It's magnificent and lavish and like something out of a magazine from a celebrity wedding.

"Wow, your company is paying for all of this? Is there a special occasion?" I whisper, still looking around in awe as I sway unconsciously to the background music.

Jared leans in conspiratorially. "Apparently, there's always a lavish party around this time, a kind of early Christmas party, but rumour has it, they pushed the boat out a little further this year because of the merger. There will be staff here from J and B and also Barr, the company we're currently in merger talks with. I would imagine this is all to impress."

I nod in understanding.

Jared motions towards the bar, and there are a few people crowded around it already. "I'll go get you a drink. Glass of rosé?" he checks, cocking his head to the side.

I smile and nod, brushing my hand over his jacket, catching a finger in his waistcoat, and giving it a playful tug. "Yes, please. I'll wait here for you."

He sighs and leans down, gently kissing my forehead. "Thank you for coming with me. I really hate these things."

I smile and rub against him. "I can tell."

Jared has stiffened since we got out of the taxi, and his body language has completely changed from the usually relaxed guy I know to this professional, hard-faced one. He looks uncomfortable, and although he fits into this sumptuous place perfectly, I know he would rather be anywhere than here tonight, socialising with his "subordinates."

"I love you," he says, tracing the back of his knuckle across my cheek, leaving a burning trail in its wake.

"I love you too," I reply earnestly.

He sighs again and walks off through the crowd, heading towards the bar as I wander around, touching tablecloths and munching on tiny entrees the waiting staff is handing out. Armed with two chicken skewers I just procured from a petite waitress who told me her name was Wendy, I stop next to a friendly-looking girl with a red dress on. She's laughing with another girl and a guy in an ugly brown suit. She looks up and catches my eye, smiling tentatively.

"Hi," I greet, waving like a dork and deciding I need to get the mingling started. Networking is what these things are usually about. "I love your dress."

She looks down at it and smiles. "Thanks! I love yours too. And your hair, oh my God, it's lovely. I wish I could go pink or lavender grey." She lets out a dreamy sigh, and I reach up to touch my rigorously styled locks that Heather teased into an elegant up-do for me.

"Thank you. It takes some work," I admit. I have to touch up my colour every four weeks, but it's worth it. I love my chalky-coloured hair.

"I'm Holly. This is Camilla and Gus." She waves at the couple she's with.

"Amy." I politely shake their hands.

"You don't work for J and B. At least, I've not seen you around. Do you work for Barr?" Holly asks, taking a sip of her champagne.

I shake my head, about to answer but stop as two more people join us.

Holly grins. "Perfect timing. Amy, this is Greg and Paul," she introduces the newcomers.

I smile warmly at them and shake their hands too.

Paul groans theatrically. "Guess who we just saw."

There's a collective grumble, and I look around, waiting to be enlightened.

"Oh great, he's arrived. I hope we don't have to talk to him," Holly grumbles.

Paul nods. "Me too. I checked the seating plan though, and thank fuck, we're not sitting with him. He's apparently bringing a plus-one with him tonight."

"A plus-one? What kind of insane idiot would date a guy like that?" Gus responds, scrunching his nose up. "Oh, did you hear I got threatened with a disciplinary today? Missed a deadline for my end-of-campaign report." He shakes his head in apparent anger.

"Who are you talking about?" I ask.

Gus blows out a big breath, and Holly answers, "Our manager. He's a nightmare."

I suddenly get a sinking feeling in my stomach. I think I've allied myself with the wrong people.

"Oh shit, he's coming over," Gus says, his eyes widening as they all stand up straighter and readjust themselves as if they weren't doing anything.

"Christ, why does he have to be so hot?" Holly complains. "Look at him, all fine and sexy in that suit. If he wasn't such a bloody tyrant, I'd fancy him something rotten."

Camilla shrugs, her eyes firmly latched over my shoulder. "I still fancy him. I like bossy, grumpy men."

Both the girls laugh, and my stomach clenches. I don't like this conversation at all.

"Jeez, he's always so broody. I think if I ever saw that man smile, I'd burst into flames. I'm not sure he's even capable of it." Holly rolls her eyes and takes a sip of her drink.

I don't even need to look around to know Jared is coming over with my drink.

"He's capable," I confirm, smiling awkwardly as she looks at me quizzically.

I see the moment the penny drops. Her eyes widen in horror, and I smile sympathetically before turning just as Jared stops behind me, holding out my glass of wine.

"Hey, there you are. Thank you," I greet.

His eyes meet mine, and I see how tense he is as he nods politely in greeting to the people I'm standing with.

"Good evening, everyone. I see you've met my girlfriend already."

I hear some barely concealed gasps behind me, and I fight the urge to laugh. It's not my fault they didn't let me say who I was before they started bashing my tyrant boyfriend right in front of me.

"Good evening, Jared," Paul says eventually.

Gus doesn't speak, just gives a polite nod with tight features, but it doesn't seem to bother Jared in the slightest as his arm slips around my waist, pulling me against his side.

The girls offer a stunted greeting, but Holly is staring at me with horrified eyes, just waiting for the moment I drop them into trouble, I'm guessing.

I clear my throat. "So, apparently, I've met some of your team," I say brightly. "The gang was just telling me that we're not sitting with them tonight; we're on a different table, apparently."

Jared raises his chin, and his lips press into a thin line. "Ah, shame."

The atmosphere is so thick that it's almost cloying, but thankfully, Wendy—the chicken skewer waitress from earlier—suddenly comes over, grinning at me as she offers me a tray of baked cheese balls. She chuckles as I rub my hands together and greedily choose three.

"Thanks, Wendy!"

I grin sheepishly and look up to see Jared shaking his head, grinning down at me—the crinkled-eyes grin that makes my heart stutter.

"I see you've made friends with the bearer of food already," he says.

"Of course. Rule number one."

"Cheese is life," he adds, nodding.

"Exactly." I reach up and pop a cheese melt into his mouth.

He playfully rolls his eyes and loops his arm around my shoulders as all five of his co-workers watch the exchange with barely concealed shock on their faces. When someone clinks a glass and asks us to take our seats in preparation for dinner, Jared catches my eye and sends me an apologetic smile.

Dinner is awkward at first, but after a while (and a few glasses of vino), everyone loosens up, even Jared. He doesn't talk much, and I get the distinct impression that he's decidedly more reserved, shy even, than he is when it's just the two of us. I don't mind too much; I chat enough for both of us.

There's a total of twelve people on our table, ranging in ages and backgrounds. Some of them work for Jared's company, some for the merger company, some are plus-ones like me, and some are clients. Dinner is punctuated with polite chitchat.

Between courses, Jared holds my hand under the table as I laugh at their jokes, exchanging ridiculous banter with them and hearing their work stories. They devour the free wine, but I, smartly, switch to water while I eat because I don't want to get drunk tonight and do or say something I shouldn't.

The food is scrumptious—though small! Even though I gorged on the appetisers and then proceed to eat all four of the tiny courses on offer (and Jared's dessert as well as my own), I will likely need to eat again before bed.

MAN CRUSH MONDAY

Almost as soon as dessert is done and it's socially acceptable, Jared stands and holds down a hand to help me from my chair. "Amy, let's go make the rounds. There are a few people I should say hello to." He looks around the table. "Excuse us."

I place my hand in his and let him lead me away from the table, as eager to make my escape as he is. Jared's first stop is to an older couple standing at the bar. The man turns as we approach and grins over at us, affectionately clapping Jared on the shoulder.

Jared tugs me to his side. "Michael, I'd like to introduce you to my girlfriend, Amy. Amy, my boss, Michael Briggs and his wife, Marnie."

Jared's introductions are polite and very formal. He's every inch the professional around these people; it's actually a real turn-on for me.

Michael's eyes land on me, and his grin grows larger. "Amy!" His hand engulfs mine and gives it a hearty shake. "How wonderful to meet you." He sends Jared a wink and then turns back to me. "Do you know what a genius you're dating? This guy!" He claps his hand on Jared's shoulder again. "Absolute whiz. Never seen anyone as hardworking and conscientious. Absolute gem he is."

"Easy, Michael. Have you had too much to drink already?" Jared jokes, raising both eyebrows at Marnie, who shrugs and nods, smiling guiltily.

Michael waves him off and leans in closer to me. "Did he tell you how he got the job here?"

I smile proudly at Jared, loving all these compliments being thrown around about him. "No, he hasn't said."

Michael laughs. "Okay, so picture this. Two years ago, I was pitching for an ad account for a well-known condiment company who wanted to branch out of their market and into making tins of baked beans. All very highbrow," he jokes, chuckling. "Anyway, I was pitching to them, my best and most well-laid-out plans. I thought I was a shoo-in. That account was practically in the bag.

Trouble was, this arsehole was pitching from the company he was working for at the time." He hikes a thumb at Jared and rolls his eyes. "I wasn't worried; the other company was small and didn't have much experience. Plus, Jared was barely out of nappies and only had small accounts under his belt. I figured the best guy would win in the end. Turns out, he did." He winks at Jared. "I lost the pitch to him. Then, over the next five months, I watched in awe and fascination as this guy and his marketing plan singlehandedly turned that company into a household name. Spectacular vision and ingenuity. I went to the board of directors immediately and told them if they didn't hire Jared Stone, I was resigning and setting up my own company, and I would hire him instead."

Jared is looking at his shoes, a frown lining his forehead, clearly uncomfortable with all the attention.

I squeeze his hand and beam over at him. "I didn't know that."

Michael nods. "Best hire of my life. The guy is a genius and has an aptitude for getting market trends exactly right. It's a talent. He'll be running this place soon." He sends Jared another playful wink that makes my stomach clench with pride and happiness. "Anyway, don't stand here talking to us old fogies. Go mingle and get some contacts." He gives us a gentle push away and turns back to the bar, ordering more champagne.

"Embarrassing," Jared mutters, shaking his head as he leads me away.

"Well, someone is a fan of yours here at least, Iceman," I joke, which earns me a laugh.

We slowly make our way around the room, engaging in polite chitchat with everyone but not lingering too long with any one person. I get the impression Jared is happier just to hover on the outskirts rather than really engaging properly with his colleagues and clients. I notice he doesn't smile. He's polite and friendly but a little stern-looking and totally professional. It's interesting, watching him be work

Jared. I can see now why Holly said she would burst into flames if she saw him smile. The knowledge that he is stingy with his smiles makes me even happier because it makes the ones I've garnered feel more special.

The whole time we work the room, the amazing big band plays swing music. When a singer takes the mic, doing excellent renditions of Frank Sinatra, Nat King Cole, and Dean Martin, my feet are itching to dance, and I can barely stand still as I sway to the beat and hum the melody.

"Why is no one dancing?" I ask, frowning at the empty dance floor.

Jared shrugs, playing with a lock of my hair. "I don't know. Maybe it's not that kind of party?"

I sigh and pout, which makes him laugh and lean down to kiss my nose. On the way to speak to someone else, we pass a toilet, and my bladder gives another dangerous squeeze. I groan. I've been ignoring it, but I can't put a toilet break off any longer. I've had too many glasses of wine and water. I'm going to have to brave the Spanx removal on my own after all.

"I need to pee," I whisper, stopping outside the toilet.

He nods. "Actually, I'll go, too, and meet you here."

I lean in, giving him a quick kiss before I head into the restroom. I'm immediately taken aback by how sleek and posh everything is in here too. It's one thing, the ballroom being all polished marble and expensive gold leaf gilding, but I didn't expect the luxury to continue into here. It's exquisite.

My full bladder forces me to abandon my examination of the swanky soaps and fluffy hand towels that are stacked on the countertops. I head into the toilet stall, groaning and swearing like a sailor, banging my head and elbows on the walls as I struggle to pull off my Spanx and pee. By the time I fight them back on again, I'm sweating and tired. Whoever said 'beauty is pain' was spot-on. When I finally manage to get my dress back into position and emerge from the stall, I spot a lady standing by the sinks, washing her hands.

I feel the blush creep up my cheeks as she's sure to have just heard the commotion I made during the struggle. "Sorry, Spanx," I say in explanation as she looks at me weirdly.

She nods in understanding. "Oh, in my day, we called them a girdle. Thankfully, I'm too old for that nonsense now."

I chuckle and smooth my dress as I head to the sinks, too, looking her over. She's likely in her late sixties, early seventies maybe, but in that rich way where people still look fifty. Her dress is spectacular yet understated—a dark grey ballgown with stones that glitter as the light hits them. She looks fabulous.

"You don't need one anyway. You look gorgeous. The hair, the dress. Wow." I let my gaze wander over her.

She looks so elegant and classy, effortlessly so.

The lady looks down at herself and laughs. "Thank you, dear. Do you work here?" She looks back up at me as I wash and dry my hands.

"Oh no. I'm here with my boyfriend." I can't help but smile at the word *boyfriend*.

She turns towards me, leaning her hip on the countertop. "And what do you think of the party?"

My facial reaction betrays me, and I scrunch my nose up in distaste. "Honestly? It's kinda boring and stuffy. Too many suits." I pull my lipstick from my clutch purse and lean towards the mirror.

The lady laughs and nods. "I have to agree."

Her agreement prompts me on, and our eyes meet in the mirror. "And why is it called a dinner dance? I was led here under false pretences. There's that great band, and no one is dancing! What a waste."

"Ah, it's always like that, I'm afraid." The lady watches as I apply a slash of fire engine–red lipstick to my lips. I bought it specifically for tonight, and it's decidedly raunchier than my usual nude gloss. "I used to be able to pull off a shade like that."

"What? You still can! Gorgeous face like that! Here." I turn and thrust the lipstick towards her, giving her an encouraging nod.

She hesitates for a second but then takes it, picks up a towel, and wipes off her own pink nude lipstick before applying mine. I shoot her a smug, knowing smile in the mirror as she nods in approval.

"Thank you. Sorry, I didn't catch your name." She hands me back my lipstick, and I pop the lid on and push it back into my bag.

"Amy."

"Very nice to meet you, Amy. I'm Gillian."

I step back and brush a couple of stray hairs back into place as I look myself over one final time. "Well, Gillian, I should probably get back to my boyfriend, or he's going to think I've fallen in. Or that I'm trapped in my Spanx." I motion my head back towards the stalls, and she laughs.

She heads for the door, pulling it open, and waves for me to go through first. I spot Jared leaning against the pillar, one ankle crossed over the other. He looks up and smiles at me.

I turn back to Gillian as we step out together. "There's my boyfriend. I'm not sure if you've met. Jared, this is Gillian. Gillian, Jared," I introduce them with a wave of the hand.

Jared's eyes widen, and his back stiffens as he stands up straight and stretches out his hand in greeting. "Ms Jenkins, it's very nice to officially meet you."

Ms Jenkins? I frown and look between the two of them, confused at the sudden change in his demeanour.

Gillian smiles and takes his offered hand, shaking it. "Jared …" She raises one eyebrow in prompt.

"Jared Stone. I'm chief advertising strategist."

Gillian smiles warmly and nods. "Oh, that's right. I've heard your name being bandied around. Didn't we steal you from another company?"

Jared nods. "You did. I joined the company about a year ago."

"That's right. Well, I've heard some great things about you. I've even seen a couple of proposals of yours pass my desk, but there never seems to be the time to take anything further. You know what?" Gillian looks at me and smiles before turning back to Jared. "I'll have my secretary schedule you some time for late next week. You can talk me through some of your ideas."

Jared's eyes widen fractionally, and his whole body stiffens, but he nods. "Okay, great. That sounds great."

Gillian steps back and smiles politely. "It was nice to meet you both. Oh, and, Jared, I think your lady friend would like to dance." She sends me a wink and a wave and turns, stalking confidently into the crowd that parts instantly for her as if she were Moses.

"Bye, Gillian," I call at the same time Jared says, "Good-bye, Ms Jenkins."

When she's disappeared into the crowd, Jared turns to me and shakes his head. "Do you have any idea who that was?" I shrug in reply, and he laughs, reaching up to rub the back of his neck. "That's Ms Jenkins, the co-owner of Jenkins and Banner …"

He raises one eyebrow, and I suddenly realise why he was so jumpy and nervous. She is his top, top boss.

My mouth pops open in shock and horror. "Oh God. I just told her the party sucked. And I told her about my Spanx."

Jared barks a laugh, reaching out to cup my face in both his hands. He tilts my head, so my eyes meet his. "I can't believe that just happened. I can't believe you just schmoozed one of the hardest and richest women in advertising in the ladies' loo. You're incredible."

When he dips his head and kisses me, my horror subsides, and my hands grip his waist for support as the kiss deepens. My body is now on high alert, as the taste of him causes my skin to have goosebumps and tingle.

When he pulls back, I let out a needy whimper and press closer to him. A smile tugs at the corner of his mouth, and one of his eyebrows arches. "So, apparently, you want to dance?"

I don't get to answer before his hand closes over mine, and he suddenly turns, giving my hand a tug to get me moving as he leads me through the crowd towards the shiny, untouched dance floor.

I gasp, my face burning with heat as I notice people's eyes following our movements. Some people even stop talking as we step onto the dance floor.

"No one else is dancing," I protest in a hushed whisper.

"Someone has to be the first." Jared shrugs and leads me to the middle. He smiles at me as he guides me to do a little twirl before he pulls me closer to him, lifting my hand and looping my arm around his neck before his hands slide down my body teasingly, slowly, holding me securely against him as he begins to sway softly to the beat of "Mr Bojangles."

My teeth sink into my bottom lip as I unleash a happy grin. This is the first time Jared and I have danced together, and it's in a place like this. I couldn't have asked for a more romantic setting. When he dips his head and kisses me, I don't even care that people are staring. Happiness consumes me, and my body softens against him, melding against him, savouring every second of it. Eventually, people follow our lead, and the dance floor fills up around us, but I'm lost in a bubble of bliss containing only him and me.

After a good few songs, it's almost midnight, and my feet begin to ache. I look up at him, and my heart thumps in my chest. This guy. I'm so in love with him that it's both terrifying and electrifying in equal measure.

I grip his tie and press against him. "Jared, take me home and fuck me until I pass out." I don't even care that people might have heard me. I'm done here, and I want to head to the after-party at my place.

He leans down, brushing his nose against the side of mine as he stares into my eyes. It's almost dizzying, my desire for him.

"Now, that would be my pleasure."

As I smile and pull back, I see the crowd around me casting subtle glances at us. Holly, Gus, Camilla, Greg, and Paul are openly watching from the dinner table they're still sitting at. The three guys seem shocked and impressed, and the girls are watching Jared with lustful eyes that make the hair on the back of my neck bristle. My guess is, they've seen a side to Jared they didn't know existed.

As Jared holds my hand tightly and we make our way out of the ballroom, I see Gillian off to one side, talking with a stuffy-looking gentleman. She raises her champagne flute in greeting and sends me a knowing smile. I wave, feeling the blush colour my cheeks as I press against Jared's side.

EIGHTEEN

When I wake on Saturday, it's already lunchtime, and I feel a little delicate, courtesy of the alcohol I consumed the night before. I'm alone in the bed, but I can hear the TV on quietly in the living room. Groaning, I push myself up and swing my legs out of bed, wincing as I realise my feet are still sore from the heels I wore the night before. My bedroom is in a bit of a state. My clothes are dotted around the floor, almost a perfect line from the door to the bed, discarded in a fit of passion. I step over my flesh-toned Spanx as I reach for my dressing gown. As he promised, Jared had no trouble whipping me out of them last night. I blush and grin at the memory. Not exactly my sexiest moment, but he didn't seem perturbed.

As I step out of my bedroom, I see Jared is sitting on the floor of my living room, his back leaning against the couch, as he works on his laptop at my coffee table. I can see spreadsheets and graphs and lots of numbers all in various columns on his screen. He's frowning at it in concentration. I smile and try to tiptoe across the room, so I don't disturb him, but he catches me.

"Good morning, sleeping beauty."

I grin and divert my course, heading to him instead as I lean down and kiss his lips. "Hi."

He smiles, one eye on the screen. "I just need to finish this, if you don't mind. Then, we can go do something or get lunch?"

"Sure." I plant a soft kiss on the top of his head and head for the bathroom, deciding on a shower after I take a look in the mirror and realise I look like Medusa's ugly sister. Sleeping in hair clips and full make-up is never a good look in the morning.

Jared is still beavering away, scribbling notes and tapping furiously on his keyboard when I sneak back to my room, dressing in my Spice Girls fitted T-shirt and a denim dungaree dress with thick black tights underneath. I dry my hair down and swipe on some eyeliner and nude lip gloss. Then, I head into the kitchen, making us a cup of tea.

When I set it down next to Jared's laptop, he looks up, seeming a little startled to see me fully dressed and ready. "Oh, thank you. Sorry, I didn't realise I'd been working that long. I thought I'd just be able to get these tweaks done, but the system has been glitching, so it's taking forever. There was a surge of clicks on social media overnight, so it's thrown my ROI off, and I've had to recalculate projections."

I grin, sitting on the sofa and pulling my legs up under me, having no idea what he's even talking about. "God, it's sexy when you get all nerdy," I admit.

He laughs and sets his laptop aside, running a hand through his messy hair as he uses one elbow to hoist himself up onto the sofa next to me. "If you think that's sexy, just wait until I start talking about algorithms and data structures."

I giggle and wrap my arms around his neck, crushing myself against him. "Stop, stop, I can't handle it!" I joke.

"You're so weird, Amy Clarke." He laughs and brushes his nose up the side of mine.

I shrug. "I can't help it if I find intelligence attractive."

His answering smile is beautiful. "Know what I find attractive?"

I shake my head in answer.

"Girls who find intelligence attractive." His thumb softly brushes across my cheek, leaving a burning trail in its wake. "I love you."

"My favourite three words in the world," I reply. My heart clenches, and I let out a happy sigh. "I love you too."

He leans in and kisses me, just a short, sweet kiss, but pulls back, smiling knowingly when my tummy rumbles. "Shall we eat?"

"Ah, my second favourite three words in the world," I reply smartly, which makes him laugh and roll his eyes.

"I don't know what to wear. Which looks better—this or the last top?" I ask, looking back at Jared, who's sitting on the edge of my bed, putting on fresh socks, watching me change from outfit to outfit, my nerves rising with each passing second. I hold the other top in front of me and then move it away again, so he can decide.

He sighs and shoots me a sympathetic look. "Amy, you look gorgeous. Please, will you just stop stressing?"

"But I want to make a good impression. I have to get it just right," I reply, my eyes flicking to my wardrobe again to see if any other meet-the-parents suitable clothing has magically appeared in the last thirty seconds.

Jared pushes himself up from the bed and walks over to me, wrapping his arms around me from behind, his bare chest pressing against my back, sending ripples of excitement through my body. His eyes meet mine in the mirror. "Amy, they're going to love you. It doesn't matter what you wear. Besides, you don't need to impress anyone, only me. And you do that on a daily basis without even trying." His eyes are sincere as they lock on to mine.

My insides dance with happiness as I put my hand over his, interlacing our fingers. "Aww, swoon!"

He laughs and kisses the side of my neck. "You look gorgeous. Wear that outfit."

I smile gratefully and turn my attention back to myself in the mirror. Black bell-style skirt and a fitted pale blue short-sleeved top. "Sure?" I purse my lips in consideration.

"Sure," he confirms, kissing my cheek before turning and walking back to the bed, riffling through his overnight bag.

He pulls out his aftershave and squirts a little on. My senses tingle with happiness as the smell wafts around me. I love it.

As he pulls a clean black shirt from a hanger and slips it on, buttoning it up, covering up his body so I can no longer sneak pervy glances at him in the mirror, he says, "You know, this whole packing-a-bag thing is getting a little tedious. I keep carting stuff over here all the time. I was thinking, maybe I should just leave some spare stuff here. What do you think?" He doesn't look at me as he says it, and I glance at the back of his head in the mirror, frowning in confusion.

"Spare stuff?" I hang my rejected shirt back in my wardrobe.

"Toothbrush, deodorant, a change of clothes or two …"

Holy shit. My mouth drops open in shock as I realise what he's talking about. He wants a drawer. A drawer in my place because he sees himself continuing to stay here often in the future. We are about to cross into the spare-toothbrush stage in our relationship. I want to fist pump the air in celebration, but I force myself to remain nonchalant as I shrug, pretending it's no big deal and that he hasn't just made my entire life.

"Sure, whatever you want."

He looks over his shoulder at me, his posture loosening a little as he smiles. "Yeah? Great. You can leave some stuff at mine too, if you want."

I smile, loving the offer, but shrug in rejection. "I probably won't stay at your place much, so there's no point."

I haven't stayed at Jared's posh palace apartment yet. My flat is just a ten-minute bike ride from my work; his place is approximately thirty-five minutes. I'm not sure I even have the stamina to ride Bessy that far. It's just easier for him to stay here. He drives; I don't. Also, since he often leaves for work before I'm even awake, staying at his place is more of a hindrance than a help.

I am staying at his place tonight though for the first time, and I'm more than excited about it. Tonight, after the party at his parents' house, he's driving us and his brother home, so it makes sense for us to stay at his place rather than just dropping Theo off and then coming back here.

"Yeah, true." He nods, seeming thoughtful, and then reaches into his bag, pulling out his wash bag and smiling devilishly at me. "I'm going to go find a spot for my stuff in the bathroom."

I laugh at his eagerness and turn back to the mirror, applying last-minute swipes of lip gloss and an extra dot of concealer on the stress-related zit that sprouted today.

By the time we're ready to leave and in the car on the way to his parents' house in Ely, I'm a bundle of nerves. It takes around twenty minutes to get there by car, according to Jared, and I spend at least eighteen of them trying not to hyperventilate. I've met parents of a couple of boyfriends before but never a whole family in one go like this. Usually, I wouldn't be bothered if they liked me or not, but I've never been so devastatingly in love with someone before. The old cliché of, *What if they don't like me?* is running through my head nonstop. Jared's parents are smart too; his mum is a chef at a high-end restaurant in

Ely, and his dad is an award-winning structural engineer. They are bound to take one look at me, ask me what I do for a living, and decide I am in no way good enough for their son—and they'd be right too. I'm not.

Jared tries to calm me, saying soothing things and putting his hand on my bouncing knee; he also tries to point out pretty architecture and Ely Cathedral in a bid to distract me, but I'm too lost in my worry to concentrate.

When we pull up outside his family home, I look up at it and don't want to get out of the car. My hands fiddle aimlessly. I pick at my manicured nails and cuticles, crunching nonstop on Jared's car sweets he keeps in the dash even though they taste disgusting because they're sugar-free.

Even in the quickly darkening evening light, I can see the house is beautiful. It's double-fronted with red ivy crawling up the walls and real hardwood windows, not the UPVC stuff. It looks huge and is a far cry from the compact bungalow I grew up in. And the gardens ... stunning.

Jared pulls into a sweeping double-aspect brick-weave driveway and parks off to one side outside a double garage.

I'm so out of my league here with these people. I feel nauseous, and I look over at Jared, silently begging him to read my mind and drive me straight home again. He reaches over and gently strokes my cheek as he smiles.

"Come on then, beautiful. Let's get this over with. They're going to adore you. Five minutes, and you'll have them eating out of the palm of your hand."

I raise one eyebrow, trying to appear confident. "You think it'll take me five whole minutes?"

He laughs and climbs out of the car, heading to the boot. I follow suit, slipping on my black silk bomber jacket and smoothing my skirt, ominously looking up at the house as I step to his side. Jared moves my overnight bag to one side and picks up the gift-wrapped present he's brought for his dad's sixtieth birthday. He told me it is a limited-edition film cell from his dad's favourite movie, *Citizen Kane*. As he picks it up, the tag flaps in the wind, and I catch sight of the writing. My heart stutters in my chest. The tag reads: *To Dad. Happy birthday from us! Love, Jared and Amy.* Us. That one little word gives me all the confidence I need to walk into the house with my head held high. Jared called us an *us*, and his toothbrush is nestled next to mine on my bathroom shelf. All is right in the world.

The front door is unlocked, so Jared lets himself in, guiding me along behind him. When we step into the house, my eyes dart around, taking everything in. It's large, high-ceilinged, and decorated beautifully. Soft music plays from out the back, and Jared's hand tightens on mine as he tugs me into the empty lounge.

"Wow," I mutter, looking around in awe as we walk through the living room and towards a set of open patio doors leading into the garden beyond.

It's like a show home. The inglenook fireplace is huge and has an old oak railway sleeper above it that matches the exposed ceiling timbers. My gaze zeroes in on the table that's been pushed against the wall and is laden with buffet food. I make a mental note on its location for later once the plastic wrapping has been removed.

As we get to the back doors, I see people, lots of people, and my nerves are back again. Stevie Wonder's "Superstition" plays softly in the background as I cling to Jared's hand for dear life. He reassuringly squeezes back, and we step into the fray.

The garden is lavish and landscaped. Fairy lights have been strung across the fence panels, and gas patio heaters and firepits glow around sporadically, banishing the slight chill of the early November evening. Bowls of cocktails with little labels in front of them garnish the table next to stacks of glasses. There's a table for gifts, and Jared adds *ours* to the pile.

"Jared, darling!"

I look around, forcing a polite smile onto my face as a lady steps out of the crowd and rushes over to us, her arms outstretched for a hug. I immediately guess this is his mother, Deborah. She's in her early fifties, I would approximate, and her hair is the exact shade of Jared's, but her eyes are blue. She's dressed impeccably in a gorgeous midnight-blue dress that I would hazard was very expensive. She engulfs Jared in a hug, and her eyes meet mine over his shoulder.

Her smile widens as she pulls back and turns to me. "And you must be Amy!"

I smile and extend my hand for a shake, but instead of taking it, she pulls me into a tight hug, awkwardly trapping my hand between us. My eyes widen in shock as I cop an accidental feel of her breasts.

"It's so lovely to meet you, dear. Jared hardly ever brings anyone home for us to meet. I think he's secretly ashamed of us." She pulls back and winks at me as she holds me at arm's length, obviously looking me over.

I feel my face flood with heat under the intense scrutiny.

"Oh, you look adorable. That skirt is to die for! You must tell me where you got it from," she continues. I look down at it and open my mouth to answer, but she loops her arm through mine and turns, pulling me forward. "Kenneth! Look, Jared brought his girlfriend!" She waves a hand at me, grinning excitedly as Jared's dad looks over at us. "This is Amy. Isn't she gorgeous?"

"Mum, take it easy, okay? You're traumatising her," Jared says, but I can hear the amusement in his tone. He raises one eyebrow at me. "Five minutes was a bit of an overestimate."

I chuckle and silently wonder what he's told her about me.

In the space of ten minutes, I'm introduced to everyone from grandads to next-door neighbours to family friends. The whole time, Deborah's arm is securely looped through mine as she parades me around the party, explaining who everyone is. Jared trails along behind us, glass of mocktail in his hand the same shade as my deadly cocktail I'm reservedly sipping on.

We've been there almost an hour when Carys, Jared's six-year-old niece, grumbles, "Grandma, when's Theo going to arrive?"

"I don't know, dear." Deborah shrugs and checks her watch before looking at Jared. "You should have brought him along with you. At this rate, he'll turn up just as the candles are blown out on the cake."

Jared shrugs. "He was working on some project. Said he'd be here once he finished it. You know what he's like when he's on a deadline. I haven't seen him for a couple of days. I've been at Amy's."

I smile at that and watch as Carys groans loudly and kicks her feet in impatience. When the song changes to Chubby Checker's "The Twist," I can't resist bopping along to the beat and grin over at her, knowing exactly how to alleviate her boredom. When I hold out my hands to her, her face lights up as she eagerly slips her hands into mine, and we both start doing the twist right in the middle of the garden. Within seconds, Deborah and a few of the other guests have joined in, and we're all twisting the night away. Jared watches from the sidelines, not joining in, but regarding me with a proud smile that I feel all the way down to my toes.

Mid-dance of the next song, Emily, Jared's older sister, walks back into the garden, sneakily popping a sausage roll into her mouth. "Theo's just pulled up in a taxi."

Carys lets out a delighted squeal and turns on her heel, abandoning the dancing as she shouts, "Funcle Theo!" and pelts into the house to see him.

I laugh at her excitement, and Deborah smiles.

"Funcle as in fun uncle," she explains.

"Something I'm not, apparently," Jared chimes in, rolling his eyes, but there's a smile at the corner of his mouth, so I know he's not taken offence to it.

Over the music, I can hear Carys talking inside the house, their voices growing louder as they approach. "Jared brought a girlfriend! Just wait until you meet her," I hear Carys gush. "She's like a pretty doll. I like her! I think she's going to be an aunticorn."

"What's an aunticorn?" Theo asks.

"Like a normal aunt crossed with a unicorn. So, like a regular aunt but better, basically," Carys explains.

"Basically," Theo repeats, laughing. "Come on then, squirt. Now that I'm here, the party can start."

I chuckle and turn towards the patio doors, smiling in anticipation. I'm excited to meet his brother; we've never actually met because he wasn't home the one time I was at their apartment. I wait a few seconds, and then Carys comes skipping out, beaming ecstatically.

My eyes flick up, and behind her, out steps ... Jared.

Except Jared is standing next to me and holding my hand. I frown, looking between the two of them, and then my mouth pops open in shock as it suddenly hits me.

"Holy crap. You're twins!" I cry excitedly.

They're the spitting image of each other, a perfect double, identical. Except that Jared is all pressed edges and immaculate neatness, and Theo is in ripped jeans, a *Little Shop of Horrors* T-shirt, and has ink stains all over his fingers.

"Did I not tell you that?" Jared asks, looking down at me quizzically.

I shake my head and continue to look between the two of them in awe. "No! When we spoke about family before, you just said you had a brother and a sister. No one mentioned anything about twins."

Deborah clicks her tongue and rolls her eyes. "You know why? Just in case you were wanting a baby, he didn't want to let the cat out of the bag about twins running in the family in case it scared you away. Would have frightened me away for sure," she jokes, winking at me.

Jared groans next to me. "Mum, seriously? Why are you like this?"

I chuckle and slip my arm around his waist, loving how I fit just right under his arm.

Theo is all smiles as he steps into the garden and greets his uncle and godfather, who are chatting by the door, offering big hugs and warm welcomes. When his eyes scan the crowd and he sees us all grouped together, his grin widens, and his eyes twinkle.

He marches over and pulls his mum and dad into a bear hug before kissing his sister on the cheek.

"Oh, finally, he graces us with his presence," Deborah teases.

Theo shrugs. "Better late than never, am I right?" He shoots her a smug smile before hugging his dad again. "Happy birthday, you old git."

I chuckle and stand back a little, not wanting to intrude, but Jared wraps his arm around me and pulls me forward again, smiling down at me.

His arm squeezes my waist as he gestures towards me. "Theo, this is Amy. The girl I've been telling you about." Jared nods to his brother.

I beam a smile at him, hoping to God I get his approval, too, because, so far, I seem to have won over the rest of them. Theo's gaze lands on me. I see his eyes tighten, and his easy grin falters for a second. His mouth pops open and then closed again as he comically looks from me to Jared and back again. He clears his throat and nods, a thin-lipped smile gracing his lips now.

"Actually, we've kind of already met. Amy is the conductor on the train I get on to London twice a month, though I didn't know her name until you just said it."

That's all it takes. Just one heartbeat for my world to fall apart. At his words, realisation smashes into me with the force of a wrecking ball. I literally feel the heat drain from my body as my eyes widen in horror.

Theo has been my Man Crush Monday all this time. Not Jared, but his twin brother.

NINETEEN

The air around me seems to disappear as my heart stops and then starts back up triple time.

Not only is Theo my crush from the train, but ... I also kissed him! Two weeks ago, on the train. I kissed him. It wasn't Jared. I kissed Theo.

The horror is building inside me, and I feel sweat breaking out all over my body.

Jared frowns down at me quizzically. "You've already met?"

I open my mouth, praying words will come ... but I've got nothing.

Thankfully, Theo jumps in and saves the day. "Only once or twice. I noticed her hair; that's all." His tone is dismissive and nonchalant, and I see Jared nod in satisfaction. Theo holds out a hand towards me, his whiskey-coloured eyes, an exact replica of Jared's, burning into mine. "It's nice to officially meet you."

His gaze is penetrating, as if he's silently trying to tell me something, but my brain has turned to mush.

My eyes flick up to Jared. He's smiling happily. He knows nothing.

Oh no, what do I do?

Around me, everyone is watching the exchange, and I become painfully aware that I'm standing there, frozen in horror, mouth agape, staring. I force myself to move, lifting my hand and putting it in his offered one, shaking it. "You too." My voice is barely above a whisper.

Tears are burning in my eyes. I need to leave. I'm about to lose it. My mind is whirling.

Jared looks down at me, his arm tightening on my waist in prompt. "Okay?"

I give an awkward nod and force a smile. "Yeah, yeah," I lie. "I just actually really need the bathroom. I think the alcohol has gone to my head." I exaggeratedly roll my eyes and look down at my empty cocktail glass.

Jared dips his head and kisses my temple. "It's at the top of the stairs, first door on the right."

He lets go of me, and I wobble on my unsteady legs as I rush inside, needing to be alone for a couple of minutes because the freak-out is creeping up on me at an alarming pace.

I set my empty glass on the table and hurry up the stairs, locking the bathroom door behind me and leaning on the sink. My breathing comes out in short, sharp wheezes. My eyes lock on my reflection in the mirror, and I loathe myself.

It is Theo that I've been crushing on all this time, Theo I've fallen head over heels in love with on those Mondays, Theo who did magic tricks and gave up his newspaper, Theo who helped old ladies off the train and shared his phone so little kids could watch cartoons.

I cover my mouth as a strangled whimper escapes. Tears well in my eyes as panic takes over.

When a knock on the door behind me sounds, I gasp and turn, looking at it in horror, praying it isn't Jared. Because ... what do I say to him now? *I thought you were someone else, and by the way, I snogged the face off your twin brother a couple of weeks ago?*

"It's occupied," I croak, watching as the handle turns.

"Amy, it's Theo. Are you okay?"

Oh God.

At the sound of his voice, my stomach clenches in anguish. "Yeah, I'm fine."

"Can I come in and talk to you real quick?"

I huff out a breath and debate on saying no. I want to put this off for as long as possible, but I know I can't. This needs sorting; it can't stay hidden.

I close my eyes and reach for the door lock, flicking it open. He opens it immediately and steps in, relocking the door behind him, trapping us in this small space together. I press back against the sink, and my eyes wander over him. He's exactly like Jared, the strong shoulders, the eyes, the mouth I kissed …

My breath catches in my throat as I quickly look away.

He laughs awkwardly and sweeps a hand through his hair, messing it up even further. "Look, I know what you're stressed about, and don't worry; I won't say anything."

I swallow around the lump that's formed in my throat and wipe away a stray tear as it silently streaks down my cheek.

"The kiss," he clarifies when I don't answer. "It all makes sense now. I'm assuming that scene on the train wasn't for me." He raises one eyebrow in question, and I nod dumbly. His lips press into a thin line. "I'll be honest with you; I was so shocked the other week when you kind of pounced on me. It came out of nowhere, and you were so different from your usual shy self on the train that I was taken aback. Now, I know why."

My heart is pounding. I need to sit down. "I thought you were Jared," I rasp.

He nods, watching as I sit on the edge of the bath and put my head in my hands. "Yeah. Not gonna lie, I did enjoy it, but it does make this a little awkward."

Awkward is the understatement of the century.

A strangled sob leaves my throat, and he crouches in front of me, gently placing one of his hands on my knee.

"Look, don't worry about it. It's happened before; you're not the first."

I look up at him through watery eyes and shoot him a disbelieving glare. "Jared's other girlfriends have kissed you and said you looked … oh God." I can't finish the sentence. My face flames with heat as I think about me pronouncing how perfectly fuckable he looked.

Theo chuckles darkly. "Not exactly like that, no," he admits. "But we've been mixed up plenty in our lives. Our own mother used to confuse us all the time until we were, like, eight."

"You're identical. I'm not surprised."

He shakes his head. "We're not exactly identical. We're mirror twins."

When I look up at him blankly, he moves to sit beside me on the edge of the bath, crossing his ankles. He seems to fill the whole space, and my own traitorous body reacts as my temperature bumps up a couple of degrees at the closeness of him. Then, another wave of loathing washes over me, and I hate myself even more for noticing how warm and hard he is while pressed against my side. I slide a few inches away before I go insane.

"Mirror twins," he repeats, turning towards me a little. "For example, I have a mole here." He reaches up and points to the small freckle he has under his right eye.

I look at it and nod. "So does Jared." I've kissed that tiny mark numerous times; it is my favourite.

Theo shakes his head. "No, Jared's is on the other side, under his left eye."

I frown in confusion and look at it again, and my mouth drops open in shock. He's right; it does look out of place. I didn't notice when he pointed before. It's such a small detail to overlook.

"We're mirror twins. It means, if we were to stand facing each other, we'd be the exact reflection of the other, like you looking in a mirror," he explains. "We're opposites in everything. He's left-handed; I'm right. He's left-footed; I'm not. Everything is the opposite, like a reflection."

I recoil and let that information sink in. It all makes sense.

Theo slaps his hands on his knees and stands up. "So, just stop stressing. I won't say anything about the kiss. I don't want to ruin what you've got going on with my brother. I've not seen him this happy in forever. Actually, I don't think I've seen him smile this much in his whole life. He's so reserved and quiet; he's a pretty guarded person, and he usually doesn't let people get to know the real him. But with you, he's able to be completely himself. He's utterly crazy about you. I know this because he's told me so."

Guilt is choking me, clogging my throat. My eyes fill with tears again.

He laughs and reaches out, taking my hands and pulling me to my feet. "Wipe those tears. Everything is fine, I promise." He passes me a wad of toilet tissue he's pulled from the roll.

I force a smile and reach up, carefully wiping at my face as I try not to smudge my make-up or make my eyes red. "Thanks, Theo."

After I flush the tissue and take a couple of deep breaths, I turn to face him. He smiles and leans in, wrapping his arms around me, engulfing me in a hug.

I gasp, shocked, but don't pull away. It's a nice hug, soft, affectionate. As I lean in and hug him back gratefully, I notice that he smells different, holds me differently, stands less stiffly than Jared does.

"Come on; it's okay. No one will ever hear it from my lips, all right? Our little secret."

He pulls back and zips his thumb and forefinger across his lips and then mimes throwing away the key, pretending to slam-dunk it into the plughole. It's so silly that I can't help but laugh.

"Get that game face on, and let's rock the shit out of this party. Someone mentioned cake and dancing. Just be warned: stay the hell away from my mum's cocktails because they're deadly."

I grin at that. "If your mum doesn't try to give you alcohol poisoning through a homemade cocktail, is she even your mum?"

He laughs loudly and looks over at me, his eyes twinkling with amusement as I follow him back down the stairs to the garden. "Look who I found. She got lost," Theo jokes.

Jared grins at me, the one that makes his eyes crinkle, and guilt hammers at my insides again.

TWENTY

N*othing's changed*, I try to tell myself.

But I know that's not true. Everything has changed.

I fight my guilt and torment, trying to pretend like nothing is wrong as Jared takes my hand and pulls me to his side.

"Okay?" he whispers, looking at me worriedly, as if he can somehow sense the building horror inside me.

No! I kissed your brother.

I force a smile and nod. "Yeah. I think it was the cocktail," I lie, pressing against his side as his arm slips around my shoulders.

One side of his mouth quirks into an apologetic smile. "I should have warned you. Sorry. I think her cocktails are, like, eighty percent vodka. They're toxic."

I chuckle and shrug. "Theo just said the same thing."

After that, I'm engulfed in the conversation happening around us. Their aunt Theresa is reminiscing about old times, bringing up tales of the twins and Emily's rebellion years and teenage angst. All the while, she's sipping on her lethal cocktail through a straw of all things. I find myself loosening up again. The ball of tension that settled in my stomach is slowly unravelling as Jared unconsciously strokes his thumb against my shoulder.

"Oh, and remember that karaoke machine you boys got for Christmas one year?" Aunt Theresa suddenly asks Jared. "You must have been about ten years old. You and Theo were the cutest things ever!" Her smile is so wide that it's almost manic.

Jared groans and closes his eyes. "Can we not, please?"

But Aunt Theresa chooses to ignore his obvious unease. "You wanted to start a boy band. Oh gosh, what was it you used to sing again? Deborah, can you remember? They'd sing it over and over for hours." She grasps her sister's elbow and gives it a little squeeze, her forehead creased in concentration as she tries to remember.

"Please stop talking," Jared begs, shaking his head.

Deborah laughs and nods. "Kris Kross. They had a dance and everything. Called themselves T and J."

My mouth drops open. *I need to see this immediately!*

"Mum. Stop. Talking," Jared says. His face is scrunched up in what I guess is mortification as he rubs at his forehead with his spare hand.

Theo laughs and playfully nudges Jared with his shoulder. "We should do it now for Amy. Revival of T and J!"

Jared scoffs, "I would rather shit in my hands and clap than do that right now."

Laughter erupts from the people milling around, and I almost choke on my drink, coughing around my fit of giggles.

Theo grins and turns to me. "You want to see it, Amy, right?"

My eyes widen as I nod in agreement, trying to stifle my laughter. "I don't just *want* to see it. I've *gotta* see it."

Jared turns and gives me the side-eye, which just makes me laugh harder. "Not happening, I'm afraid."

"Oh, come on," I tease, pouting at him.

He's saved from answering by a loud bang that echoes into the night.

I jump in fright, and Deborah squeals and claps her hands. "Ooh, the display is starting!"

I look up as more fireworks crackle and fizz into the sky.

Jared leans down, talking into my ear over the din, "There's a fireworks display at the local playing park. That's why we're outside most likely—free entertainment."

"Oh, okay. Frugal party planning. I like it." I nod and tap my finger to my temple.

He grins and sets down his empty glass, stepping behind me, wrapping me tightly in his arms, his chest pressing against my back as we both watch, oohing and aahing in all the right places. Turns out, his favourites are the loud ones that make your stomach quake, and mine are the ones that sizzle as they fall.

Where his arms are around me, he feels me shiver. It's getting colder now, and my thin bomber jacket is more for looks than practicality. The patio heaters aren't banishing as much of the cold as they should as the temperature drops.

"Are you cold?"

When I nod in reply, he pulls away and unzips his own jacket before leaning back against me and tugging the sides around me, so I'm cloaked in his delectable scent, trapped in his jacket with him. I can feel the warmth of his body that's seeped into the material, and it's wonderful. His arms go around me, tugging the jacket, so it covers us both as much as possible as he leans down, planting a kiss on my cheek. His breath and mouth are warm on my skin, and I press back into him further.

I hear his mum, "Aww," but I don't look over at her.

I just enjoy the moment and pretend that he's not making my heart ache with guilt.

When the fireworks finish and the last light from them fades away, leaving smoke trails in the sky, Jared turns to his dad. "Maybe we should move the party inside now? It's getting cold."

Kenneth nods. "Good idea. It is getting a bit nippy." He claps his hands to get everyone's attention. "Let's move inside now before we all catch our deaths."

I smile gratefully at Jared.

Deborah steps to our side. "Jared, can you help your father turn off all the patio heaters and put the covers on the firepits, please, darling?"

"Yeah, sure." He nods in reply, and the warmth of his body disappears as he steps away.

I try not to whimper at the loss of contact. I instantly feel a little vulnerable and lonely. As he walks off with his dad, Jared glances back over his shoulder, catching my eye and winking at me before he proceeds to do the Kris Kross legs-and-jump dance combo, and then he just carries on walking as if nothing happened.

I burst out laughing just as Deborah smiles and loops her arm through mine.

"Come on; you can help me unwrap the food."

My mood is immediately lifted. She said the magic word.

"So, Jared tells me you're a chef?" I ask as I start removing the plastic wrap from the trays and trays of food loaded onto the dining room table.

My mouth waters at the sight and smell of some of them. There are all sorts of posh nibbles on offer, not just your basic sausage rolls and cheese and pineapple on a stick (though those are there too). There are assorted sliced cooked meats and sandwiches, antipasti, various flavours of chicken skewer, dips, sliced breads, cheeses. It all looks homemade. I'm in heaven.

"I am. I love to cook. Do you?" she asks.

I scrunch my nose and shake my head. "I'm a disaster in the kitchen."

The next tray I unwrap contains some sort of bacon-wrapped potato bites, and a little groan of desire slips from my mouth. Just as I'm wondering if it's impolite to start eating them, Deborah pops a honey-glazed sausage in her mouth and winks at me.

I follow suit and eat a potato bite. My eyes drop closed as the flavour explodes on my tongue. "Oh God, this is amazing. Deborah, you are officially my new hero."

She chuckles, her eyes glowing with pride. "You know, you're probably not a disaster. Maybe you've just been cooking the wrong things," she suggests. "We should exchange numbers. I have lots of simple, easy recipes. I could WhatsApp them to you."

She raises one eyebrow in question, and I nod enthusiastically.

"That would be great. Can I have the recipe for this?" I ask, picking up another bacon-potato thing, which is like an orgasm in the mouth.

She smiles and nods.

People are starting to crowd around us now, eagerly picking over the food. I'm jostled as an uncle reaches over and grabs a handful of pork belly skewers.

"Come with me, Amy," Deborah says, nodding behind her.

I follow her into the kitchen, watching quizzically as she digs in a drawer.

When she finds what she's looking for—a pen and paper—she smiles and hands it to me. "Here, put your number on there."

I do as I was told, jotting my mobile number down.

She's watching me, her head cocked to the side, her eyes shining with affection. "You know, you're not Jared's usual type," she says as she pockets my number.

I frown, unsure if that's a bad thing or a good thing. "Oh, really? What's Jared's usual type?"

We haven't really discussed exes, only in passing when he told me his last girlfriend was more interested in his money than him.

Deborah scrunches her nose in distaste before quickly catching herself and schooling her expression. I feel my affection for her grow even more. "I've only met two of his previous girlfriends, neither of whom I liked very much. Both of them were tall, leggy, bimbo types with not very much personality."

I frown down at my very much *not* tall and leggy self.

Deborah must catch my expression because she steps closer to me and laughs, setting her hand on my arm, squeezing reassuringly. "Don't worry; I can tell by the lingering looks he gives you that he's *very* happy with the length of your legs," she says playfully.

I feel my cheeks warm and drop my eyes to the floor, my insides squirming with both pride and unease at this conversation. "Well, I'm glad to hear it."

"I'll be honest; you're more the type of girl my Theo would bring home. If you'd arrived with the both of them and I didn't know who you had come with, I would have bet my life on it that you were with Theo. He always goes for lovely, happy, chatty girls like you." She reaches out and cups my cheek with one hand.

Her words hit me like a punch to the chest because Theo was my usual type of guy too, not Jared. I don't have time to expand on that thought though because Jared sticks his head around the door.

"There you are. I've been looking for you. You're not talking about me in here, are you?" he asks, smirking at me as he steps into the kitchen.

I teasingly raise one eyebrow. "Yes. Are your ears burning?"

He grins and waves a hand towards his mother as he steps to my side. "Don't believe a single thing this woman tells you. She lies."

"Cheeky." Deborah laughs and swats him on the back as she heads out of the room. "Don't be too long in here, you two." She winks at me over her shoulder and pulls the door closed behind her.

"She likes you," Jared says as soon as we're alone. A proud smile twitches at his lips, and he steps closer, his eyes wandering my face in such a way that my insides quiver with anticipation. "They all like you. My aunt Theresa wants to keep you forever. I said I'd have to see what I could do." His finger traces across my cheek and follows the line of my jaw achingly slowly.

When he presses against me, one arm wrapping around my waist, pulling me flush against him, I can feel every hard inch of him, every coiled muscle, every bit of his power and strength. His eyes meet mine, and I'm so lost that I even forget to breathe. When he dips his head and captures my lips in a kiss, I soften against him. My hands go to his chest, sliding upwards until they rest on his shoulders as his teeth give a gentle scrape across my bottom lip. I whimper into his mouth as my lips part, and his tongue sensuously caresses mine. His hands slide down to my bum, squeezing before tickling their way down my outer thigh, sending ripples of desire through me so strong that I accidentally bite his lip. He chuckles but doesn't pull back; he just trails little kisses across my cheek until he gets to my ear. I'm almost panting with desire, my fingers digging into the solid cord of muscle on his shoulders.

"We should go rejoin the party before I pick you up and fuck you against this counter." His voice is a husky growl in my ear that sends a shot of desire to the pit of my stomach, and I can't think of a single good reason why he shouldn't do exactly that. "Amy, you're so bloody hot. Sometimes, I just can't stand it."

I gulp and gently push him away from me, trying to get some space to calm my racing heart and raging hormones. "Jared …" It's barely above a whisper, more like a plea, but I don't know what I'm pleading for—for him to stop or for him to never stop.

I shake my head, trying to clear the fog of lust that's settled over me as my fingers curl around his shirt, not letting him get too far away from me. He's driving me insane.

"I just need a minute." He blows out a big breath and steps back another step, running a hand through his hair.

My eyes instinctively drop down to his crotch. I can see how excited he is, his lust matching my own, just thankfully mine isn't noticeable from outside, unlike his.

Our eyes meet, and we both laugh.

By the time we both calm down enough to join the party again, it's in full swing. People are dancing and chatting, laughing and eating, scattered around the living room in large groups. Off to one side, Theo is dancing elaborately with Carys, swinging her around, and the pair of them are being generally outlandish with their crazy, over-the-top dance moves. It's clear that Theo is the life and soul of the party and is happiest being the centre of attention. I can see now why she said he was Funcle Theo.

I can't take my eyes off him. It's so weird, seeing it. This is what I imagined my crush was like—the happy-go-lucky guy on the train who chatted to everyone. This is the type of guy I usually go for, the loud one who makes everyone laugh by being the clown and is happy in his own skin, outwardly confident. Seeing a guy who looks exactly like Jared being so silly and free makes it even more thrilling to witness. My skin prickles with sensation, and I rub my hand up my arm, feeling the goosebumps there.

I gulp and sneak a glance over at Jared. He's in the middle of a very grown-up-sounding conversation with an uncle about his job and how it's going. He's the opposite of his brother. He's quieter, more reserved, seeming content to stay in the shadows and let other people shine. Tonight, he's more like what he was like last night with his work colleagues—polite and a little standoffish. There are none of the free smiles that Theo is throwing around like they're going out of fashion.

The difference between the twins is so stark that I silently wonder how I didn't know they were two different people. The extraverted train guy who I fell so completely in love with and the quiet, introverted, OCD, organised guy I've been dating for the last six weeks. I swallow the lump that's rapidly forming in my throat. How did I not notice? Even the way they hold themselves is different. Jared is all straight back and stiff shoulders, exuding quiet confidence, looking like he is ready to reason through any problem. Theo is more relaxed, his shoulders looser, more casual, like he has no idea where life will take him but he's excited for the ride.

They are the complete opposites. Mirror twins. I muse it over. Not just in looks, but in everything, they seem to be the opposite of one another.

The party comes to a close around eleven with all the older members of the family leaving not long after the last bite of food is devoured. As we say our good-byes to his parents and promise to come back soon, Jared wraps his arm around me tightly and leads me towards his car, pressing the key fob to unlock it.

Suddenly, Theo streaks past. "Shotgun!" he calls, heading for the passenger side, wrenching the door open, and climbing in.

Jared groans. "Theo, don't be a dick all your life. Let Amy sit in the front."

Theo shrugs, grinning at me. "Can't, sorry. I already called it. Snooze, you lose, Amy. Better luck next time."

"Theo, you're not five. Get out of the car and let Amy sit in the front. You're a grown-arse adult; you can't call shotgun!"

I wave a hand and stifle a laugh at the incredulity in his voice. "It's fine. I only have little legs anyway; you two giants take the front."

Jared scowls at his brother for a few seconds, and when it becomes apparent that Theo's not going to move, he groans and reaches for the driver's seat, collapsing it forward so I can climb over it and slide in the back.

Once I'm in, he rights the seat and climbs in, his eyes meeting mine in the mirror. "Do you have enough room?"

"Yep." I nod, buckling up my seat belt and wriggling to get more comfortable on the leather seat.

Theo turns and smirks at his brother. "Maybe if you didn't have such a ridiculously small car, I wouldn't mind sitting in the back. No one needs a tiny sports car unless they're compensating for a small dick." He quirks one eyebrow at Jared, who sighs deeply.

"If I did, you'd have the same affliction, wouldn't you? You literally just insulted yourself, genius." He rolls his eyes and puts the car into gear, pulling out into the road and flashing his lights at his parents, who are standing on the doorstep, waving enthusiastically.

I send them a wave even though they likely can't see me in the dark.

As Jared makes the twenty-minute drive back to his place, I look between the two of them. My brain won't switch off. Theo is so chatty that I'm reminded of why I fell in love with him in the first place. His personality was why I was so attracted to him on those Mondays on the train. He is so my type that, on paper, I couldn't have made up a more perfect man for me. Jared, on the other hand ... isn't my type at all.

The guilt of that knowledge is crushing and painful. I'm with Jared; we've been dating six weeks now ... but it was his brother that I fell for. How do I reconcile that? My life went from fairy-tale to horror story in just a couple of seconds.

I feel awful. My head is beginning to hurt. It's all becoming too much, and I just want to go home and have some alone time, maybe cry myself to sleep over this whole catastrophic situation.

Tears prickle in my eyes, and I know a meltdown is imminent. But I can't think of a single good reason to get out of staying with Jared tonight.

When we pull up outside their building, Jared tips the seat again and holds out a hand to help me out of the car. Ever the gentleman. Then, he grabs my overnight bag from the boot and leads me inside the building.

Theo opens their apartment door, and Jared's body immediately stiffens against mine.

"Theo, ugh, what is that smell?" He turns his nose up and reaches for the light switch.

The scent wafts over me too, and I recoil. It's some sort of gone-off, stale, greasy food smell.

As the apartment is bathed in light, Jared groans. "Bloody hell, you're a slob! I was only gone one night! What even is that?"

I look in the direction he's looking—the kitchen. Their beautiful marble worktop is covered with dirty saucepans, used plates with congealed food and ketchup, crumbs, spillages, and a sink full of washing up.

"Blimey, calm down and eat a Snickers or something," Theo teases. "I made burritos; that's all. I'll clean it; don't worry."

Jared turns back to me and shoots me an apologetic smile as he leads me into their apartment. He tuts noisily as he catches sight of the living room too. There are more used plates and cups in here, and their coffee table is covered in paper and art materials.

I step out from under Jared's arm and can't help but look around their place with fresh eyes. Now that I know they're twins and the complete opposites, my gaze wanders over the things in his apartment that I noticed when I was here before. The stuff that is so *me*—the Marvel statues, the books, the posters. How much of the stuff that I love in here belongs to my boyfriend and how much of it belongs to the guy I've been in love with for five months before I even met my boyfriend?

I decide I need to ask. It seems important.

"Who has the Marvel collection?" I ask, nodding to the statue collection on the shelf, praying that it's Jared's. Just some redeeming feature, something to hold on to of the things I thought I knew and loved about him.

Theo steps closer to them and grins like a proud father. "You like them? They're mine."

It's like another little jab to the heart. Something else to add to the tally list of things I've gotten wrong.

Jared flops down onto the sofa, leaning forward and starting to tidy away Theo's pencils and charcoals into the tin, piling up the loose papers and sketches, stacking up the empty, dirty plates that Theo let build up while Jared was staying at mine.

"He started collecting them years ago. They're slowly taking over the place." Jared sighs and shakes his head, but I can tell by his playful tone that he doesn't dislike them too much.

Theo notices the one I'm looking at—Storm from X-Men—and smiles. "Ororo Munroe. Or Storm, as she's better known. Omega-level mutant, absolute badass in the comics."

He picks it up and hands it to me. I take it carefully, turning it this way and that, looking her over. She's gorgeous, mid-spell, hair flying everywhere, white eyes, her white-and-gold cape flowing. It's stunning.

"She was always my favourite as a kid," I admit. "Plus, she was married to Black Panther for a while too. Power couple alert." I grin over at him as I cautiously put it back down.

Theo smiles down at me, seeming both shocked and impressed by my knowledge. "Ooh, you know your stuff." He nods over his shoulder at Jared. "Dumbass doesn't like superheroes."

Jared bristles and shrugs. "I don't mind them. I'm just not all jizz my pants about it like you are."

I chuckle and point at Theo. "Burn."

Jared laughs behind me and stands. "Shall we go to bed, Amy?" He raises one eyebrow, a playful smirk on his lips, the meaning clear.

Theo obviously catches the hidden meaning, too, because he makes a scoffing noise in the back of his throat and rolls his eyes. "Try to keep the noise down, huh? Remember I have to look you guys in the eye tomorrow."

I force a smile as Jared playfully punches his brother in the arm before holding out a hand to me. With one last look at Theo, I put my hand in Jared's and allow him to pull me to his room.

As we step inside, my eyes widen. I've been thinking about what his bedroom would be like for the last few weeks, wanting to see inside, to really get to know Jared, but the room is … disappointing. It's practically bare. There are no personal touches around at all. The king-size bed and the large padded headboard mounted on the wall are the focus of the room. There are no pictures or art on the wall, no colours splashed around. It's plain and neat and a little bit boring. The fitted furniture blends into the background and is barely noticeable. It's almost as if he only just moved in and put his clothes away in the wardrobe. The only thing that screams lived-in in this bedroom is the dressing table; instead of being a dressing table, he has the area set up like an office. There are neat stacks of files with colour-coded notes paper-clipped onto them on his desk, a pot of pens, a packet of the strawberry sweets the same as his car ones, and a corkboard with lots of stuff pinned on it. It's all so methodical and tidy and so Jared.

I turn back to make a joke about what a neat freak he is, but as the door clicks closed, he immediately starts making those eyes at me. The ones that make my tummy flutter, my panties wet, and my thighs weak as my hormones go into overdrive.

But I'm just not in the mood tonight. My mind is still spinning, and my heart still aches. There's a pounding starting behind my eyes—either from too much thinking or from the alcohol, I'm not sure which—but as Jared approaches me, his eyes all sultry and predatory, I shoot him an apologetic look and shake my head.

"I'm sorry. I have a headache. Do you mind if we don't tonight?" I ask, taking his hands as he reaches for the bottom of my shirt.

I'm so confused. I just need to sleep and turn my brain off. Hopefully, I'll wake in the morning with a fresh perspective, and I can stop this horrible, sinking feeling inside me.

His expression changes immediately, his eyebrows knitting together in concern as he steps closer to me and gently cups my face in his hands. "Of course. Are you okay? Why didn't you say anything?" He dips his head and plants a soft kiss on my forehead.

I close my eyes and melt against him, wrapping my arms around his waist and pressing my face into his chest. His smell is calming, soothing. I can hear his heart thumping steadily in his chest, and I feel an ache settle over me.

Why did tonight have to happen? We had been going so well, ticking along so nicely, and our relationship was blossoming into something amazing, but then Theo had to come along and pull the rug out from under us. Nothing is the same now, not even hugging him. My guilt is eating me up, ruining the moment, ruining everything I thought I knew.

Jared eases back from my embrace, but I'm not willing to let go yet, so I tighten my arms around him, locking my hands around my wrists so he's trapped in a little cage-like grip. He kisses the top of my head, his hot breath tickling my scalp, causing my skin to tingle.

"Amy, if you let me go, I'll get you some tablets." He reaches behind his back and pries my hands apart, stepping back and shooting me a sympathetic smile. "I'll be right back. You get in the bed."

He steps away from me before I can voice my protest and heads out of the door, leaving me alone in his bare, immaculate bedroom, where there's not a single thing out of place. Tears well in my eyes, and I look up at the ceiling, blinking rapidly to try to banish them.

By the time he comes back into the room, carrying a glass of water in one hand and two pills in the other, I'm just changing into my Bagpuss shorts and T-shirt pyjamas. He patiently watches me as I swallow the pills and then slip into his bed. His smell engulfs me; it's exquisite and painful at the same time. I love it; I hate it. I want to smother myself in it and run away from it in equal measure. I'm so conflicted that my head gives another throb. I can't even keep my eyes open to watch him undress, which is something I would never normally miss.

He turns off the light and slides into the bed next to me, wrapping me tightly in his arms, his hand softly stroking the back of my hair. I feel my chin wobble as emotion crashes over me. I press my face into his chest and cling to him.

"I love you," he whispers, his lips press against my hair as his legs tangle with mine.

My favourite three words in the world now feel like they stab a hole in my heart. My throat is clogged with guilt. "I love you too," I mumble against his skin.

But the thing that hurts the most is the question that keeps revolving around my head: *Do I love him ... or is it his nerdy, magic-performing twin I am really in love with?*

TWENTY-ONE

I barely sleep. Instead, I spend most of the night lying awake in Jared's arms, my mind whirling a mile a minute, plagued by questions I don't know the answers to.

By eight a.m., I feel absolutely wretched and slightly sick. There's no fresh perspective this morning, just more confusion and uncertainty. My sleepless night has not helped in the slightest. All I can be positive about is that I hate myself. I hate the situation. I hate that I lied to Jared when he asked me if everything was okay. I hate that I kissed his brother by accident yet still told Jared I loved him, too, last night before he fell asleep, cuddling me so intimately. But mostly, I hate the fact that I know, deep down, that Theo was the one I fell in love with, not Jared.

I tilt my head and look up at him. He's still sleeping peacefully, and he looks like something carved by angels. My gaze wanders his face and settles on the little mole under his left eye. It used to be my favourite thing about his face—it still is—but now, that little freckle makes my heart ache for a whole different reason. I long to reach out and touch it, but I don't want to wake him, so instead, I carefully ease myself from his bed and tuck the covers up around him, tiptoeing out of his room and into the hallway.

I nip into the bathroom, doing my business and then wincing at my reflection in the mirror because I look like Gene Simmons from Kiss where I haven't taken my make-up off before bed last night. I use my hands and roughly scrub at my face until I'm semi-presentable. Then, I pad into the kitchen, searching out my first priority—coffee, strong and lots of it.

"Morning."

I jump so hard that I hit my head on the kitchen cupboard and let out a little yelp of surprise and pain as I whirl on the spot. Theo sits at the dining room table, sketchbook balanced on his knee, pen in his hand.

"Dammit, you scared me," I wheeze, putting my hand over my heart to quell the thumping.

He smiles apologetically. "Sorry."

"What are you doing up already?"

He shrugs and pushes himself up from his seat, coming over to the other side of the kitchen island. "Couldn't sleep. Plus, I'm behind on a project I have to hand in tomorrow, so I'm trying some last-minute catch-up."

He sets his drawing pad down on the counter, and I can't resist a sneak peek. It's an exquisite picture of a scruffy cat, sitting on a tiled roof. It's simple yet full of so many intricate details and pen strokes; it's incredible. I can't look away from it.

"Is Jared still asleep?" he asks. When he notices I'm staring at his drawing, he pushes the pad away obviously.

I drag my eyes away and nod in answer to his question.

"Wow. He never normally sleeps in. You must have worn him out last night." He suggestively wiggles his eyebrows, and I can't help but laugh.

My eyes take him in. He looks good in the morning, as I knew he would. Jared wakes up, looking like one of those just-rolled-out-of-bed models, so it is only fitting that his brother does too. He's wearing black shorts and a loose-fitting white muscle-vest thing that guys wear to the gym. The kind that has the low armpit holes, so you can see the muscles on their ribs when they move. I don't want to notice that Theo has those rib muscles, but I do.

I gulp and force my eyes away. "I'm making a drink. You want one?" I turn back to the kitchen to keep myself busy.

I pick up the grey canister labelled *Coffee* and pull off the lid, frowning at the contents. Instead of the instant granules I'm expecting, I'm confronted by little pods.

"Ugh, what in the fresh hell is this?" I turn and show him. "Where's your coffee, dude? This is a catfish."

Theo chuckles behind me. "Jared's idea of luxury. They go in that beast." He points to the scary-looking silver machine on the countertop.

"Seriously? You don't just have instant?" I ask.

Theo shakes his head, his eyes glittering with amusement as he folds his arms over his chest and watches me.

"It's too early for this kind of fuckery," I grumble, reaching into the pot and pulling out one of the pods.

I take a deep breath and head over to the machine, ready to tackle it. I need my coffee. This thing is going to give up the goods, or I'll just chew on the granules from the pod. Either way, I'm getting my caffeine fix.

I try everything, lifting the lid, trying the pod this way and that, pressing on buttons, but when it beeps angrily at me, I let out a little growl of frustration and stamp my foot like a petulant child.

"Here, let me." Theo laughs and steps up behind me, reaching around my body and pulling off a plastic canister from the back of the machine. As he does so, his side bumps against mine, and the bare skin of his arm brushes against mine.

My pulse immediately jumps, and my stomach clenches.

I flinch back and blink at my body's reaction. "Sorry, sorry. Thanks." I hand him the pod and step to the side.

My body temperature has bumped up a couple of degrees, and I can't stop my eyes from raking over his back, over the muscles in his arms, in his shoulders, his long legs. As he leans over the sink and fills the canister with water, the armholes in his shirt expose the tanned skin on his sides and stomach. My fingers itch to reach out and touch him, to see how warm he is, how solid.

Suddenly, my eyes widen in horror as I realise what I'm doing. *I'm perving on my boyfriend's brother. I'm so going to hell.*

I shake my head at myself, turning away and putting my head in my hands. But was it really that bad? After all, he looks *exactly* like Jared. Who's to say that isn't the reason I'm attracted to him? Jared turns me on something rotten and almost drives me mad with lust, so it is surely perfectly acceptable that his exact body double would too?

But the guilt doesn't subside as I try to convince myself I'm not a horrible person. Because it isn't just the body I'm attracted to in Theo's case. It was his personality that first made me attracted to him—and to Jared!

Personality is always my first priority in a partner. Personality is what I've always sought in a boyfriend and coveted as precious. It doesn't matter what they look like. I've lusted after guys with potbellies and a hairy back all because they made me laugh hysterically. Intelligence, kindness, and a sense of humour are traits I find most attractive. Actual looks are way down my list. It just so happens that the Stone twins have good looks in abundance too.

To distract myself, I decide to probe on a question I've been wondering for months: what does my train crush actually do? When I guessed something arty before, I was surprised when Jared told me he was in finance. Now, looking at Theo with his ink-stained hands, I'm thinking I was right about my Man Crush Monday's profession all along.

I point to his sketchbook. "Is that what you do for a job? Draw cats?"

He smiles over his shoulder. "At the moment, yes. I'm a freelance book illustrator. I draw whatever I get contracted to. I'm currently working on a children's book series about a homeless cat and his adventures. I'm supposed to have finished the art for book three by tomorrow when I go to London to meet with my publisher, but"—he shrugs and clicks his tongue—"I'm behind."

I raise my eyebrows at the revelation. A book illustrator. So, all those trips to London were to meet a publisher.

"Wow. Can I …" I look at the sketchbook hopefully and then immediately regret asking. "Sorry, never mind. It's private. You probably don't like showing people your work in progress."

The coffee machine whirs into life, and he grins at me before picking up his pad and holding it out to me. "I don't mind. Fill your boots."

Excitement bubbles up inside me, and I turn to the first page, gasping at the beautiful illustration of a tattered, scruffy cat sitting on a fence, looking at the moon. This one has been coloured in bright watercolour type inks and is spectacular. "Wow."

I carefully leaf through the pages, in awe of his talent. They're all the same cat in different scenarios that obviously go with the words of the book. As I flick through, I notice they're not all work-related. Some of them are just random sketches of everyday life: a bus, a lamppost, a coffee cup, a caterpillar, someone's shoe, a homeless man, a fountain.

Theo scoffs and rolls his eyes, "I get distracted easily, as you can see." He turns away to make my coffee.

"Clearly." I grin.

As I'm happily turning pages, examining his art … suddenly, there's *me*. A pencil sketch of my profile from my shoulders up. I'm wearing my work uniform. It's shaded beautifully in pencil, highlights and all, my eyeliner the perfect Cleopatra flick. There is some colour on the sketch, standing out bright and bold against the shades of grey. Some pink streaks in my hair, giving depth to the braid it's tied into, and my eyes have been inked in a bright, startling blue.

My mouth drops open, as I don't quite understand what I'm seeing.

"Wait. Is this me?" I say it before I can think through if I even want to know the answer.

He whirls around, and I see the horror on his face as he snatches the book from my hands and literally throws it across the room. We both watch as it flutters to the ground, and some of his pages get bent as it skids across the floor, coming to rest, leaning up against the wall of glass.

"Shit. What? No. What?" His mouth opens and closes like a fish, and I can't stifle the bubble of laughter that rips its way up from my chest. He groans and closes his eyes. "Okay, yeah, that was you," he admits.

I chew on my lip, fiddling with my hands as I look over at him. "Why would you draw me? When did you?"

He sucks in a ragged breath. "Couple of months ago, I guess. And why wouldn't I draw you? You're gorgeous."

It's my turn to make the fish mouth this time as I lose the ability to speak.

He takes my cup from under the coffee machine as it lets out one last burst of steam and then puts another under for himself. "Okay, just so we put all our cards on the table, want to know a funny story? Well, it's not actually funny; it's kinda tragic when you think about it." He laughs nervously and rakes a hand over his face as he shakes his head. "For months, I've sat on your train and thought you were amazing and cute as hell. I tried several times to ask you out, but it never quite computed with you."

I frown, confused by his words. "What? No."

Theo reaches up and rubs at the back of his neck, his eyes firmly latched on the floor. "Yep. Several times. Remember those tickets I had to Comic Con and I told you my friend had dropped out last minute and that I was going on my own? And I asked what your weekend plans were?"

A lump has formed in my throat. I nod. It was about two months after he first started boarding my train. I remember when he was telling me about it. I was so nervous around him that I barely managed to hold myself together that day.

He shrugs, and his eyes meet mine. "Yeah, obviously, I didn't want to go on my own."

Oh my God. My eyes widen in shock.

He smiles awkwardly. "And remember that time I told you that the train coffee sucked and that there was a really good bakery I knew in the city that you needed to try?"

I gasp.

He sighs. "Admittedly, I should have just come right out and asked you on a date. I was working up to it but never quite had the balls. I always thought, *I'll get her number next time.* But then, a few weeks ago, you weren't on the train, and I was worried you'd been transferred or left or something and I'd missed my chance."

"I was on holiday for two weeks," I croak.

Understanding crosses his face, and he nods. "Ah, okay, that explains that then. And then, of course, the next time I saw you on the train, you kissed me."

I wince and press my hands to my cheeks as they flame with embarrassed heat.

He chuckles wickedly. "I really thought my luck was in that day. But then you just kind of ran off after and shouted you'd speak to me later. I waited around for as long as I could to see if you'd come and find me on the platform, but you didn't, and I had no way of contacting you. Fast-forward almost two weeks, and imagine my surprise when I show up at my father's sixtieth birthday bash and meet my brother's new girlfriend, and it turns out that she's the girl I've been secretly fantasising about for months."

Oh Christ.

He fancies me too.

I don't know what to do with this information. I just look at him with wide eyes, feeling like someone is gripping my heart with an icy-cold hand.

He shrugs. "But it's too late now. You're with my brother. And I'm happy for you both. Jared is my best friend as well as my brother. I love him to death, and I want to see him happy even if it makes me jealous as hell."

I can barely breathe as this all sinks in.

He smiles boyishly and shrugs one shoulder in a *what're you gonna do* gesture as he puts on a funny voice. "The moral of the story, kids … if you fancy someone, just ask them out before someone else does and you miss your chance."

It's on the tip of my tongue to tell him that when he was noticing me on the train, I was noticing him too. That I thought I was dating *him* all this time. But I don't. I can't do that to Jared.

"I … I …" I wince, not knowing what to say. I clear my throat and try again, knowing I need to put a stop to this. "I don't think we should continue with this conversation."

He nods in agreement, pressing his lips together. "I agree. Here, a peace offering."

He turns and reaches into a top cupboard, bringing down a round metal tin. As he turns back to me and pries the lid off, I smile gratefully and reach into the tin, picking out a biscuit.

"Ah, she likes a digestive. Interesting choice," he says, choosing a custard cream. "Let's dunk on it and agree never to mention it again."

I chuckle and nod, knocking my biscuit against his before breaking it in half and dunking it in my coffee for a couple of seconds before eating it, watching as he does the same with his.

I'm on my third biscuit when two arms close around me from behind.

I squeal in fright, and Jared laughs, his chest rumbling against my back as he nuzzles into my neck, saying, "Good morning, beautiful." He looks from me to the biscuit tin to Theo, who's boosted himself up on the kitchen worktop, chewing noisily, brushing crumbs onto the floor from his lap. "Ah, the breakfast of champions. How healthy," Jared muses playfully.

Theo scrunches his nose up. "Hey, I know what your underlying problem is here. It's envy. You watch what you eat and exercise every day and look like that. I eat whenever I want and look exactly the same." He holds up his hands and smugly tilts his head. "I'm just saying, don't hate the player, hate the game."

Jared laughs. "I don't even know what you're talking about. It's too early for your riddles." He plants a soft kiss on the side of my neck, and I turn to look at him over my shoulder as his hands slip under my T-shirt, gently caressing my stomach. "Are you feeling better today?"

His eyes are my undoing. They're so sincere and caring that it makes my heart ache. The weight of everything comes crashing down on top of me again. Looking at him makes me feel awful, and I'm silently berating myself for something I didn't have any control over. Looking at Jared makes me feel so shameful that I want to punch myself in the face because he is wonderful, a thoughtful, caring man … but he isn't the one I first fell in love with all those months ago.

Looking into his eyes, I honestly don't know if I am just with him because of who I *thought* he was or if I am actually in love with *him*. When you take all the quirky, nerdy Theo stuff away, do Jared and I have anything in common at all? We're direct opposites, not each other's types at all.

"Amy?" he prompts, raising one eyebrow when I don't answer.

I grind my teeth and nod. "I'm fine today, thanks."

"Good." He smiles and dips his head, planting a kiss on my lips, his hands tightening on my waist as he presses himself against me.

A feeling of cold mortification grips my stomach because Theo, who not ten minutes ago admitted that he was jealous, has to watch this. It isn't right. Not in front of Theo. And maybe not even at all. I don't know what I want. The swirling confusion is back, made worse by the easy, fun time I had with Theo in the kitchen. That was our first real proper chat—something I would have given anything for a couple of months ago—and now, I'm kissing his brother.

I'm hurting everyone right now, including myself, but I feel powerless to stop it. Guilt and horror consume me, and I pull away, putting my hand on his chest and pushing him back a little to get some space.

He doesn't notice my unease and lovingly brushes my hair behind my ear with one finger. "What shall we do today?"

I shake my head and say the first excuse that pops into my brain, "I'm going to my mum's house. She called Friday and asked me to come over today. I forgot. I just remembered." As I say the words, I realise how much I need them to be true. I need to speak to my mum, talk things through with someone who won't judge me, someone who knows Jared and can help me see sense in this whole clusterfuck situation. I also need one of my nanna's hugs.

He raises one eyebrow. "Yeah? Okay. I could come? Drive down there, save you getting the train?"

"No." But I'm too quick to answer; it comes out a little aggressive and forceful.

Both of them notice, and Jared's forehead creases with a frown that I long to smooth away with my finger.

"Is everything okay?" His eyes are searching mine.

I can see the concern there, and it makes me feel worse because he shouldn't have to worry about me. I don't deserve his concern. I hate that he's worried about me. I want to throw my arms around him and tell him everything's going to be okay, but I can't because I don't know if it will be.

I force a smile and set my hand on his bare chest, feeling the heat of him under my palm and the steady thump of his heart. My own heart gives a sympathetic squeeze in time with his. This is painful.

"Sorry. Yes, everything's fine." I go up on my tiptoes and kiss him, hating myself, loving the kiss, loving his taste, hating that Theo is watching. What an oxymoron. My guilt is overwhelming, and I can feel tears prickle at the backs of my eyes.

With Jared's arms wrapped around me and his mouth on mine, I silently wish I hadn't gone to that party at all last night, that I'd never had the truth revealed about Theo. Jared had been making me blissfully happy for weeks before I knew that he wasn't the man I thought he was. Doesn't that count for something? Or is what we have not enough now that I know Theo has been there, waiting in the wings, my perfect man?

I pull back and put on a brave face even though my heart is breaking inside. "I should go get dressed. Would you drive me to the train station?"

Jared's eyes are locked on mine. I can tell he's trying to drag the hidden truth from them, sensing something's wrong but not knowing what. He blinks a couple of times and sighs before giving me a little nod. "Course."

His arms drop from my waist as I step away. I miss them immediately.

TWENTY-TWO

After kissing Jared good-bye outside the station, I'm crying so much that I give myself hiccups, and the lady I'm seated opposite on the train buys me a cup of tea and a jam doughnut to try to cheer me up. I can't seem to stop myself. The kiss was so beautifully bittersweet. I wasn't sure if it was just on my end, but it felt like it was weighted with sadness. It felt like a last kiss. And that knowledge felt like someone was slowly cutting my heart out.

By the time I get to Mum's, my nose is blocked, my forehead is red and blotchy, and my throat is sore. I didn't call them to tell them I was coming, so when I let myself in the back garden, they both look up, startled.

"Amy? What's happened, sweetheart?" Mum asks, dropping the gardening tools and throwing off her gloves as I rush to her and throw my arms around her, fresh tears wetting her shirt.

I cling to her, unsure of where to even start.

Nanna walks up, wrapping her arms around the both of us. The warmth and comfort of their combined hug is like sinking into a warm bath after a long day.

"Has something happened with Jared? Have you two …" Nanna asks, trailing off.

I whimper and pull back, my chin wobbling as I struggle to catch my breath. "It's all ruined," I croak.

MAN CRUSH MONDAY

Mum strokes my hair, her forehead wrinkling in concern.

Nanna cups my cheek with her hand, and her eyes wander my face. "Is this why they call it an ugly cry?"

"Mum!" Mum elbows Nanna in the side in reprimand, but the joke lightens the mood fractionally, and I suck in a deep breath, trying to articulate this whole horrific misunderstanding.

"The guy I fell in love with isn't the guy I'm dating." My words come out husky and broken from all the crying.

"What do you mean?" Nanna asks.

Mum and Nanna exchange a confused glance before Mum tilts her head, looking at me so I can tell she's trying to get a read on the situation.

"Let's go sit down. Amy, you need to calm down, sweetheart. I can feel you trembling. Take a few deep breaths," Mum suggests.

I allow myself to be led to the table, and I sink down on one of the plush chairs, catching Puzzle as he makes a leap for my lap.

"Now then, what's this all about?" Mum asks, softly stroking my knee.

I snuggle my face into Puzzle's neck and absentmindedly stroke him. "I went to the party last night at Jared's parents' house. His brother, Theo, turned up a bit late, and when he walked in, I found out that he and Jared are twins! Almost-identical twins." I look around with wide eyes, expecting gasps of horror, but judging by the blank looks they're giving me, they haven't gotten it. I gulp. "Theo is the one from the train, not Jared."

That does it. The penny drops.

Mum's eyebrows shoot up into her hairline as she sits back in her chair, her breath coming out in one long gust.

Nanna clicks her tongue and points at me excitedly. "Gemini! I told you I got some Gemini vibes, didn't I? I thought it was a star sign I was feeling, but Gemini is twins. Ha! Called it." A smug smile creeps on her face as she looks from me to Mum and back again, not understanding the importance of the information. I press my lips together and watch the realisation slowly settle over her face, and her smile falters. "Wait, the twin brother is the one from the train?"

I nod, swiping at the tear that falls down my cheek.

"Oh," Mum sighs, slowly shaking her head. "Well, this is a mess. So, you really did meet Jared in that coffee shop?"

My head is aching from all the crying, so I reach up and massage my forehead with one hand. "Yeah. And it gets worse." My voice is almost a whisper now. "I kissed Theo."

Mum gasps. "Amy! What were you thinking? I've never known you to cheat before. What is this all about?"

Her reprimand along with her scowl of disapproval make my stomach hurt. I've not seen her this disappointed in me since I got in trouble with the police for accidentally kicking a football into a neighbour's greenhouse and running away. I was eight at the time.

I adamantly shake my head. "I didn't know it was him. I thought the guy on the train was Jared. I kissed him a couple of weeks ago, but it turns out, it was Theo. I didn't even know he existed at the time. I thought they were the same person."

Does that make it better, more acceptable? I think so, but I'm not sure.

"Was it a good kiss?" Nanna asks.

Mum scoffs and turns her disapproval to Nanna, "What's that got to do with anything?"

Nanna shrugs. "I'm just asking."

Mum sighs and rolls her eyes. "Amy, sweetheart, I don't think this will ruin things. You could just explain to Jared, tell him the truth that you accidentally kissed his brother and that you thought it was him. Obviously, he might be a bit upset about it at first, but he'll be fine. It was an accident. And it's half his fault if he didn't tell you he had an identical twin out there."

She still isn't seeing the big picture.

I can barely look at her, so I look down at the dog's back as I speak, "Mum, I fell in love with the guy on the train *months* before I even met Jared. It isn't Jared that I fell for; it's his twin."

The silence is deafening. Even my nanna, who I've never seen lost for words, is mute.

I clear my throat. "Everything is ruined." My voice breaks as I say it, my tears are back in full force, my body racked with sobs.

Mum reaches out, placing her hand over mine, squeezing supportively. "So, you're telling me, it's Theo that you're in love with, not Jared?"

I scrunch my eyes shut. "I don't know. I really don't know. I fell in love with him on the train; I can put my hand on my heart and tell you that I did. Theo is literally everything I've ever wanted in a guy. He's funny and dorky, nerdy and outgoing. We're a perfect match." I swallow my emotion and chew on the inside of my cheek before I finish, "But being with Jared for the last few weeks has been amazing."

Mum nods. "But Jared isn't your type."

"You know he's not. You said so yourself last week."

Memories of her *but* spring to mind. Even she saw it when I didn't. I think about Jared now—shy, quiet, businesslike, serious. There is not a single thing we have in common.

"Jared is amazing. I adore him; I really do." That is the truth. Every time I think of him, my insides flutter, and my skin prickles with sensation.

Nanna cocks her head, intently looking at me. "But it's Theo you want."

"I don't know what I want. All I know is that I fell in love with the guy who collects Marvel statues, does magic tricks, and chats with people on the train. That guy isn't Jared."

Nanna stands. "I'm going to make some tea. I'll put a dash of whiskey in yours; it'll calm your nerves."

I watch as she walks off towards the house.

Mum is chewing on her nails, thinking, her eyes firmly latched on me. "Okay, let's look at this from another angle," she says. "Pretend you hadn't even met the guy on the train, so you're not already in love with him. You meet a hot guy in a coffee shop, and he asks you out. Would you have said yes?"

I think. I really try to put myself in that situation. But I just can't because I don't know what I would have done because I *did* know him before, and I *was* already in love with him. I shrug in answer.

Mum continues, "Okay, so think back to your dinner date. Did he do enough—that guy you went on the date with—for you to want to go on a second date with him? Would you have noticed on that date that you had nothing in common and just called it a day then? Did you let things slide because of what you thought you already knew? If you'd met him on a night out—straight, dependable, quiet Jared—would you have gone on a second date with him?"

My head is swimming with all her questions. I put my hands in my hair and want to scream. "I don't know, Mum. That's the problem I'm having. This is just horrible."

Would I have even given Jared a second look if I hadn't known him from the train? I don't know the answer. That's what's tearing me apart.

She leans forward, wrapping her arms around me, gently rocking me like she used to when I was a child. "Sweetheart, I think you need to be brutally honest with yourself here. You need to try and separate what you felt and when you felt it, so you can work out who you feel it for." She strokes the back of my head. "I will say this, I've never known you to stray outside your type. You always go for the weird, nerdy guys. Always. When I've met your boyfriends before, I always knew what to expect before they even walked through the door. A loud, chatty male version of you. Jared is … not that."

I nod in understanding. He definitely isn't that.

She continues, "But it doesn't mean that you and Jared aren't suited though. After all, opposites attract. And if you think about it, these nerdy guys you always go for … where are they now if they're so right for you?"

I blink up at her hopefully.

"Chemistry. That's what matters. And I saw that between you and Jared."

I nod. I know the chemistry is there. "But is the chemistry there because I was already in love with him before I even met him?" I sniff and wipe my nose on the sleeve of my jumper in a very unladylike fashion as Nanna comes back and sets down a tray of tea on the table. "Now that I've met Theo, he's everything I thought he would be. He's extravagant and quirky, funny, loud, confident." My mind flicks to him dancing with Carys, how carefree and silly they were. "He's ridiculous." I roll my eyes and smile. "He's exactly what I thought my crush would be like, but then I got with Jared and assumed I had just gotten him wrong. Now, I find out, all along, my crush *is* actually like that … and I've just been dating the wrong brother."

Nanna's eyebrow arches, her hand stilling midway through pouring out milk. "Dating the wrong brother?" She picks up on my words. "That's a strong statement."

I groan and shake my head. "I didn't mean it like that. I mean, Jared isn't who I thought he was."

Mum cocks her head to the side and looks at me. Her eyes boring into mine. "Really? Because for a second there, it sounded like you were insinuating that you should be or want to be with the brother."

I open and close my mouth, but nothing comes out.

Her eyes widen fractionally, and her lips press into a thin line.

"I don't know what I want. I'm so confused; I don't even know which way is up right now." I drop my head back on my shoulders and stare at the sky, wishing my head would stop pounding. "Our whole relationship was built under false pretences. He isn't who I thought he was when we first met in that coffee shop. I mean, should we even be together? I don't know. I don't know how much of the love I feel for him is actually for the carbon-copy version I fell for on those train rides and how much of it is from the guy I've been getting close to for six weeks. How do I know?" I ask, pleading with them for help.

I just need someone to help me split the two apart, so I can formulate my feelings. At the moment, they're so jumbled; it's like there's still one person. *Oh, why couldn't they just be the one person? Someone up there hates me.*

Nanna passes me a steaming cup of tea, and I wrap my hands around it gratefully. "Can you pinpoint when you fell in love?"

I nod emphatically. "Clear as day. The magic trick on the train. It was four months ago. Two and a half months before I even bumped into Jared at the coffee shop."

Mum presses her lips together, and I can tell she's disappointed in my answer. She likes Jared more than I realised.

Nanna nods. "Okay. On another note, has the brother made any indications that he's interested in you? Did he remember you from the train?"

"Yeah," I croak, my eyes burning with tears again as I think about mine and Theo's conversation in the kitchen this morning. "Turns out, he liked me, too, and was working up to asking me out."

"And do you fancy the brother?" Nanna checks.

I close my eyes and think back to the kitchen, that split second where his arm brushed mine. I was physically attracted to him, yes. "Yeah, but …"

She raises one eyebrow. "But?"

MAN CRUSH MONDAY

I flick my eyes to Mum, seeing she's gone quiet, reflective, just listening to my words and silently making judgement. My stomach constricts. "But they look exactly alike. I fancy the pants off Jared, so it surely means nothing that I'm attracted to his exact body double?"

Nanna sips her tea, watching me over the rim, as Mum asks, "Question for you then. If they were both available, both wanted to be with you, and you could be with either of them with no consequences or hurt feelings, which would you choose? The nerdy one or the quiet one?"

I can't answer. That's the exact thing I don't know.

Nanna answers for me, "Well, that's hardly a fair question. She's only spoken to this Theo properly, what, two, three times?"

I nod.

Nanna purses her lips. "Then, you need to get to know him. Make an informed choice," she says.

"I can't do that to Jared." I adamantly shake my head.

I don't want to hurt him. He doesn't deserve any of this; neither of them does. My thoughts flash to Jared saying he was falling down the rabbit hole with me, that he loved me. Inside my head, I can hear those three spectacular words spoken in his voice, clear as day. My skin prickles, and my insides swirl with guilt and mortification. I am going to hurt him, I know it, and that thought makes me hate the very essence of myself even though none of this is really my fault.

Mum blows out a big breath. "Here's my advice."

I look up at her, waiting for her pearls of wisdom, praying she has something that can make this all right again—maybe a magic wand or some sort of spell?

"You've always been an honest person. I think you should be truthful with Jared, tell him what's happened. You've not cheated, and none of this is your fault. Maybe he'll understand."

Nanna snorts indignantly, making Puzzle jerk in his sleep. "And maybe, when you tell him, he'll run a mile, and the choice will be taken away from you. Maybe you won't ever see him again."

I gasp, horrified. Her words are like a knife to the stomach. The mere suggestion of not seeing him is painful. My heart squeezes in my chest with grief at the thought of the loss of him. It doesn't bear thinking about. I don't know what I feel for whom, but I know that I don't want to lose him. What if I could somehow work it out, pick them apart? What if it is Jared I am supposed to be with and I ruin everything with the truth?

"When are you due to see one of them next?" Nanna asks.

I swallow around the lump in my throat, tightly wrapping my arms around myself. "Tomorrow. Theo is due on my train." My chin wobbles. *My crush, not my boyfriend. Two separate entities.*

"And when are you seeing Jared?"

I sniff, wincing as I take a swig of the spiked tea. "Not until Tuesday after work. He's got a dinner meeting Monday night with clients."

Nanna nods. "You have a bit of time then. Talk to Theo tomorrow. If there's nothing there between you, problem solved."

Mum raises one eyebrow. "And if there is?"

"Problem doubled," Nanna replies, looking at me as she squeezes my knee sympathetically.

We lapse into silence, and I stare into my cup, wondering how all this got so messed up, so quickly. One minute, I'm floating on a cloud with an amazing boyfriend who has confessed he loves me. Next minute, I'm trying to cross traffic at rush hour, my heart in my mouth and my stomach twisted in knots.

Suddenly, it hits me. I look over at Mum. "Crossroads. You saw it in the cards. You said I would have to choose a path." I close my eyes and groan.

Mum nods, and I can tell she already came to that conclusion a while ago while I was talking. "I don't think there is a wrong choice here, sweetheart. You just have to work out what you want and then go for it."

"And not break anyone's heart in the process," I mutter, knowing it's too late.

My own heart is already splintered and fractured after this; it's just a matter of damage limitation now.

TWENTY-THREE

I've barely slept for two days. My body aches with tiredness, my brain hurts with confusion, and my heart aches because it's fundamentally broken.

I'm not looking forward to today. I have the dreaded Monday blues that everyone else has but for good reason. Today, I will be seeing Theo on the train, and I don't have the first clue what I'm going to say to him.

I spent the day yesterday talking with my mum and nanna and arrived home in the early evening none the wiser. After that, I called reinforcements, and Heather came over to talk me down too. She basically agreed with my family; it wasn't my fault, but I needed to try and work out what I was feeling and for whom before it went any further with Jared.

So, that's what I'm going to attempt today. I want to work out three things:

> 1. If I am physically attracted to Theo.
> 2. If we have better chemistry than I do with Jared.
> 3. If I am with Jared because I thought he was Theo, or did I, somewhere along the line, fall in love with Jared for himself?

I don't know how I'm going to work out those things. I'm just going to have to wing it. My nanna suggested just simply getting to know Theo a little more, so that is as good a place to start than any. A harmless chat to see if it sheds any light on the situation.

When I see him rushing towards the train, my heart sinks. He looks great in a black suit with a *Thanks for the memories* Stan Lee T-shirt underneath—so different to Jared's usual tailored splendour.

I realise then that this is going to be harder than I thought to decipher. I hate that I think he's cute when I see him. I was hoping to see him and for it all to be clear one way or the other. But them looking identical makes the physically attractive point impossible. Of course I think he's hot. I think Jared is hotter than wasabi-coated peanuts, so it's a no-brainer that I fancy Theo too.

As I somehow knew he would be, Theo is late and barely makes it aboard and in his seat before the doors close.

As the train departs, I take a few deep breaths, trying to prepare myself as I begin my job, collecting tickets and working my way through the train.

My feet falter as I step over the threshold of the refreshments carriage. My eyes widen, and my palms grow damp with sweat. Theo is in there, leaning casually against the counter as he waits for his drink to be made. Elaine, the barista, bustles around, chatting over her shoulder while he nods along and throws her smiles. I stop, watching the exchange, noticing again how free Theo is with his smiles; he hands them out like they're flyers to a circus. So different to Jared, who is more serious. His smiles are earned and meaningful.

My stomach is churning with anxiety. I long to just run away, to jump off the train to avoid this conversation and situation, but I know I can't. This isn't just going to blow over or go away if I ignore it long enough. Unfortunately, I have to face this one head-on, and I'm the only one who can make up my own mind.

Before I can work out what my opening greeting should be, Theo looks over his shoulder and spots me. "Hey, Amy. How are you?" He smiles his thanks at Elaine as she puts his drink down on the counter, next to a Kit Kat.

"Hi. I'm good. How about you?"

He shrugs one shoulder and pulls the lid from his tea, adding a couple of sugar packets. "I'm okay. Tired. I had to pull another all-nighter for work." He reaches up a hand and covers his mouth as he yawns.

I nod a greeting at Elaine as I step to Theo's side, acutely conscious that she's listening. Elaine is the one you go to for train gossip; she hears all the juicy stories in the refreshments cart. I don't want to give her any ammunition on me.

"And did you get your drawings done?"

"Illustrations," he corrects. "It makes what I do sound more professional and less of a job I took just because I can work in my pyjamas and I'm too lazy to work a full day," he jokes. I chuckle. "But no, I didn't. It'll be okay though. I'll ask for an extension at the meeting today. They love me there, so it'll be fine, I'm sure."

"Ah, fingers crossed."

He nods and waves a hand at the counter full of confectionery and snacks. "Can I get you anything?"

"No, thanks."

He picks up his drink, and we both walk towards the door.

"So, are you okay, really? You kind of ran off a bit sharpish yesterday morning. Jared was sulking all day; he's worried something happened at the party. He asked if maybe someone had said something to upset you. He said you had a headache and were a bit off when you went to bed, and then you ran off in the morning." He looks at me from the side of his eye, watching for my reaction.

A lump forms in my throat, and I will myself not to cry. I hate that Jared's worried about this. It makes the guilt intensify. "Ah, yeah, everything's fine. I just forgot I was supposed to go to my mum's; that's all," I lie. "I'll speak to him later on."

I deliberately didn't call him last night. He'd texted to check in and asked me to call when I was free, but I was still in a state, and by the time Heather left, all I wanted to do was curl into my bed and sleep. So, instead of calling him, I just sent him a message, saying I'd only just seen his messages and I was now in bed. I felt awful, fobbing him off like that, but I didn't know what to say to him. Ignoring the issue was the easier option.

As we step into the next busy carriage together, Theo smiles, and I reach down to my ticket machine.

"I'd better let you get on." He winks at me before heading off, through into the next carriage.

Through the glass in the door, I see him flop into his seat at the table at the very end. He will be my last passenger. I silently wonder if he's done it deliberately.

I try to keep my eyes averted from him as I serve the other passengers, but it's hard. It's like they're magnets; they keep swinging back to him, watching him as he scribbles in his notebook, a look of deep concentration on his face.

By the time I work my way through the two carriages and get to his side, he's drawn a beautiful sketch of a dragon.

My eyes widen in appreciation. "Wow, that's amazing."

He grins up at me and shrugs as if it's nothing. "Forgot my book today, so I've gotta amuse myself somehow."

It's on the tip of my tongue to ask what he's currently reading. But I don't.

"Got your ticket?" I ask instead.

He nods and produces his prepurchased ticket from his pocket, as usual. He clears his throat, shifting in his seat, his eyes on the table as he asks, "So, if I wanted to get the last train home from London before you finish your shift, which one would I have to get?"

"Um … the 3:12 is always my last train." My hands fumble with his ticket as I hand it back, and I almost drop it.

He nods thoughtfully. "Okay. I'll see if I'm finished on time and if I can get that one. If I do, maybe we could go for coffee when you've finished your shift? Or are you seeing Jared after work?"

I shake my head. "He's having dinner with clients tonight." I chew on my lip, my guilt hammering me like a battering ram.

His eyes light up. "So, maybe then? I'm not sure I'll be able to get there on time though. It depends on how long my meeting goes on for. But if I'm done on time, we could go catch up, get to know each other a little better?"

That is exactly what Nanna suggested. Maybe it's fate, but my guilt at the situation doesn't fade one bit. "Okay." My answer comes out stilted, and I shuffle my feet and fiddle with my machine to cover my awkwardness and unease at the situation.

"Great. Maybe I'll see you later then."

I wave over my shoulder as I walk off. I can't decide if I hope he makes it onto my last train or not.

I spend the rest of the day worrying about it. Ninety-nine percent of me wants him to miss the train, but that one percent …

It's so busy on the afternoon train that I don't actually see him board, and I'm quietly pleased about it. Well, ninety-nine percent of me is.

I'm happily going about my duties when I spot him. He's in the last carriage, crammed in among the standing commuters. He grins over at me as I check people's tickets.

My stomach clenches, and I'm not sure if it's from happiness or horror.

I force a smile and talk to him over someone's shoulder as I check the tickets for the standing passengers. "Hey, you made it then?" *Stupid Question of the Day award goes to …*

He nods and passes me his ticket. "Just. Had to run all the way here from my meeting."

He wipes a hand across his forehead and flicks fake sweat as he blows out a breath. I can't help but laugh.

"Still up for that coffee? Would seem rude to jilt me after I just ran all the way here. Despite appearances to the contrary, I'm not actually fit at all, so I hope you appreciate the effort."

I see people side-eyeing us, watching this play out with interest.

I nod and shrug. "Sure. I need to just finish up, and once we pull in, I need to go sign out and drop off my machinery. I'll meet you out front after a few minutes?"

"Sure, Amy."

By the time I'm done and ready to leave for the day, he's already standing at the front entrance. He's leaning against the wall, on his phone again. As I approach, I see he's playing Wizards Unite, completely consumed by the game. The goofy grin slips onto my face as I sneak up beside him and glance over at his phone.

"Wow, I'd use a potion before it departs."

He jumps and laughs as he rakes a hand through his hair. He turns the phone around to me and raises one eyebrow. "You catch it. I've tried three times already today and not managed it. I'm jinxed."

I grin, and we begin to walk, me tracing the swirly pattern on his phone to catch the confoundable and him watching where we walk and tugging me out of the way when I almost trip over someone's suitcase. When I've caught it, I whoop triumphantly, and he gives me a high five before slipping his phone back into his pocket.

"So, how was your meeting? Get your extension?" I ask as I follow obediently along at his side as he walks down the road.

He nods. "Yeah, I got another week. I'll meet with them again next Monday now."

My body twitches. I'll see him again in a week instead of two. I'm not sure if it's excitement or trepidation that I feel swell in my stomach.

As we approach the café, I grind my teeth. It's the same one I met Jared in for the first time when I thought all the stars had aligned and I'd actually just spoken to my crush for the first time. Now, I'm here with my real crush … my boyfriend's brother. This is so awkward that a ball of anxiety forms in my stomach, making me feel slightly sick.

Theo reaches for the door, pulling it open and gesturing for me to go inside first. The café is half-full, warm, and noisy. I look around, hoping I don't know anyone, and to my relief, none of the baristas who know me are working. I usually make my trips here in the morning, so the evening staff is probably always different.

"What do you want? You go grab a table, and it's my treat," Theo offers, unbuttoning his suit jacket.

My eyes flick down to his T-shirt. I love it. I want it for myself. My mind is already comparing him in the T-shirt to Jared in his fitted, pressed shirts that he has laundered at the dry cleaners.

"Um … I'll have a caramel coffee cooler with cream, please."

He raises an eyebrow. "In this weather?"

My mouth drops open in fake indignation. "I'm taking that as a personal attack."

He laughs, and his eyes sparkle with amusement. "You're ridiculous. Go sit down."

He motions to an empty table that's secluded and off to one side. It's the kind of table you choose when you're on a date and want to talk privately. I nod and walk off, deliberately choosing a different table that's more central and closer to other people. Yes, I need to get to know him, but that doesn't mean I have to get cosy with him in a private booth.

As he stands in the queue to order, I pull out my phone, seeing a text from Heather. It's basically a moral support pep talk. I messaged her earlier that Theo had asked me for coffee. She is now just telling me to relax, just see how it plays out, and to try to notice the things I claim made me fall for him in the first place, so I can make an informed decision.

After a few minutes, Theo walks over, carrying a tray. I smile and push my phone back into my pocket as he sits opposite me and slides the tray onto the table.

I look down at it and notice he's also bought chocolate pastries. My mouth waters at the sight of it. He nudges a plate towards me, and I smile gratefully.

I watch as he rips open three packets of sugar and dumps them into his hot chocolate, stirring absentmindedly. It's weird, watching him eat sugar and cake. It's like I'm watching Jared do something I've never seen him do before.

He catches me staring and raises one eyebrow. "Don't judge me. You with your caramel cooler and cream. Hypocrite." He laughs and takes a bite of his pastry, shrugging nonchalantly. "My mum once said my blood type is maple syrup."

I laugh. I can imagine Deborah saying that.

"Not like Jared's. His is the tears of his employees," he jokes.

I feel a squeeze of my heart at the mention of Jared. An awkward silence descends over us, and I begin to wish I hadn't agreed to come. Yes, I need to see if there is something here, but sitting at this table with him feels a little like cheating. It makes me uneasy. From the outside, it looks innocent. But it's not innocent when, every spare second, I'm comparing him to my boyfriend to see if I'm more suited to this brother or the other.

As he looks down at his drink, my eyes wander over him. They latch on the little mole on his cheek. The more I look at it, the more I realise how obvious it is that he wasn't Jared. How did I not know? It looks so out of place there, under his right eye.

"So, do you usually go for the strong, brooding type then?" Theo asks, eating cream from his drink with a spoon.

I raise an eyebrow in question.

He clarifies, "Strong, broody type. Like Jared."

"Is that how you'd describe him?" I chuckle.

He nods and carefully blows on his drink. "Yeah, I mean, he has the resting bitch face nailed and everything."

I snort a laugh. "I'd call it a sexy smoulder."

"Oh, really?" He narrows his eyes at me, his jaw clenching in a moody, thoughtful expression, and it's so Jared that my heart clenches.

"I think yours needs more work," I force out, looking down at the table because I can't look at that face without guilt eating me up inside. "To answer your earlier question, no, I don't usually go for the broody type. I usually pick the loser guy, the real nerdy one who lives at home with his mum still. My last boyfriend was everything Jared isn't. He was a streamer."

"A streamer?"

I nod. "Yep. He literally played video games for a living and streamed his plays online."

"Wow. Living the dream," Theo jokes.

I chuckle and nod. "What about you?"

"I'm not a streamer, but now, I'm thinking a change in profession is in order." He looks up at me, and his eyes twinkle with humour. "My tastes are kinda refined. I like fun girls who know who they are in life and aren't afraid to show it. Like you. You're a bit of me."

My face heats up at his words. I don't know how to answer, so I just press my lips together and squirm on my seat. My mind is whirling a mile a minute. I don't really like that he's flirting with me—I'm his brother's girlfriend—and while I technically met *him* first, it seems inappropriate. Though, I reason, maybe he isn't even flirting. I could just be misunderstanding his friendliness for flirting. It's obvious that I suck at reading this guy. I mean, I didn't even notice he'd been hinting at us going out for months, so I can't claim to be an expert on Theo Stone. Flirting could just be in his nature for all I know.

He sighs deeply and continues, "You're not like the girls Jared usually goes for."

"Your mum said that too," I admit.

"Oh, really? And is that why you've been avoiding him?"

My mouth pops open. "I haven't been avoiding him. I told you this morning, I forgot I'd agreed to go to my mum's." The lie burns my throat on the way out, and I try to hold eye contact to give it more merit, but I can tell he knows it's not true.

Eventually, he purses his lips. "Let's change the subject. This is awkward."

I snort a laugh and nod. "You took the words right out of my mouth."

As his eyes drop down to my lips, my body goes rigid as my mind starts imagining things it shouldn't—things like what he tastes like and how his body would feel pressed against mine. I silently wonder if I would like it more than when Jared is pressed against me.

"Favourite movie ever?" I blurt the question, forcing my mind from distinctly naughtier places.

That lightens the mood immediately, and we spend the next hour talking about comic books, movies, our favourite superheroes, and who would win in a fight—Wonder Woman or Captain Marvel. It's nice, relaxed, chilled and fun. I find myself laughing a lot, and my cheeks ache from all the smiling by the time we've finished our second drink.

"Maybe we should move on to somewhere else? A bar maybe, get a proper drink?" Theo suggests hopefully as the baristas start closing off sections of the café and tidying up around us in a clear message for us to get a move on.

The twinkle in Theo's eye makes my back straighten. This is fast beginning to feel like a date, and I don't like it. I need to leave.

I look obviously down at my watch and wince. "I can't. I should actually make a move home."

A frown line appears between his eyebrows, but he nods in understanding. "That's okay." He reaches into his pocket and pulls out his phone. "Here, stick your number in. Next time I'm at that comic book shop in London I told you about, I'll text you to see if you want anything."

I take the phone, my thumbs hovering over the keypad, knowing that if I put my number in here, I'll be stepping over a line. A line that will very likely end with Jared hurting.

I swallow and put the phone back on the table. "Nah, it's okay. I won't want anything anyway." I slide the phone back across the table in clear rejection, and I see the disappointment in his eyes as he picks it up and pockets it.

"Okay." He stands and politely smiles down at me.

I stand, and we walk side by side out of the café. When my hand accidentally brushes against his, my face flames with heat, and I whip my arm away, wrapping my arms around myself, pretending it's due to the change in temperature as we step into the chilly night air.

"Well, this was really nice. We should do it again next time. Maybe next Monday—if my meeting doesn't go on too long, that is," he says, pursing his lips in question.

"Yeah, maybe." I shrug and give a half-nod.

When he leans in and hugs me, I close my eyes and try to soak up every ounce of information and feeling that I can from it. I notice the tiny, subtle differences. It's completely different to being hugged by Jared. The smell of him is different, the way he holds himself, the pressure of it. When Jared holds me against him, there's affection that goes into it, like he doesn't want to let go, versus Theo, who's just hugging good-bye as friends. The discrepancies are small but stark. It's startling and a little disorientating, and it makes my shame flare inside me again.

When the hug breaks, his eyes shine down at me, and I catch the obvious flick of his gaze to my lips. My breath catches in my throat as I realise he's contemplating kissing me. I quickly pull back and laugh awkwardly, getting some personal space.

"Well, thanks for the drink. I'd better get home," I mumble, kicking the toe of my work shoe into the gap between the paving slab.

Theo nods and steps back, too, his arms dropping down to his sides. "Yeah, see you next week then. If I don't see you before, that is."

"Why would you see me before?" I ask, frowning in confusion.

He laughs and reaches up to tousle his hair. "You know, if you come around with Jared or anything."

I blink. "Oh. Oh, right, yeah. Of course."

He bobs his head. "Well, see ya." He waves and turns, walking up the road and glancing back over his shoulder, sending me another of those heartbreaking smiles.

I feel the tears welling in my eyes as I turn and head back towards the station, so I can collect my bike. I'm absolutely none the wiser after that conversation. I think back to the three questions I set out answering this morning.

1. Am I physically attracted to Theo?

Answer: Yes. He is gorgeous, so of course, I am attracted to him. I didn't melt when he smiled at me like with Jared, and my insides didn't fizz with lust when he touched me or gave me the bedroom eyes—but that could be easily explained away. The guilt I'm feeling inside overrode everything. It's possible that my guilt for the situation is preventing me from thinking about those things too deeply. Maybe, once I let it go, the lust would come, just like with Jared? After all, I only felt the instant attraction to Jared because of Theo's personality on those train rides. Yes, I looked at Jared and was attracted to him when I met him in that café, but was that only because I was already attracted to Theo's personality before that?

2. Is there more chemistry with Theo than I have with Jared?

Answer: Unsure. We certainly have more in common than I do with Jared. We're into the same things, laugh at the same jokes, love the same movies. But does that equate to chemistry? I'm not sure.

3. Am I in love with Jared because I thought he was Theo all along?

Answer: I still have no idea.

I try to think it through again as I stroll back to the station and collect my bike. Then, I wheel her home instead of riding her because I'm mentally and physically exhausted from the situation.

I honestly can't say with much certainty which one of them I am in love with. And that makes my mind up for me. I can't keep on with this the way it is.

Tomorrow night, I will speak to Jared and explain everything. I know it won't go well. What guy wants to hear that his girlfriend, whom he's been dating for six weeks, has been dating the wrong guy all along? But I can't continue with this pretence. Neither of us deserves that, and it can't be swept under the carpet. It isn't fair to keep him in the dark about this.

If I tell him and I lose him over this, then maybe it was never meant to be in the first place. Only time will tell.

Jared is a level-headed guy; maybe he'll even be able to help me see the answer here.

TWENTY-FOUR

I'm so nervous; I feel sick. My heart races in my chest as I look up at the clock, watching the second hand tick around. I have just got off the phone with Heather. She had tried to talk me out of this, suggested I might lose them both if I tell the truth. But I don't care. I need to tell him. I can't keep something this important from someone I'm supposed to care about.

Just before seven thirty, the doorbell rings, and my heart sets off in a gallop. I push myself up on wobbly legs and head over to open the door. I'm greeted by Jared's grinning face, and I feel another fissure tear my heart. He looks amazing in jeans and a thin grey pullover, and a breathy sigh leaves my lips.

"Hey you," he greets, stepping into my flat. He reaches up and cups the side of my face with one hand, stepping so close to me that it makes every nerve ending in my body wake up and sing with pleasure. When he dips his head, his lips capture mine in a soft kiss.

My knees weaken, and my eyes drop closed as I lean in, putting my hands on his chest for support as the kiss deepens and his tongue traces my bottom lip. A whimper leaves my throat, and his other arm wraps around my waist, turning us so I'm pressed against the wall, trapped in a little cage by his hard body. His smell fills my lungs, the heat from his body pulsing into mine as his tongue strokes mine, all of it combined coaxing my excitement, drawing my passion into a frenzy.

Everything else is forgotten. Theo, the train, the coffee shop, the twin thing. It's all gone. All that's left is Jared and the deep feelings he's evoking in me.

He breaks the kiss and presses his forehead to mine; his breath blowing across my mouth makes it water. I stare into his eyes, and it's like we're in a little private bubble where nothing can hurt us. He's carved us a little place where we can just … be.

I cling to him, not wanting him to step back, not wanting this moment to break because I know the instant he moves away from me, our problems will come back again.

"Are you crying?" he asks, his voice husky and filled with concern as he bends his knees so we're on the same level, reaching over to wipe a thumb across my cheek.

Am I?

His eyes bore into mine, and I can see the alarm there.

I swallow and close my eyes, dropping my head forward into his chest, breathing him in as my silent tears continue to fall without my permission.

His arms wrap around me, holding me against him. "Amy? What's happened, baby?"

He tries to pull back, but I cling to him, so he has to pry me away from his body. I don't want this moment to end. I know as soon as I tell him, everything will be ruined, and I'll never be able to take it back. I want to put it off as long as possible before my life implodes irrevocably.

His eyes meet mine as his fingers grip my shoulders, holding me away from him as he studies my face. I can see the panic building inside him as he imagines the worst.

"I need to talk to you." My voice is barely above a whisper.

He nods, not taking his eyes from me as he releases one hand and shoves the front door closed. "Okay."

I gulp and step back. "We should go sit down."

I take his hands in mine and nod towards the sofa. The misery is building in my chest, making it hard for me to breathe as I lead him to the couch and sit. He sits close to me, his hand covering mine. It makes me feel both hot and cold at the same time. He's confusing, overpowering, intoxicating.

My mind flicks to Theo. He doesn't make me feel like this, but is that simply because I'm not comfortable with him like I am Jared? I've had weeks to get over my nerves, weeks to learn every curve to his body, every small imperfection to his skin. I know what it feels like to be physically close to Jared, so of course, he is going to whip my body into a frenzy like this with one kiss.

Jared reaches out and wipes another tear as it slides down my cheek. "Amy, tell me what's wrong."

I gulp. "I don't know where to start."

Concern knits his eyebrows together as he inches closer to me on the sofa, his hands rubbing my thighs soothingly. "Are you in trouble with something?" He blinks, and his lips pop open before he says, "Oh shit, are we pregnant?"

The *we* hurts my heart. It's like being dropped from a great height. My heart stammers in my chest at the sweet word.

"No."

When I quickly shake my head, his body loosens, and he huffs out a sigh. But at the same time I see relief, I also detect something else in his eyes ... maybe disappointment? But I decide to let that one go. I can't even think about that now.

"Good. That's good," he replies, licking his lips, his eyes still boring into mine.

I can't look at him. "Do you believe you can fall in love with someone without even knowing them?"

His hand closes over mine, his thumb rubbing my knuckles. "I never used to. But when I first met you, I felt a connection straightaway. I don't think it was love, but it was definitely something."

His answer is like a punch to the stomach. It *was* something.

His skin brushing mine is driving me mad. I pull my hand from his, twisting in my seat and folding my legs between us like a little barrier as I hug my knees to my chest.

"I need some space. I can't think straight when you're this close to me. You make my mind spin like a record player." I sniff loudly, swiping at the rogue tears that seem never-ending.

When I look over at him and the concerned worry I see building like a storm in his eyes, it makes the hate that I have for myself intensify. I detest myself for what I'm about to do and say. Jared doesn't deserve any of this. He's amazing, sweet, funny, and one of the best men I have ever met in my life. He deserves unconditional love, not a girl who is confused about her feelings for him.

My chin wobbles. "I'm so sorry."

"Amy, you're scaring me a bit now. What's happened?"

I nod, taking a deep breath. "I need to just say this. Please don't interrupt me; it's hard enough in the first place. I just need to get it out."

His back straightens, and the muscle in his jaw twitches over and over as he grinds his teeth. But he doesn't say a word.

"Before I met you, I fell in love with a guy who got on my train. He was everything I ever wanted in a man, but every time I saw him, I was so nervous that I barely said more than two words to him. For five months, he got on my train every other Monday, and I'd just fall more and more in love with him each time. Then, one day, I bumped into that guy outside a coffee shop. We talked, and he asked me out for dinner. I thought I was the luckiest girl in the world because everything was finally working out for me and the guy I'd been crushing on."

His body has gone still. I can't even see him breathing as he works it out.

I swallow my guilt. "I'm so sorry."

"Theo?" His voice is a husky growl, so he clears his throat. "Theo gets on your train."

I nod, my breathing hitching with sobs now. "I'm so, so sorry, Jared. I never meant to hurt you. I didn't know you had a twin. I didn't do this deliberately. I thought you were the guy from the train all along, the guy I'd been falling in love with for months. Then, when he turned up at the party …"

He blows out a big breath and rakes a hand over his face. "I think I would have preferred you telling me you were pregnant."

I whimper, "Me too."

He shifts on the sofa, the cushions squeaking under his weight as he rolls his neck on his shoulders and then scowls at the floor. "So, you were in love with Theo, and then you've been dating me all this time, thinking I was him?"

I nod.

"So, it's Theo you want to be with, him that you're in love with, not me?"

My heart crumbles at the pain I can hear in his voice. I reach for his hand, squeezing tightly. "I … I don't know. Maybe. My brain is a mess. I'm so confused. This all just came out of nowhere on Saturday. I love you. My heart aches; my body goes crazy when you're around me." That is the damn truth. I can feel the residual ebb of lust he created in me from just a simple kiss.

"But do you actually love *me* or the guy you fell in love with on the train? Because news flash: we're not the same person." His tone is loaded with sarcasm, but I don't blame him. He's hurt; I'm hurting him.

I groan, and my eyes fall closed. "I don't know. I'm so sorry."

He sighs, and quiet descends over us. He hasn't let go of my hand; we're still gripping each other for dear life.

Eventually, he breaks the deafening silence. "You know, I kind of knew something would come along to fuck this up."

I frown and look over at him. "Really?"

He nods, shrugging nonchalantly. "Yeah. I've never really had much luck with girls. Before you, I'd never met anyone I wanted to really be with; they were all just someone to pass the time with, someone to warm my bed.

"Funny thing is, my last girlfriend, even she preferred Theo to me. She tried it on with him a couple of times. I couldn't even blame her. Theo's great. He's the life and soul of the party. You could drop him in Trafalgar Square, and he'd be best friends with someone within ten minutes. It's a gift. Something I've been jealous of since as far back as I can remember.

"We're the complete opposites; we always have been. Mirror twins in every way. Everyone prefers Theo when they get to know him. He's always been the popular and sought-after one. Even at school, we hung in a big group, and he was the favourite twin—the one who was always first choice for a night out or wingman, always in the thick of it all. I just tagged along on the outskirts because I was his brother. He knows just what to say at the right time, how to act to make people love him. It comes easy to him. He's better than me at everything, even life in general." He snorts a laugh, but it's humourless and full of indignation.

I can barely breathe as I watch him closely, taking it all in.

"The only thing I've ever been better at than Theo is working hard. I did better at school than him. He's more creative; I'm more academic. I have a better work ethic than he does. I work harder and achieve more. It's the only way to surpass him. He even beat me to being born; I'm the younger twin by nine minutes. Even my mum has a favourite; she won't admit it, but it's obvious. I'm not winning the popularity contests against him."

As his eyes meet mine, I can see the sadness he's trying to disguise.

"I've felt second best my whole life." He laughs and shrugs, but I can hear the pain in his words. "I guess I finally felt like I was winning at something with you. That we were winning together as a team. Building something we could have that was just our own. I've never really had anything that was just mine before. Turns out, I'm even your second choice."

I shake my head. "Jared, no, that's not what I said." The guilt of it feels like it's crushing me. My tears double, and I rub at my chest because my heart is physically aching for him.

He turns to face me, reaching out, putting his hands on my knees, rubbing gently. "Look, this isn't your fault. You didn't know we were two separate people; you couldn't have known. If I had met you first, maybe we wouldn't have this problem now. If only I got the fucking train!" He jokingly waves his fist in the air in mock anger, and it seems to lighten the mood.

I can tell he's putting on an act that he's fine though. His words about being second best have resonated with me, something he can't take back. It's like a window into his soul, and no matter how much bravado he tries to put around this to disguise what he said, it's out of the box now, and it can never go back in.

I sniff and push myself up, wrapping my arms around his neck, tightly crushing myself to him. He sighs, his breath moving my hair, as he wraps his arms around me, too, pulling me onto his lap. I have to finish this. I haven't even told him the worst bit yet.

"There's something else. Please don't hate me," I whisper into his neck.

His hands stroke my back. "I won't. I never could, Amy."

His smell is beautiful; it's so comforting. I don't ever want to let go. But I know I need to get this finished. We can't just leave it there; this needs to be resolved somehow. I pull back and look into his eyes, sitting on his lap, my chest pressed against his, our faces inches apart.

My chin wobbles with emotion, but I take a deep breath and just say it, "I kissed him a couple of weeks ago."

I feel his body stiffen against mine. His hands curl into fists at the small of my back, and his eyebrows pull together into a scowl.

"It was a couple of weeks ago, when I went back to work after my holiday. He was on the train, and I thought it was you. I … I …" I don't want to say anything else, and I silently pray that's all the details he needs. I grip my hands into the back of his hair. "I'm so sorry. I thought it was you." I will him to believe me. "I don't want you and Theo to fall out over this. He didn't know who I was. I just kind of jumped him. He didn't even have a choice in the matter. He was so surprised; he barely even kissed me back. I don't think he knew what hit him."

A sad smile tugs at the corner of Jared's mouth. "I've been on the receiving end when your passion goes haywire, so I can imagine how shocked he was."

"I'm sorry," I whisper, closing my eyes as shame and disgust wash over me. "I hate myself for this whole situation. None of this is Theo's fault, and it would kill me if you two fell out. He didn't know any of this. When he walked into the party, he was just as surprised to see me as I was him." I gulp. "Theo said we should just keep the kiss to ourselves, not tell you because he didn't want you being upset over a mistaken identity. But he doesn't know the whole story. He doesn't know that I'd fallen in love with him on those train journeys. I couldn't keep that secret from you."

Jared's eyes lock on mine, his face a mask of steel. "So, I guess you're feeling pretty fucked up in here." He taps my temple with his index finger, his other hand pushing on the small of my back, so I press tighter against him.

I nod and gulp, reaching up to brush my thumb over the little freckle under his eye. "Yeah."

He sighs deeply, a resigned sigh, and I find myself tightening my grip on him because I know he's about to pull away. "I value your honesty. It's one of the things I love about you the most. You wear your heart on your sleeve. I just want you to be happy, Amy. I thought I was making you happy, but ..." He groans and shakes his head.

"You were," I say quickly.

"But it's not enough?"

My breath catches. "It *is* enough. It's just ... look, Jared, I'm crazy about you. I love you. You're the most amazing man I've ever met. But how do I know if I'm in love with you for you or because of all the time I spent falling for your brother? We're so different. Would we have even gotten this far together if I wasn't *already* in love with you? How do I work out my feelings when everything is so jumbled?"

He nods. "I'm not gonna lie; I hate this. It hurts like a kick to the balls, but I don't blame you. You didn't know."

His grip on me loosens, and I let out a needy whimper.

I shake my head, already knowing what he's about to say. "Don't say it."

"I have to." He strokes my hair. "I think we need to take a break. You need some time to think about this properly. You need to know how you feel. If you figure it out and it turns out you want Theo, not me, then you two should go for it." He grits his teeth, and I can see how much it pains him to say it.

My heart gives another squeeze.

"If you figure out it's me you want, great. I'm here. I'm all over this. I'm done for when it comes to you. I'm totally fucking smitten to the point of ruin, Amy. I'm still free-falling down that rabbit hole. But you need to figure it out first. I don't want to be your second choice. I can't go into a relationship that I hope is long-term, only for you to realise in a year's time that you're with the wrong brother. I don't want to live in Theo's shadow when it comes to you. He can have everything else—none of that is important to me—but I'm not content to be second best where you're concerned. You need to get your head straight, figure it out. I want you to choose me, but I'm not stupid. Everyone prefers Theo; it's the story of my life. And if that happens, then that's okay. I'll be okay."

I whimper, and my insides twist. My breathing is shallow, and I have no words. "Jared," I breathe his name and wrap my arms around him, holding him so tightly that I'm probably strangling him, but I just can't let go.

His arms wrap around me, too, and we cling to each other. His hug is luxurious. His smell, the feel of him, the way his breath tickles down my neck, the heat of his hands as his fingers dig into my sides—it's too much.

"We need a break," Jared says again. "Some space. Take as long as you need."

He scoots forward on the seat, but I don't let go. I clutch him closer.

"I really should go, Amy."

He pulls his head back, and I do the same, our eyes meeting.

He forces a smile, but it doesn't reach his eyes. "I can't help you with this one. You need to figure it out yourself. We need to make sure this is right before we go any further. If we're meant to be, we'll be. If not …" He trails off and shrugs sadly.

His words feel like he's gutted me with a blunt knife. I'm hollow, empty, just a raw, ragged mess. He eases me off his lap, and I stand on my weak legs, wrapping my arms around myself for comfort as my whole world feels like it's falling apart.

Sadness consumes me, and when he leans down and presses his lips against mine, I kiss him back with all the passion that I have, putting all my feeling into it. The kiss is beautiful, poignant, and heartbreaking.

I don't want him to go, but he's right. I need to fix this mess myself. There's no one else who can untangle this but me.

He breaks the kiss and presses his lips to my forehead. They linger there, and I close my eyes, savouring the feel of them.

"Bye, Amy." He pulls away, and I hear the hitch in his voice, but he's already walking away towards the door, pulling it open.

He strides through it, leaving me alone in my flat with my heart breaking and big, fat, devastated tears rolling down my cheeks.

TWENTY-FIVE

Two days pass, and they feel like the longest two days of my life—worse so than when I had that stomach bug where I didn't even move from my bathroom floor for thirty-six hours. Before this, that was the pinnacle of worst time of my life. I thought that was rock bottom. I was wrong. Now, that low seems like a distant memory and a far cry from the depressed state I've slipped into.

I've barely slept. I'm walking through life like a zombie. My emotions are all over the place, and all I can think about is Jared, Theo, and how the hell I can try to distinguish my feelings between the two of them. Where do my feelings for my train crush stop and my feelings for Jared begin? Or are they one and the same? Was what I had with Jared ever real? It felt so real at the time, but now, I can't be sure.

Through my confusion ... I miss Jared. I miss his voice, his smile, his sarcasm, and just the way he makes me feel when he holds me at night.

It doesn't help that there are little reminders of him everywhere. Even dreary, monotonous stuff like showering and brushing my teeth are tinged with memories of him. The stuff that he left here on Saturday (before my life imploded with the big twin reveal) still sits on the neat little spots he chose for them in my bathroom.

Even my bed is betraying me. What used to be my favourite place in the world is now a shrine to my on-a-break boyfriend. His scent is all over it, agonising and torturous as it lulls me to slumber where I dream of a magic-performing Jared, who turns and suddenly splits into two. And then, when I wake, I'm surrounded by his smell, and I'm reminded again of what I've lost. Because that's what it feels like, as if I've lost him, and it hurts more than I even care to admit to myself. I could change my sheets, get rid of the smell, but I can't bring myself to do that. I love it and hate it in equal measure. When the smell begins to fade slightly, I even find myself spraying his deodorant around the room like air freshener and spritzing my spare pillow—his pillow—with his aftershave just to torture myself further. I deserve it.

We haven't had any contact since he walked out of my flat and called time on us. The no-contact thing makes the time drag into one endless bad day and even worse nights where I cry myself to sleep.

Today is Thursday. I am seriously contemplating bending one of the fundamental on-a-break rules. I'm considering texting him.

His meeting with Gillian Jenkins was today, and I haven't been able to stop thinking about him all day long. I stare at my screen, seeing the message that I just typed out sitting there. I delete and type again. My thumb hovers over the Send button as I debate on if I can send it or not. Does on a break mean no contact at all? Most likely. But I am desperate to know how his meeting went.

I groan and read the message again.

Hey. How did your meeting go?

Light, friendly, just a question.

Before I can change my mind, I press Send and then drop my phone down next to me on the sofa and frown, waiting for his reply. Suddenly, a thought occurs to me: what if he doesn't reply? What if Jared isn't interested in speaking to me again after the pain I've caused, driving a wedge between him and his brother?

I groan and push my microwave meal around its little tray with my fork. The TV is on, but I can barely see it or concentrate on it.

When my phone beeps to life, I jump so hard and pick it up so quickly that I almost drop it in my food.

It was good. Thanks for asking.

I chew on my lip, worrying over the lack of a kiss on the end. Does that mean anything? Has he done a Ross from *Friends* and found himself a copy-place girl he can spend his "break" with? Is she getting the kisses from the end of his texts? Is that the type of break we're on? I seriously hope not because the thought of him with other girls makes my insides ache and my blood boil with jealousy.

I hit Reply, wanting to keep this small line of communication open.

Great news! Did anything come of it?

I debate on adding my own kiss on the end and decide against it.

Almost as soon as the status of the message changes to read, the phone rings in my hand. Jared's face appears on my screen, and my insides jolt. I could weep; I'm so happy.

I put the phone to my ear. "Hello?"

"Hey." The sound of his voice makes the hairs on my arms stand on end and my tummy flutter. "It would take too long to type it out, so I thought it would be easier just to call you," he explains.

I nod, savouring the sound of his voice. "How are you?" It's all I've been wanting to ask for the last two days, ever since he walked out of my flat and didn't look back.

"I'm okay. How are you?"

"Good," I lie, and it really is a total lie. I'm not doing good at all. All I can think every second of the day is the fact that I might have made a terrible, terrible mistake, but I just have no clue if that is right or not. "So, tell me about the meeting. I've been thinking about you all day, sending all the good vibes and Karma at you."

"Oh, is that what I was feeling, good vibes and Karma? I thought it was nerves," he jokes.

I smile and clutch the phone closer to my ear.

"Meeting went well. Really well actually. She loved almost all my ideas. She wants me to put together a proposal for the new specialist team and present it to the board in a couple of weeks. If that goes well and they approve it, I could be heading the department and taking on new staff, branching out, and expanding."

Pride swells in my chest, and I grin from ear to ear. "Jared, that's amazing. I'm so proud of you."

"Thanks." I can hear the modest embarrassment in his tone. Jared isn't one who likes to have a fuss made of him. "She asked about you. Remembered your name and everything."

I shift in my seat and wince. "Did she mention my Spanx?"

He laughs a loud, throaty laugh, and I feel it vibrate in my tummy.

"No. She just asked how you were. She said you were positively charming. Those were her exact words. She liked your honesty and asked if you wanted a job there."

"Ha! They couldn't afford me," I joke.

"I told her you probably wouldn't enjoy being bossed around either."

"Unless it was by you." The flirtation slips from my mouth before I even knew it was coming.

Jared laughs again.

"I hope you don't mind, but I didn't mention anything about what's going on. To be honest, I wouldn't even know where to start. I just said you were fine and that I'd pass on my regards to you," he says.

I close my eyes, hating that I put him in that position. "Of course that's fine. Next time you see her, tell her I said hi."

"We don't exactly hang out together in the tearoom or anything, but if I happen to see her around, I will." I hear the smile in his voice. "So, what time are you meeting Heather? Is she coming to yours, or are you two going out?"

I play with my food, stabbing the pasta and squishing it with the back of my fork. "We're not doing Tequila Thursday this week."

"Oh, really? Is she out of the country or dead?" he teases.

I love the fact that he remembers something I once joked weeks ago.

I shrug. "Neither. I just didn't fancy it tonight."

This is the first time in five years we've not had a BFF tequila night, but I just couldn't face it. I'm not in the mood to socialise. I know she would want to talk about Jared, and I'm just not up to it yet. It's too fresh and raw. I'm still too confused. We'd just end up going over the same old stuff until my head ached. Instead, I just want an early night and to snuggle in my Jared sheets.

"Really?" he asks, his tone concerned. "Are you all right? You're not dead, are you?"

I feel dead inside; does that count?

"I'm good," I repeat my earlier lie.

"Okay, so if you're not drinking margaritas tonight, what are you doing?"

"Right now, I'm just eating dinner."

"What are you having?"

"Microwave mac and cheese from Marks and Spencer."

"Ah, top-end, processed shit."

I laugh at the disgust and disapproval in his tone. "Yep, it's delicious."

I look down at the congealed mess in front of me and scrunch my nose up. It is categorically *not* delicious. Leaning forward, I push my plate onto the coffee table and decide not to even attempt to eat the other half of it.

"What are you doing?" I ask, changing the subject.

"Current status: sitting in bed, working on my laptop, talking to you," he replies.

My eyebrow rises. I can picture it clear as day, and my stomach clenches. "Do you want me to let you go, so you can get on with whatever you're working on?" *Please say no! Please say no!*

"No, it's fine."

I smile and look down at my nails. "So, how are things? Are you ..." I clear my throat. "Are you and Theo okay? You haven't fallen out over this, have you?" I wince, waiting for his answer.

"We're fine," he replies. There's a tough edge to his voice, but it doesn't sound like a lie. He's just finding it difficult, and it's probably a little awkward. "I told you, it's not anyone's fault."

I nod. It's not my fault, but I still feel guilty about it.

"Did you finish *Stranger Things*?" he asks—his turn to change the subject this time.

I raise one eyebrow. "No. I pinkie swore, remember? Why? Did you?" My mouth opens in shock as I think about him skipping ahead without me.

He laughs quietly. "I knew you wouldn't have. Seeing as you're not drinking your weight in margaritas and I have nothing on that can't wait until tomorrow, do you want to watch the next episode now?"

My eyes widen. *He wants to come over?* Panic surges through me as my eyes dart around my flat, seeing all the mess—the unwashed plates in the sink, the crumbs from my biscuits still sitting on the table, my neat pile of Dr Pepper cans I've been stacking on my worktop like a carnival ball toss game, my dirty clothes in a bundle next to my washing machine where I lost concentration earlier when I meant to put a load on. And my very much unshowered self, whose current best friend is a can of dry hair shampoo.

"Um ..." I know I'd need to delay him at least an hour, but the excitement at the prospect of seeing him is bubbling in my stomach.

Jared continues, "We can watch at the same time and talk on the phone. It'll be kind of like watching together. I don't think that constitutes a break in the pinkie-swear rules."

I smile in understanding, a little more disappointed than I care to admit that I'm not going to see him in person. But at least I won't have to rush around like a madwoman on crack and tidy up now.

"Okay," I agree.

"Great. Open Netflix and select the next episode," he instructs.

I do it, finding the place we made it to before everything went so wrong.

"Got it?"

"Yep."

I hear him tapping keys on his laptop. "Okay, I'm ready. Press play in three ... two ... one ..."

I hit play, and we synchronise the episode. Grinning, I put Jared on loudspeaker and sit back on the sofa, getting comfy. If I turn to the side slightly and try hard enough, I can imagine him sitting next to me and that nothing is messed up. It's nice. Really nice.

TWENTY-SIX

By the time the weekend finishes, Jared and I are over halfway through the new season of *Stranger Things* with just three episodes left. By my calculation, we will be finished on Wednesday night. I'm not looking forward to not having an excuse to talk to him after that. We've spoken every day, watching episodes together on the phone, chatting and laughing as we synchronise watching. We pretty much have it down to a fine art now. It works better, we've discovered, if we listen to the phone call with one earbud in rather than loudspeaker. Less echo that way from the TV, and we can still talk freely while watching.

During those hours of phone calls, neither of us has mentioned seeing each other again or even spoken of the situation at all. I love that he's giving me time to get my head in the right place. I appreciate it more than I can articulate. But the trouble is, nothing is getting any easier or clearer. I am beginning to wonder if it ever will. Or will it always be a murky mess? Will Jared and Theo always be interwoven and inseparable in my brain?

I've tried so hard to split them. I lie awake for hours, going over our separate interactions. Replaying memories of my crush on the train—him sharing his phone, chatting happily, reading his books, drawing. And I replay my time with Jared—our dates, our lazy Sundays, him meeting my mum and helping my nanna. And just the quiet moments we shared when the rain was pattering on the window and we snuggled on the sofa in our own little bubble or how I'd be perfectly content to watch him work when he was on a tight deadline. The little look of concentration that would create the line between his eyebrows that made my tummy fizz.

My mum's question keeps popping back into my head. *Would I have given that good looking, well-dressed man a second look if the first time I'd met him was at that coffee shop?* I have to admit … probably not. If it wasn't for Theo, I wouldn't have been with Jared. How do I know this? Because I remember the first time Theo got on my train all those months ago. I remember doing a double-take, thinking he was fire, but it was more in a celebrity-crush type of way, not a serious *I want to date that guy* type of thing. What made me really notice him was when he climbed off the train and turned back to help a lady lift her buggy down the step, all the while pulling silly faces at the toddler in the pram. I noticed it, stored it, and remembered him two weeks later when he got on my train again.

Of this, I am one hundred percent sure: Theo is the reason I was even with Jared in the first place. If that guy on the train had walked up to me that first day and asked me out, I would have likely said no. It took a while for me to become properly attracted to him, a lot of train journeys before I noticed I was slowly falling for him.

I am very specific in what I am attracted to, and on first glance, the Stone twins aren't that.

Theo was the reason I agreed to the dinner date with Jared. And the deeper I delve into it, the more I realise it wouldn't have happened if it wasn't for my crush on Theo. The chemistry on that date with Jared was off the charts; a small touch of his hand made my insides erupt with passion *because* I was attracted to him already. If I took away the sizzle from that date, would I have noticed that Jared and I had nothing in common? Would I have agreed to a second date, kissed him in that stairwell, thought about him all night long? No, I probably wouldn't have seen him again. I certainly wouldn't have slept with him on a second date. That knowledge hurts.

But the other side of the argument I keep having with myself is, maybe it was supposed to happen like this. Maybe *I am* supposed to be with Jared, but fate knew I wouldn't have given him a chance, so she sent in Theo to butter me up and mellow me out before she threw the real prize at me. It seems unlikely. And if that is somehow true, fate has one seriously messed up sense of humour. It seems to me like I am reaching a bit here with my explanations, trying to justify chemistry where there should be none.

One thing I know for sure though: I love talking to Jared. I love that, after watching TV together for the last few days, before he hangs up the phone, he promises to call the next night, so we can watch some more. Not least because it means that, if he is on the phone with me, he isn't out screwing other girls. That knowledge makes me deliriously happy.

My weekend breezes by, and before I know it, it's Monday again, just an average, dreary Monday. I'm on my last trip, the London to Cambridge 3:12 p.m., when I step into the last carriage and stop short. Theo is sitting there, chilled and relaxed, his book open in his lap, his feet stretched out and propped on the seat in front of him. I didn't see him get on the train. In fact, this isn't even one of his weeks. He went to London only the week before, so he isn't due again until next week.

I step to his side. "Hey."

He looks up from his book and gives me a cheerful smile, sitting up in his chair more, his feet dropping to the floor. "Hi." He reaches into his pocket, pulling out his ticket.

"I didn't see you this morning?" I say, glancing at his ticket.

Theo blows out a big breath and rolls his eyes. "I missed the usual early train. Had to get the next one. Always knew it would happen eventually." He shrugs. "My bed is too warm and comfy to get out of, especially this time of year when it's all dark and depressing in the mornings at that time. Early starts should be illegal."

I smile, my eyes discreetly raking over him. Eight in the morning isn't even that early compared to how early some people start—Jared, for example.

"I thought your week was next week?" I pass him back his ticket.

"I got an extension on my deadline, remember? I told you last week. Because I hadn't finished my illustrations, I was meeting my publisher again this week."

Understanding washes over me, and I nod quickly. "Oh, yeah. I remember you saying that now."

He smiles and closes his book after dog-earing the corner to mark his spot. "You're finishing your shift now, right? This is your last train? Want to get a drink now or some food?"

He remembered when my last train home was? Did he deliberately get on this train to ask me out?

I chew on my lip and shrug. This might be my best chance at working out my feelings once and for all. "Okay, sure. I'm starving actually. I dropped my lunch today when I was swooped by a pigeon that looked like it had rabies." I indignantly scrunch my face.

He bursts out laughing, and I narrow my eyes in reprimand. It really wasn't funny at the time. I screamed and basically tried to ninja-chop it, all while looking extremely stupid, much to the amusement of my colleagues and people nearby. Classic Amy.

"Yeah, laugh it up, arsehole," I joke, rolling my eyes.

He shoots me an amused smile, fighting for control. "I'll meet you out front then, shall I? Like last time?" he offers when he finally stops laughing and the train starts to slow because we're approaching the last stop.

I nod and smile. "Sure. See you in a bit." I wave over my shoulder and head back to work, strangely excited but at the same time dubious about the plans I've made. Again, it feels like I'm somehow cheating on Jared by just hanging out with his brother even if it is just an innocent friend thing.

By the time I'm finished and ready to go home, I fiddle with my bag strap and head out through the station to see Theo is standing by the main entrance, waiting for me again. He beams over at me as I walk to his side.

"So, where do you want to eat? There's a place down the road that does, like, barbeque food. They serve all day. I think it's even happy hour at this time," he offers, looking at his watch.

I know the place he means, and my mouth waters as I nod emphatically. "I love it there! Let me just grab my bike, and I'll wheel it there—saves me coming back this way after."

The restaurant is halfway home for me.

He watches as I unlock Bessy, hefting her upright and pushing her along with us as we keep pace on the short journey. When we get there, I carefully lock her up outside. It's weird, walking with him. He walks differently to Jared, I've noticed. Less stiff, his arms just kind of swing, his body lollops along rather than the measured strides I'm used to. His hair is less styled too, as if he half-heartedly attempted to tame it this morning and gave up because he was too tired. It's almost comical, their differences.

When we're seated and looking over the menus, the smell in the air makes my tummy grumble, and I put my hand over it, silently cursing the pigeon again. "What have you been up to? Other than working?" I ask as he comes back from ordering our food and drinks.

He sits back in his seat and takes a large gulp of his beer. "Went to the Lake District this weekend with a couple of friends. It was one of their birthdays, so it was basically just a piss-up weekend in a cabin. Trouble is, they're both quite sporty and into exercise and fresh air and all that crap."

He wrinkles his nose, and I laugh.

"So, they decided early one morning—after we'd been doing shots the night before, I might add—that it'd be a great idea to hike up one of the mountains. Picture me, absolutely hanging, climbing a damn mountain. Never felt so rough. I think I actually died twice on the way up. So, basically, my friends are now dead to me."

I chuckle and watch as he pulls out his phone, scrolling through the screen before turning his phone so I can see. In the first picture, he's sitting on the top of a mountain on a pile of rocks, pale, his head in his hands. Behind him is a beautiful backdrop of scenery, but as he flicks through the photos, it's just him in various stages of dying at the top, and his friends ripping the absolute life out of him for it.

"Claim to fame: I puked up there. I'm probably the first ever to," he says confidently. "I can probably find an actual action shot of that if you want?" he jokes.

"Hard pass," I scoff, shaking my head in amusement. I chew on my lip and take a sip of my drink. "Jared didn't go with you?"

I know he didn't because he was talking to me last night, but Jared had told me he shared friends with his brother, so it surprises me he didn't go away with them for the weekend.

Theo shakes his head. "Nah, he said he had work and was invested in watching some show or something. He was invited but said no. I was surprised though. Climbing mountains is the type of thing Jared would enjoy. The weirdo."

I smile, my insides clenching at his answer. Invested in watching a show—is that because we were watching it together?

The food comes over then, and I gasp down at mine in excitement. I've chosen the chicken wrap with fries, and it looks incredible. My mouth waters.

Theo watches as I take a bite and then says, "So, it turns out, you thought I was cute on those train journeys too, huh?"

I choke on my shock. The food that was delicious now tastes like cardboard in my throat as I look at him with wide eyes. I chew and swallow. His eyes don't leave mine the whole time.

"We made it a full thirty minutes without that coming up. Then, you had to go and ruin it." I try to make light of the conversation as embarrassed heat burns from my neck to my hairline. I squirm on my seat.

He shrugs casually and picks up his knife and fork, cutting into his burrito. "It needs airing. Dirty laundry just festers if not washed."

I chuckle at his stupid analogy. "That's true."

He nods, thoughtful. "So, you and Jared are currently on a break, I heard, because you're not sure if you like him or me."

I suck in a breath and sit back in my chair. "That's not exactly it." *Or is it exactly that?*

He raises one eyebrow and waits.

"I … I noticed you on those train journeys," I admit, fiddling with my napkin. "I liked you." Understatement. "So, when I met Jared, I thought you were the same person."

He nods in understanding. "So, where do feelings for me come into this? Jared said you confused things and weren't sure if you were in love with me or him."

Oh God, kill me!

My mouth opens and closes like a fish. He's putting it so simply, but this isn't simple.

"I was attracted to you. I'm not sure if that's love or not. We hadn't even really spoken." I grind my teeth. "I love Jared. I'm just worried that …" I sigh, not having the right words. "That maybe it's not real. Maybe my feelings I had for you messed everything up, clouded things in my brain. That maybe what I thought I'd felt for you got tangled with what I thought I felt for him. And now, I'm not sure what I even feel at all."

"Sounds like quite a conundrum."

I nod. "And I've always been shit at puzzles."

He laughs and reaches up to rub at the back of his neck. "And what can I do to help you make up your mind?" His tone is flirty and suggestive.

His eyes bore into mine, and I can see the passion there. It makes my back stiffen.

I drop my eyes to the table and shrug. "Nothing."

"Are you and Jared going to work it out, you think?" he asks, stuffing in a forkful of burrito.

"I don't know."

"Maybe we could, you know, go out again this week or at the weekend. See how it goes? I did see you first. Rules are rules. I should have called dibs. Though if I said that to Jared, he'd probably reply he licked it, so it's his."

I feel the blush creep onto my cheeks. He certainly did lick it.

Coming back to his question, I think about it. Theo is so easy to get along with. Like Jared once said, he knows exactly what to say at the right time to make people love him. It's so easy to see why I was so won over on those train journeys. And we're so compatible; our humour is the same. No, he doesn't make my panties wet with a smile like Jared does, but is that because there's all this guilt inside me and a horrible feeling that I shouldn't even be here? If I were willing to let that go, I could probably build something with Theo and have fun while doing it. But my mind shoots back to Jared and how much that would hurt him. I'm not willing to do that.

"I don't think that's such a good idea, Theo."

"How are you ever going to know then?" he asks, cocking his head like a curious puppy as he regards me with interest.

"I don't know."

Maybe I never will know. At this point, I'm still so confused over it that I have even considered not seeing either of them again. Maybe they would both be better off in the long run. I don't want to ruin their relationship by choosing one over the other. Maybe I should just request a transfer to another route at work so I don't see Theo and then just delete Jared's number from my phone. A clean break from them both. Move on. I could take a vow of celibacy, adopt ten dogs, and become the local crazy dog lady. Lonely forever. I would rather that than hurt Jared.

The rest of my week has been pretty dull. After parting ways with Theo on Monday night—and rejecting his offer to swap numbers again—I went home and just had time to shower and slip into my comfy lounge pants before Jared called, and we watched more of the season.

The trouble now is, Jared and I are all caught up on the show. We binged it all, and there are no more episodes to watch. The last one was viewed during the week, and I am extremely disappointed about it. I miss Jared and his closeness and his crinkle-eyed smiles that make my insides flutter. The phone calls have taken some of that loneliness away. But because the show is finished, we have no excuses to talk; therefore, when we hung up the phone last time, we didn't agree a time to speak again.

It's been three days since my last Jared fix. I am unreasonably disappointed that he hasn't instigated contact again since then because I haven't felt like I can. I hope he is just busy with work. I know he had a big project on, some hotshot company that has a massive ad budget, because he told me about it and how important it was. I just have to hope that's the only reason he's not called and not just the fact that he's had enough of hanging on a shoestring, waiting for me to make up my damn mind.

It has been almost two weeks now since we began our break, and there is no end or solution in sight.

When my phone rings, I jump for it, suddenly thinking it's Jared. I grin and pick up the phone, only to see it's a mobile number I don't have saved and not his handsome face lighting up my screen.

My disappointment is all-consuming, and I scowl down at the phone in anger.

I sigh and debate on not bothering to answer it; it's likely one of those accident firms.

Hello, we've been told you were recently involved in an accident. Is that right?

But the trouble is, I'm lonely. It's a Friday night, and I'm sitting in my pyjamas, eating Ben & Jerry's straight from the tub, watching reruns of *90 Day Fiancé: The Other Way*, and trying to justify how my life could be worse because at least it's not as messed up as some of these people on the show!

So, I answer the call, expecting an automated voice.

Instead, I'm greeted by the sounds of someone crying—hysterical crying at that.

"Hello?" I frown.

"Amy? Amy, it's Deborah."

The name means nothing to me for a split second, and then I blink in understanding. Jared's mother. Dread settles over me, and I feel my body go cold.

"Deborah? Is everything okay?"

"There's been an accident!"

My mouth goes dry. "What? When? Who?" My hand flies up to my chest as horror builds within it. Everything stops as I wait for her to speak.

"Both of them!"

TWENTY-SEVEN

"What?" My eyes widen, and I jump to my feet. "What's happened, Deborah, please?"

"I don't know!" she wails down the line. "I just got a call from a nurse at the hospital. I'm listed in Theo's phone as the emergency contact. It's both of them. Both!" She's crying so much that I can hardly make out her words.

I swallow my horror, my body going cold at her words and the sound of her distress.

"Are they okay?" My grip on the phone is so tight that my hand aches.

I hold my breath and wait for her reply, but it doesn't come. Instead, there's jostling and crackling on the line, and a new voice comes on.

"Amy, it's Kenneth."

Panic is beginning to consume me. "Kenneth, what's happened? I don't understand. What kind of accident?" My heart is racing in my chest.

"Deborah just received a phone call. There's been a car accident. Both the boys were in the car. One has a broken leg and some other injuries but is relatively stable."

He stops talking, and I can hear Deborah's wails grow louder in the background.

"And the other?" I prompt desperately.

"The other one has head injuries and some internal bleeding. They've had to rush him into surgery."

Oh God, no. Please, no.

Surgery. My legs give out at the word, and I drop onto the sofa, putting my head in my shaky hand. "Which?" I croak, unable to form a full sentence. My brain hurts, and my stomach clenches as I wait for him to answer. My mind is still messed up, my feelings for them both so tangled that I don't know what I want him to say.

"We don't know which is which. They were on their way back from the gym, so both had workout gear on and their wallets in their gym bags. Because they had no ID on them, they don't know which wallet or bag belongs to which one."

Kenneth clears his throat. "Amy, I need you to go to the hospital. Can you do that for me? We're on our way there now, but we've been away, visiting family, and we're still an hour out at least. I need you to go there and see if you can tell which one is which. The doctors want to know. Please? Amy, can you …"

"Yes," I whisper my reply. I'm already on my feet, grabbing my handbag and keys, slipping my shoes on.

"Thank you! Thank you, Amy! They're at Addenbrooke's. Go to A and E department. Can you let us know? I'll be driving, but if you could, call Deborah as soon as you know anything."

"The one in surgery, is he going to be okay?" I ask, squeezing my eyes shut as I wait for him to answer. Abject terror is building like a storm inside me.

"We don't know. They told us to hurry and that it was serious," he answers.

His words feel like they're killing me.

Serious. How serious? Is one of them going to die? Which one?

I nod and say my good-byes, running out of my flat so fast that the door bangs shut and flies open again.

"Shit! Come on!" I hiss, grabbing for it and yanking it closed again before thrusting my key in the lock and angrily twisting it.

I turn and bolt for the stairs, taking them three at a time, almost face-planting as I get to the bottom where my body is going too fast for my legs.

I fumble with my keys again, finding the one that fits the communal storage cupboard at the bottom of the stairs. After wasting precious seconds attempting to get my key in the lock with my hands shaking like jelly, it finally opens, and I wrench out Bessy, throwing my leg over her and pushing away from the wall in one smooth movement. My panic is taking over, I'm losing it, my brain is spinning so fast that it's making me feel dizzy, but I have to hold it together. All that matters is getting to the hospital. Jared and Theo are hurt, one of them seriously so, and I need to get there.

As I join the road, my mind not really on the task at hand but more on the two men in hospital, a car horn blasts behind me, and then it overtakes me, the guy opening his window to flip me the bird. I wobble precariously and wave an apology, pushing my legs faster on the pedals, wishing I had a car.

The hospital is a good fifteen-minute bike ride away, but I make it in nine. By the time I arrive, I'm sweating, exhausted, and gasping for breath. Tears are streaming down my face, and at some point on the manic ride over here, I've realised I'm in my Winnie the Pooh pyjamas and am not wearing a bra. But none of that matters as I jump off my bike, unceremoniously dumping it against the railings and not even bothering to lock it up. I run for the A&E department so fast that I almost trip over my own feet.

I'm almost frantic by the time I race up to the reception window and skid to a halt. I reach up and swipe the tears from my face. The receptionist looks up, startled.

"Hello, can I help you?" she asks, shooting me a worried smile.

I nod, gulping in lungsful of air. "Car accident. Two men brought in. Twins." I can barely get my words out. My mouth has gone dry, my tongue sticking to the roof of my mouth as I pant for air.

Understanding crosses her face, and she nods. "Just wait there a second. I'll buzz Beverly for you. She's the nurse who called the next of kin." She holds up one finger and then picks up the phone, pressing the buttons frustratingly slowly.

I lean against the counter for support as I glance around the waiting room. It's only half full, and some of the people watch me with interest. I must look a sight, a girl hyperventilating and covered in a sheen of sweat, wearing pyjamas. I can't bring myself to give a damn.

Finally, the receptionist puts the phone down and smiles at me. "Beverly will be out in just a moment."

I step back, my eyes darting around, unable to stay on one thing for more than a second as I wring my hands and chew on my lip. The wait is like torture. Thoughts rush through my head so fast that I can barely process them before they're gone.

It takes a couple of minutes before the receptionist waves over my shoulder. "Beverly, this is the lady you've been waiting for. With the twins."

She nods to me, and I turn, seeing a petite lady with mousy hair walking towards me. There's a sad smile on her face, and my heart sinks.

"Hi, are you Amy? I was told you were coming in because their parents are a while away." She reaches for me and nods towards the double doors at the end of the corridor. "Come with me."

"Are they okay?" The words hurt my throat on the way out, and I look over at her with wide eyes.

She purses her lips, seeming to choose her words. "I'm afraid I can't tell you too much, as you're not next of kin. One of them is up in surgery. It's touch and go; he was very badly injured. But they're both in the best place. We're doing all we can. It would really help us though if we could identify them. I'm not sure if you were told much, but it was a car accident, a pretty bad one. Neither of them had ID on their person. The paramedics found their wallets and phones in the car, but as they're identical, it's impossible for us to tell from their licences which is which."

She shoots me a sad smile, and I nod in understanding.

I blindly follow her down corridors, past closed curtains and open ones where people sit or lie on beds, their faces scrunched with pain. My head is swimming, my stomach churning so much that I wonder if I actually need to vomit. The adrenaline of the phone call is wearing off now, and my exhaustion is making my legs feel like concrete blocks as I try to keep pace with the petite little nurse, who's surprisingly fast, her shoes squeaking on the linoleum floor.

"The one who's down here has a fracture of the tibia, two broken ribs, and some cuts and bruises. He's unconscious at the moment, and we're going to get him up into surgery to set his leg as soon as possible."

As we approach the end of the corridor, a doctor looks up.

Beverly waves to get his attention. "This is Amy. She's here to identify the Stone twins if possible." She turns to me. "Do you think you can? Is there some kind of distinguishing mark?"

I nod, unable to speak, my chin wobbling as more tears fall.

"Great." The doctor nods and steps to the side of a blue curtain, tugging it back.

I drop my eyes, taking a couple of deep breaths, trying to prepare myself. I study a little black mark that stains against the cream floor, wanting to put this off as long as possible. I'm not sure who I want to see lying in the bed. Whichever one is here, it means the other is fighting for his life in surgery. My feelings are still interwoven for them both. Either way, this whole situation is awful.

I can barely force my eyes up, but I make myself. The figure on the bed is smashed and still. There's blood smeared on his face, tubes sticking from his hand. His leg is strapped in some kind of blue boot thing, and I can see bloodstained bandages over it. His head is strapped to a red board, blocks stuffed around his ears, holding him still. The heart rate monitor beeps steadily next to his bed.

A whimper cracks out of my throat, and I reach up to cover my mouth. Looking at him lying there is like torture.

The doctor clears his throat, and I look up at him, seeing him watching me expectantly. I glance back at the man in the bed and force my heavy legs forward, leaning over so I can see his face.

My eyes search among the grime, seeking out the little mole. There it is … under his *right* eye.

What's left of my heart breaks even further as emotion so powerful washes over me that I have to grip the edge of the bed for support as my knees almost give out.

"This is Theo Stone," I croak. The words feel as if they rip my throat on the way out, and I sink down into the chair next to his bed and weep.

TWENTY-EIGHT

I'm broken, fundamentally broken inside. Nothing works. My body is uncoordinated and jerky, and my breathing comes out in ragged gasps as I sob into my hands. All I can see when I close my eyes is Jared, alone, fighting for his life. The thought of losing him is killing me, tearing me apart inside.

When I'm finally able to breathe again, I dial Deborah. She answers on the first ring, her voice a desperate plea as she says my name.

I clear my throat. "Hi, I'm here. It's Jared who's in surgery. Theo's okay." My voice breaks, and I can't say anything else as my vision blurs with tears.

Deborah lets out a pain-filled wail that I feel in my gut, and we basically cry together down the phone for a good five minutes, neither of us saying a word.

"Deborah, tell Amy we'll be there soon. Maybe half an hour. Deborah!" Kenneth says in the background.

But all that comes down the line from Deborah is a pitiful squeak.

I nod in understanding, my breath hitching. "I heard. Half an hour," I mumble, just needing to be off the phone. "I'll see you soon. Drive safe." I disconnect the phone and swipe at my tears.

"Amy?"

I jump and turn, seeing a familiar face tentatively poking around the end of the curtain.

Tim frowns at me and pulls the curtain back some more when he sees it is me. "I thought I heard your voice! What are you doing here?" He steps in the cubicle, and his gaze drops to the bed, his eyes widening in surprise. "Oh shit! What happened?"

With one arm, he engulfs me in a hug, pulling me against his body. With the other, he picks up the chart from the end of the bed and starts looking over it.

I press my face into his chest, wrapping my arms around him in a bear hug, ignoring that he smells slightly of stale sweat and cheese and onion crisps. He's probably coming to the end of a twelve-hour shift. It's so good to see him and be comforted that I don't even care.

"It's not Jared," I croak, crying into his neck as he rubs my back. "It's his brother. Jared is …" I whimper and squeeze my eyes shut. "Jared is in surgery. They … they …" I'm hyperventilating, and I can't finish my sentence.

Tim pulls back and drops the chart on the bed, tightly gripping my shoulders. "Breathe. You need to chill. Take a deep breath. In through the nose, out through the mouth, like this."

He shows me how, his breath blowing across my face as I force myself to copy him, my eyes latched on his. My heart is jackhammering so fast in my chest that it feels like it's about to explode.

When I'm finally more in control, Tim pulls me into a hug again. "Amy, I have to go for a bit. I came down here to collect a patient. I thought I heard your voice, so I came to check, but they're probably waiting for me right now. I'll go get my patient and take her up to my ward, and then I'll come back down here, okay?"

I sniff and pull back, putting on a brave face even though I feel like I'm slowly dying inside. "You don't have to. Jared's parents will be here soon."

He waves off my protests with a flick of his hand. "I'm due a break anyway. Give me ten minutes, and I'll come sit with you until his parents arrive." He leans in and kisses the side of my head before squeezing my hand and slipping out of the gap in the curtain again.

Once alone, I can barely look at Theo. It's too painful. Guilt and shame swirl in my stomach with the agony and worry, and every glance at his face just makes that intensify.

For something to do, I pick up the chart and clip it back on the end of his bed, and then I fiddle with the hand sanitiser lotion bottle. Eventually, when there's nothing else for me to busy myself with, I watch his heart rate monitor until Tim arrives back downstairs ten minutes later.

When he pokes his head around the curtain, I smile at him gratefully. Having him here doesn't make anything easier; it just means I have someone to cling to. I feel lost, like I'm stuck on a rock in the middle of the ocean with waves crashing around me, growing more intense and terrifying with each one.

Tim takes my hand and looks over at Theo. "Heather told me about the twin thing. It's crazy how much they look alike. Now, I see why you didn't know."

I nod and chew on my lip. "Tim, can you ask them if there's any news about Jared? I asked them earlier, and they said they can't tell me anything because I'm not next of kin." I look at him pleadingly.

He nods and leaves, coming back a couple of minutes later and shaking his head. "No news yet. He's in surgery."

His eyes are alight with concern, and my body goes cold.

"What aren't you telling me? What else did they say?"

He shakes his head. "Nothing. They didn't say anything else. It's just … he's in a bad way, Amy. He might not …" He shakes his head again, and he doesn't need to finish the sentence.

Jared might not make it. I can see the sorrow and anguish on Tim's face.

I blink rapidly when my eyes burn with unshed tears. I refuse to let myself believe it. "He'll be fine. He has to be." *Because I don't know what I'll do if he's not.* I shake my head and lift my chin. "He'll be fine," I repeat, more confident this time, pushing down my inner voice that isn't quite so sure.

Silence lapses over us. He just sits with me and holds my hand until Jared's parents arrive. They bustle in, a hysterical sobbing mess, and Deborah leans over Theo's unconscious body, fussing with the sheets and stroking his face. Kenneth looks down at me sadly, and I stand.

Tim squeezes my hand. "I'll leave you to it now. I should get back to work."

Kenneth turns to him, his eyes wide with urgency as he spots his nurse uniform and name tag. "Can you tell us anything? How are they? Have they given any indication how the surgery's going?"

Tim clears his throat, and his eyes flick to me and then back to Kenneth again. "I'm sorry. I don't work in this department. I'm a friend of Amy's. I saw her come in, so I've just been keeping her company, waiting for you. You should ask at the nurses' station; they'll call upstairs for you and get an update."

"Oh." Kenneth nods and steps aside, so Tim can pass. Then, he steps to my side and puts a supportive hand on my shoulder. "Have they told you anything? Why is Theo still out?" His fingers dig into my shoulder, and Deborah looks up at me hopefully.

I shake my head. "They won't tell me anything. I'm not next of kin. Every time I ask, they just say they can't tell me anything. They just said I could wait in here with him until you arrived."

Deborah's distraught eyes flick to her husband in a silent plea, and he nods in understanding.

"I'll go find someone." He leaves, and I go to Deborah's side, wrapping my arm around her shaking shoulders.

She turns in my arms and hugs me tightly. We cling to each other like we're both on that rock in the middle of the ocean, just waiting for a lifeline to come save us.

Kenneth is pale when he comes back, and my muscles tense. He swallows a couple of times.

"Okay, so Theo has a broken leg, couple of ribs. They're going to send him up to surgery soon to set his leg. The doctor thinks it needs to be pinned."

My eyes flick to his leg, and I wince, a cold shiver trickling down my back.

"Other than that, he's doing okay. Scans and tests all came back good. They're just keeping the head blocks on as a precaution, as he's likely to have muscle damage in his neck."

I nod. Waiting.

He clears his throat again, reaching up a shaky hand to wipe at his face. "Jared is in surgery now. He was driving and hit the steering column hard. There's ... some damage to his heart."

His heart? Oh God.

A whimper slips from my mouth, and I clench my fists, digging my nails into my palms, trying to fight for control when all I want to do is scream and wail.

"They're in surgery now, fixing the blood vessels or something. There's some other stuff, but it's the heart they're most concerned about." Kenneth's voice cracks as he says it.

He'll be fine. I repeat it silently, over and over in my head. I can't bear to think about any other outcome.

Jared Stone is not allowed to die. I simply forbid it.

Kenneth goes to Deborah's side and holds her while she cries. I feel a little like I'm intruding in their moment, but I can't seem to make myself move. My whole body is numb and frozen to the spot.

"When they bring him out of surgery, they'll place him on the cardiology ward upstairs. They said there's a waiting room up there we could sit in, or they'll call down once he's out."

Deborah pushes Kenneth away from her. "You go. You go upstairs and wait for Jared. I'll stay here and wait for Theo."

Their eyes meet in silent conversation, and Kenneth nods, his arms dropping to his sides.

"Okay." He turns to me. "Would you like to come upstairs with me, or would you rather …"

He looks back to his lifeless son lying in the bed, and I know in that instant that they know about the whole situation and the mistaken identity, my confused feelings.

I swallow around the lump in my throat. "I want to see Jared." My words are confident, and I lift my chin, expecting some confrontation about the whole thing.

But Kenneth just smiles sadly and nods, leaning in to kiss his wife on the top of the head before stepping to the curtain and pulling it aside to make a gap. I force a smile and step to Deborah's side, rubbing her back as she fusses over Theo again, brushing the hair away from his face, dabbing and wiping at his dirty face with a tissue she's produced from her bag.

She pats my hand but doesn't take her eyes from Theo. "Let me know as soon as you hear anything, okay?"

I nod and turn, following Kenneth as he strides from the room. I follow him out on my wobbly legs, trying to match my outer demeanour to his cool and calm one. He reminds me a lot of Jared—fearless, unfazed by life, ready to take on the world. I try to tap in on that strength because I feel like I'm two seconds from having a full-blown mental breakdown. The air around me feels thin, and I feel a little light-headed.

When we get to the ward, a nurse shows us to the waiting room, promising to let us know as soon as she hears something. Kenneth and I sit. The TV is on, but I just can't concentrate on the words. We don't really speak other than the odd mumbled pleasantry. Neither of us has polite chitchat in us as the worry builds and builds. My eyes flit up to the clock on the wall every three minutes, which makes the time drag even further.

It's a very long two hours before a woman walks in, wearing surgery scrubs. My heart stutters in my chest. Kenneth jumps up, his features alight with worry. I'm watching the lady's body language, trying to second-guess what she's about to say. Is that expression one of sorrow, or is that small smile a good sign? I feel sick as I push myself to standing, too, and wait.

"Mr Stone?" she asks, looking at Kenneth.

He nods quickly, reaching up to scrub at his face. "Yes. Yes, hello."

"Hello, Mr Stone. I'm Doctor Prince, one of the surgeons who was working on your son Jared." Her eyes flick to me. "Is it okay to talk to you now or …"

Kenneth nods quickly. "Yes, this is Amy, Jared's girlfriend."

Jared's girlfriend. The words are so sweet that I feel emotion clog my throat and sting my eyes.

The doctor smiles at me. "Ah, okay. It's nice to meet you both. I just wanted to let you know that they'll be bringing Jared down here to the cardiology ward in a few minutes. Has anyone explained his condition to you?"

He's alive! He's okay. I reach up and grip fistfuls of my hair, my stomach loosening a little at her words. I close my eyes and focus on that. *Baby steps. He's out of surgery.*

Kenneth clears his throat. "No." His voice is hoarse, as we sat in silence for so long.

The doctor nods. It's then that I notice her smile is still tight. "Well, during the crash, Jared sustained multiple injuries. The one we were most concerned about was his chest. He must have hit the steering column quite hard. That caused what we call a myocardial contusion, kind of like a bruise to the heart. It can be serious, depending on how much damage was caused. In Jared's case, we had to rush him up to surgery to repair some of the blood vessels around his heart." She looks from Kenneth to me and back again. "We're happy with the way the surgery went. He seems stable now. We're going to keep him sedated for a little while and keep him on a ventilator, just to let things settle so his heart doesn't have to work too hard. Give him a bit of a rest and some time to recover. There's a chest tube in, just to stop any fluid that might build around the area."

My whole body is numb as I just stare at her, taking in her words. Kenneth reaches over and wraps his arm around my shoulders.

The doctor smiles sympathetically and continues, "He also had some lacerations to his liver and some internal bleeding, which we've managed to get under control. There was also an open fracture to the skull, or compound fracture as it's also known, but tests we've run so far indicate there's no damage to the brain. We'll keep a very close eye on him for the next few hours. All being well, tomorrow, we'll schedule more tests."

"Skull fracture?" Kenneth repeats.

I close my eyes as I feel the warmth drain from my body. The list of his injuries is alarming, and my stomach begins to ache.

"Like I said, we've done scans, and there doesn't appear to be any damage to the brain. We'll scan again tomorrow to make sure there's no change. At the moment, we're more focused on getting his heart in good working order. The surgeons are optimistic, but it is early days."

Early days. Code for don't get your hopes up and be prepared to say good-bye just in case.

Impossibly, my heart breaks a little bit more.

"Once he's all settled on the ward, one of the nurses will come and get you, and you can go in and see him," the doctor says.

Kenneth sticks out his hand, and they shake. When the doctor turns to me, my arm weighs so much that I can barely lift it to return her polite gesture.

As she leaves the room, I turn to Kenneth, who blows out a relieved breath and runs a hand through his hair.

"I should call Deborah real quick." He fumbles with his phone, and I slump back into my seat, listening to him reassure his wife that everything went well and promising to call once we have seen him.

All I can think is the words the doctor said. *"Early days."* It's swirling around and around in my head, the worry building in intensity.

After another few minutes, we're ushered along the corridor and into a side room containing just four beds. Kenneth rushes to Jared's side, and I stop at the foot of his bed, looking down at him in sheer dismay. He looks so broken and vulnerable. My hand flies to my mouth to stifle my whimper. He's attached to all manner of machines and IV lines; tubes are strapped to the side of his bed with bags of blood and fluid collecting in them. There's a machine squeezing air into his lungs and another showing each precious pump of his heart. His face is bruised and swollen; his chest and head are bandaged. It's like something out of a nightmare, a nightmare where the love of your life is so dangerously close to leaving you that you can barely stand it.

I let my eyes wander over him, taking him in, watching his chest rise and fall. My six-foot-two giant looks so tiny in the bed. My chin wobbles as silent tears streak down my face. I long to crawl up onto the bed with him and give him some of my strength.

Please, please be okay, I send him a silent plea, hoping he can somehow magically hear me and know I'm here.

I can't lose him. I just can't.

TWENTY-NINE

I sit there for twenty hours straight. The doctors don't even kick us out at the end of visiting; they just pull the curtain around us and let us sit in the chairs at his bedside through the night. We don't talk. I have no words. Depression has stolen every emotion from me. I'm numb as I just stare at Jared in the bed, willing him to be okay, willing him to wake up soon and come back to me, willing his heart to keep beating.

Kenneth and Deborah take turns in sitting up here with me and swapping to be downstairs with Theo.

He woke after having his leg set yesterday and told his parents and the police more about the accident.

Apparently, a truck had veered onto their side of the road and hit them head-on. There was nothing they could have done to avoid it; it was just an accident. Jared was driving, and they'd just been for a workout at the gym. The driver admitted he was trying to adjust his satnav to direct around some roadworks and took his eyes off the road for too long. He didn't even realise he'd veered into the other lane until the collision.

Until that moment, everything had been normal, just a normal day and trip to the gym they'd done a hundred times before. The truck had come out of nowhere. It really put things into perspective, how fragile life was and how we shouldn't ever take it for granted. A freak accident had almost wiped them out.

Nothing is guaranteed in life. After this, I vow to never take another day for granted again.

Before his shift starts this morning, Tim comes up to give me a hug and a much-needed change of clothes that Heather sent in for me. In the bag are also a packet of biscuits and a flask of coffee, which Kenneth and I share for breakfast. All the waiting around and dozing in the chair has given me neck and backache. Time seems to be stretching on forever. Now, I know what they mean when people use the phrase *longest night of my life*.

The worst of it is the nothingness. The waiting for news. It mingles with the worry and anxiety and churns like a ferocious monster in my stomach. As I sit there, staring at him, it feels like I'm grieving. Grieving for him even though he's still here.

What I keep coming back to is how stupid I have been. Looking at him now, how did I not know how I felt about him? Why did it take nearly losing him for me to see he is everything I need? Jared—the adorable, smart, hardworking, lovable, thoughtful, funny, sweet, OCD, underwear-folding, sexy guy—is the love of my life. He is the yin to my yang, the Ross to my Rachel, the Bert to my Ernie. Yes, we probably are opposites, but just like a puzzle piece, he completes me. And it took all of this for me to see it. So what if I liked Theo first? So what if liking Theo was what made me give Jared a chance in the first place? All along, I have just been fooling myself into thinking I was in love with Theo, worrying that my feelings for Jared were somehow wrong, confused, tangled with what I thought I felt for his brother. When in reality, they weren't at all. I was just overthinking it.

I know now that Theo was merely a fixation, a crush, a craze. It wasn't ever love that I felt for him. No. *This* is love. Only love can make you feel this absolutely terrified. Only love has the power to gut you completely like this.

Theo is great. But Jared … Jared is special. And he's mine. Well, he was anyway. Now, our fate is hanging by a thread.

At lunchtime the next day, the doctors discharge Theo, and Kenneth and Deborah leave to take him home. Kenneth vows he'll be back soon, but I tell him to take his time, have a nap, catch a shower, and I promise to call them if anything happens. He looks exhausted and is no good to anyone, sitting here, just waiting.

I'm left sitting by the bed on my own, chewing on my nails and picking at a loose thread on the sleeve of Heather's jumper. My routine is stilted and repetitive. I can't bring myself to leave, even to go down to the food court to eat even though my tummy rumbles so loudly that it's almost embarrassing. So, I just sit in the uncomfortable chair, stand, walk around the bed, look out of the window at the roof of another part of the hospital, read the posters on the wall, watch the nurse do their checks. Sit, stand, repeat. My gaze never strays long from the heart monitor, watching the numbers and the rhythm, checking it's still working and he's still fighting.

A little while later, a porter and a nurse come in to collect Jared. They're taking him to get a couple of scans to see how he's doing, and once they have everything back in a couple of hours, they'll make a judgement if he can start coming off the machines. The nurse refuses to let me accompany him and assures me they'll be gone at least half an hour, so when they leave, wheeling him off on the bed, I dash to the concourse, stuff a Burger King down my neck in just a few short bites, and call Deborah, my mum, and Heather to give them an update before heading back upstairs. I'm back in the ward, waiting, before he is.

An hour later, the doctor comes in and gives me good news. The scans look clear, there's no build-up of fluid around his heart, and he's doing really well. The X-ray on his head shows no bleeding on the brain. They are ready to start taking him off the machines.

They remove the ventilator and tube from his throat, seeming very pleased with how he responds. The nurse, Kelly, sits in with me for half an hour, keeping an eye on his blood saturation and pressure. She chats away about Christmas and her plans she has with her boyfriend, seeming completely unaware that she's slowly killing me inside because my boyfriend was so close to death just a few hours ago and I have yet to see his beautiful eyes open.

My gaze stays focused on Jared, and when Kelly leaves a little while later, satisfied that he's stable, I sit forward in my chair and clasp my hands together under my chin, watching for any signs of movement. They took him off the sedative drip. It is now just a matter of time.

When his finger flutters a full two hours after they stopped the drip, my eyes widen, and I jump to my feet, looking down at him expectantly. He squeezes his eyes shut before they blink open, and relief washes over me in droves.

Those eyes, those beautiful brown eyes, flit to me, and I feel the hair on the back of my neck prickle as the tension loosens in my shoulders.

"Hi," he croaks, his voice husky from the tube that was lodged in his throat for hours.

"Hi." I smile, my eyes filling with relieved tears.

He reaches up towards his head, so I catch his hand and shake my head.

"Careful. Don't move, okay?" I reach for the call button and press it.

His eyebrows pull together in a frown as he looks around, clearly confused. "Shit. What happened?" His voice is sore-sounding and cracked.

"You were in a car accident. You're okay. You're pretty banged up though, so you need to be careful. Stay still. The doctor will come in a minute. We've been waiting for you to wake up."

He blinks rapidly. I see his lips silently repeat the words *car accident* as his frown deepens. Suddenly, his eyes widen. "Oh shit. Theo? Is Theo okay?"

I can see the panic building in his eyes and hear it in the hasty beat of his heart on the monitor as he turns his head, trying to see his brother.

I put my hand on the side of his face and lean over the bed more, trying to quell his panic and keep him still before he hurts himself. "He's fine, I promise. He has a broken leg and some other minor stuff. They've sent him home already."

His gaze comes back to mine, and I can see the question there.

I force a smile. "He's fine, Jared, I promise. He's home now. Your parents took him home; that's why they're not here." I softly stroke his face, and the curtain is yanked to the side behind me.

I step back and look over my shoulder as the nurse who's been checking on him steps in and looks from me to Jared.

Her mouth pulls into a warm smile. "Oh great, you're awake!" She's so cheerful that I feel a grin slip onto my face too. "How are you feeling?" She steps to his side, looking down at him, pulling out her penlight, checking the reactions of his eyes again for the hundredth time.

Jared goes to answer, but his throat cracks, and he coughs instead.

She smiles sympathetically and reaches for the jug of water, pouring a glass and popping a straw into it. "I know; your throat is sore. It's from the tubes. It'll ease off soon. Here." She offers him the straw, and he takes a couple of pulls on it, his eyes moving from her to me and back again, as if he's checking I'm not leaving.

He sighs and pulls his head back. "Thanks."

When he reaches up to wipe his face, I wince and watch as he touches the bandages around his head, his eyebrows pinching in bewilderment.

"So, my name's Kelly. I've been looking after you today," the nurse says. "I'm glad you've finally woken. You gave everyone quite a scare."

Understatement of the century.

She checks his blood pressure, writing down details from the heart monitor, and takes his temperature. "How's your pain? You've not long had a dose, but I can give you a top-up on your pain meds if you need some?"

Jared shakes his head. "No, it's okay. It's not too bad. What happened?" His hand moves to his chest, feeling the bandages there too.

"The car accident caused some damage to your heart. We had to take you into surgery and fix you up," she answers.

I notice she's not giving him many details, likely trying to keep him calm and still.

"Heart surgery?" Jared repeats, his eyes flicking to me.

I press my lips together and nod.

"We'll have you good as new in no time. Just try not to move too much, all right? I'll let the doctor know you're awake, and she'll come down and have a chat with you, answer any questions you might have." She steps back and puts her hand on my shoulder, giving it a supportive squeeze.

When she leaves, I move back up next to Jared's head and smile down at him. My hands wander over to him, one on his neck, the other on his forearm—two of the few places left on him where he has no scratches and bruises. I revel in the warmth of his skin. His hand closes over mine, and our eyes lock.

"You scared me. Don't ever do that to me again as long as we both live, okay? Promise me," I say sternly. I don't think I'd live through anything like this again.

He tries to smile, but it's more of a wince. "Okay. Promise." He lifts one hand, closing his fist and leaving his little finger sticking out.

My heart squeezes in my chest. I smile and mirror his movement, wrapping my little finger around his as we pinkie swear. That's all it takes to make me lose it. The sobs come again, and I press my face into the side of his neck, crying with relief. His hand comes up to the back of my head, winding in my hair.

"Amy, it's okay. I'm all right."

"I nearly lost you. You almost died," I whimper and pull back, my eyes meeting his as his other hand comes up to cup my cheek. "I couldn't stop thinking about it. Thinking what if you died, not knowing how I felt about you."

His eyes search my face. "I thought you didn't know how you felt."

I close my eyes and savour his touch. I never thought I would hear his voice again, feel his hands on my skin, see those eyes looking at me with so much hope that it feels like I have his life in my hands.

"I know," I whisper.

"Yeah?" His voice is hesitant yet desperate.

I nod and open my eyes, looking down at him as I say the words, "Yeah. I'm crazy in love with you, Jared Stone. Just you. I love everything about you. You're perfect to me. I love everything from your OCD-cleaning brain, right down to your *Love Island*–hating toes. I love every single part of you. I'm so sorry I doubted that, even for a second. I was confused, but I know now. I love you. Just you. Only ever you." That is the truth, my soul laid bare.

Theo might have started out as my Man Crush Monday on those train journeys, but Jared is my Man Crush Every Day. I love the very essence of him.

A devastatingly heartbreaking grin slips onto his face, and there are the crinkles around the eyes that I love so much. They're scratched and marred with a bruise, but they're there.

"Are you sure?" he asks, stroking my face, his eyes lighting up with undisguised hope.

"Yeah," I confirm.

He presses his lips together, thinking. "But how do you know? How do you go from not knowing to being sure? I need you to tell me you're sure because I can't go through this again. I need to know you're one hundred percent mine because I don't want to have to worry about this for the rest of my life, baby. Tell me how you know. What changed?" His eyes are so vulnerable that it pierces my soul.

I gulp, dropping my eyes to the freckle on his cheek. "I don't want to tell you how I know. I'm ashamed to say it out loud."

"Amy, please?" There are tears in his eyes, and I can see how much he needs this reassurance.

As the man who has always felt second best in his life, he needs to know that what we have is real, that I choose him. I can see the doubt there, the disbelief; he'll always worry about it otherwise.

So, I look into his eyes, and I tell him the truth. I can't lie. I never have been able to, and I don't want to start now, especially not to him. "When you were brought to the hospital after your accident, they didn't know which twin was which because you'd both put your wallets in your gym bags," I begin.

He swallows, watching me, enraptured. "Okay?"

"Your parents were an hour away at your auntie's house, so they asked me to come to the hospital and see if I could tell which was which."

I'm crying again now, and he softly brushes away a tear from my cheek with the pad of his thumb.

"They took me to see Theo. He was unconscious; you were already in surgery. When I saw him, I could tell."

His lips pop open, and he nods in understanding. "The mole."

"The mole," I repeat, reaching out and gently touching it. A wave of shame washes over me, absolute revulsion for myself. I don't want to admit the rest out loud, but he needs me to. "When I saw that little mark on his right cheek, I've never been so devastated in my whole life. It broke my heart. And I knew right then and there that if I had the chance to swap you both—have you safe downstairs with a broken leg and Theo upstairs, fighting for his life in surgery—I would do it in a heartbeat. I wouldn't hesitate for a second if it meant you would be okay. You were all I cared about. That's how I know."

Jared has gone quiet and still.

I chew on my lip and fight another wave of loathing for myself. I will never forgive myself for wishing Theo in harm's way, but I can't and won't take it back. If the decision had been mine, Jared would have been the one home already with a broken leg. No question.

I sniff. "So, there you go. Now, you know I'm a despicable, horrible person."

He nods slowly, his eyes burning into mine in understanding. "Yeah, but you're *my* despicable, horrible person."

He smiles, and my heart stutters in my chest.

"Really?" I whimper.

His smile widens. "Amy, just shut up and kiss me."

And so I do.

EPILOGUE

I close my eyes and let my head drop back on my shoulders as I inhale the sweet, almost sickly scent of the hundreds of white roses and lilies that have been purchased and expertly woven into beautiful displays and arrangements for today. Quiet music plays from inside the church, hauntingly drifting out, making the hairs on my arms stand up on end. I smile as the May sunshine warms my face. I feel completely at peace and deliriously happy.

Today is a good day to get married.

Sighing in contentment, I open my eyes and lean forward, peeking through the open doors into the church. My eyes land on Jared, standing up at the front with Tim and a couple of other groomsmen. He looks both relaxed and eager. My gaze wanders over him in his suit, and I bite my lip in appreciation. He looks worthy of an actual, legit swoon, and I can't wait to get down to the end of the aisle because, as nice as the flowers smell, I know he will smell even better. He looks ridiculously handsome today, decked out in his wedding attire. I smile and feel sorry for the rest of the wedding party, having to stand next to Jared and pale in comparison.

My love for him is overwhelming; sometimes, it really does feel too much, too scary, too perfect.

MAN CRUSH MONDAY

I haven't seen him since yesterday. Per tradition, last night was the stag and hen nights, and I spent the night with Heather and the girls in a beautiful hotel room, drinking margaritas and eating pizza and M&M's. I missed him something rotten.

When the elderly church helper sticks her head out and spots us, she smiles. "Ooh, you're here. I'll give them the signal!" she chirps excitedly and turns to give the vicar a wave.

The soft music stops, and the wedding march starts up.

My breath catches in my throat, and I grip my pretty bouquet of roses, turning to look back at the girls standing with me, sending Heather a wink. My feet are itching to race me down the aisle, and I can barely stand still as I wait for my turn to walk up the little carpet and get to the front. My heart is racing.

When it's finally my turn, I step around the corner and beam a smile, loving how everyone is turned to watch me walk. I feel stunning in my dress with my hair all up in an impossibly cute up-do with loose curls around my face.

The church looks beautiful as I focus on putting one foot in front of the other and not to stumble in my two-inch heels. (Heather insisted I wasn't to wear my Converse.) The guests murmur how gorgeous I look, and I glow with pride as I walk down the aisle.

When Jared turns, catching my eye and sending me that wonderful crinkle-eyed grin, my stomach flutters.

It's been six months since the accident, and he's doing great. His heart is strong, and there are no ill effects from the crash at all, apart from a few scars. But even those I like; they're part of him, a reminder that life is fragile. Jared is as strong as an ox and is even entered for another half-marathon next month. Only this time, instead of the money he raises just being for the dementia charity, he's splitting it, donating half to the hospital that saved his life.

The way he's looking so lustfully at me makes a blush creep onto my cheeks, and I drop my eyes to the floor, trying not to think dirty thoughts. As I pass my mum and nanna, they grin at me widely, and Nanna sends me a dorky wave, which I return.

When I finally get to the front, I see Jared's teeth are sunken into his bottom lip as his eyes rake over me in my dress. I giggle at the lust I see there and step to my left, away from him. My eyes slip from Jared to Tim, seeing him fidgeting nervously with his hands. He looks a little pale.

I grin and turn to the back of the church, watching as Heather and her dad step around the corner. She looks exquisite in her white princess ballgown, and I feel pride swell in my chest. My best friend is getting married to my other best friend today. I couldn't be happier even if it were my own wedding day.

Tim and Heather decided two years was long enough to be engaged, and after Jared's accident, we all made a pact not to take things for granted or put off things. They booked their wedding a couple of days after he was released from the hospital. That crash scared and touched all of us in different ways.

I turn back to watch Tim as he watches Heather. The look on his face makes my heart clench. His nerves are gone now; it's just sheer love that I see shining from his eyes. I hold in a little squeal and shuffle on the spot in jubilation.

When I look back at Jared, I see he's still looking at me. He grins and raises his hands, telling me he loves me, using sign language. My heart melts a little more. This is the new language he has been learning in his spare time. At work, his proposals to the board have been funded, his department has expanded, and more people have been recruited for the specialised division he's spearheading. His most recent hire is a partially deaf graphic designer. He uses sign language as well as lipreading to communicate, so

MAN CRUSH MONDAY

Jared decided this was his new project. He is always trying to better himself, always striving to be the best person he can be. He awes me. Every. Single. Day. I've been learning it too. I'm not a fast learner like he is, but he is a patient teacher. *I love you* was one of the first things I could sign.

As Heather gets to the top of the aisle, she hands me her flowers, and I give her a nod and a wink of encouragement before she turns back to Tim.

The wedding ceremony is beautiful, just as I imagined it would be. They have their own vows they prepared. Tim's makes everyone laugh; Heather's makes me cry happy tears. The rings are exchanged, and the kiss has the perfect, respectable amount of tongue for church. They've pretty much nailed it all.

As they turn and walk down the aisle, arm in arm, I grin and step to the side, letting the other bridesmaid, Heather's cousin Hailey, walk behind them with the best man, Tim's childhood best friend. When it's my turn, I step to Jared's side. Along with another friend of Tim's, Jared has acted as an usher for the day. As my arm links through his, I smile up at him and sigh contentedly.

Outside the church, we throw rice paper and rose petals as the camera clicks, catching the confetti explosion and the newlyweds' ecstatic faces.

The crowd thins, and people start making their way to their cars, so they can make the short trip to the wedding reception. The party is being held in a marquee, set up in the breathtaking grounds of the hotel we stayed at last night. I went down to the marquee this morning to make sure everything was in place, and it looked magnificent. Heather is going to love it.

As I follow behind the rest of the wedding party, meaning to get in one of the posh cars they hired for the bridesmaids, Jared's hand tightens in mine, and he pulls me to a stop.

I turn and look up at him, seeing him looking down at me with *that look*. My insides clench at the unadulterated lust I see in his eyes as he steps closer to me, his arm snaking around my back and pulling me flush against him.

He looks like he wants to eat me, and my whole body is begging for it too.

"You look absolutely stunning." His voice is hoarse with arousal as his hand slides down to my bum, squeezing gently. "I can't wait to get you home later. Have you got some sexy underwear on under this?"

A heavy ache settles between my legs at the promise in his voice. I wince, knowing I'm wearing an ugly flesh-coloured pair of Spanx again. "I hate to tell you, but I'm wearing those ridiculously massive hold-me-in knickers again."

He chuckles and leans down, putting his forehead to mine. "Even better."

I squeal and kiss him. I now can't wait to get home either.

Jared and I have been living together for the last three months. Things have been moving fast between us, but when you know, you know. And we *definitely* know. We now have a lovely little two-bedroom flat with his and hers sinks in the bathroom and a cute little balcony that we often watch the sunset from. It is nothing like Jared's old wraparound grand balcony, but this one is even better because it is ours. When we decided to move in together, it quickly became apparent that negotiation and compromise were in order. My flat was too small, and his flat was too posh and clinical, so we settled on somewhere new. We now reside in a recently renovated, second-floor flat in a gorgeous building not far from where I work. Jared had the final say on which flat we picked, and I got final say on the decoration inside. Give and take. Perfect.

Us taking the next step and deciding to live together meant that Theo had to find somewhere else to live—no longer able to freeload off his twin. He now shares a flat that's not too far from ours with one of their other friends. He's doing well, still trudging along through life as if it were a comedy show, and generally being his awesome self. We see him often, and I'm pleased to say, the little mistaken identity blip hasn't soured their relationship in the slightest.

As Jared's tongue slips into my mouth and I get my first taste of him for the day, I grip his waist and press myself closer to him as the lust builds inside me. We've been together almost eight months now, and I still can't get enough of him.

A throat clearing from behind me makes me pull away, a little bit dazed as I realise where I am. Jared smiles sheepishly over my shoulder as his arms loosen on me, his hands sliding up from my bum to the small of my back. I blink, coming back to reality as I turn and spot my mum and nanna standing there, watching us.

Nanna is grinning at us like we're the cutest thing ever, and Mum rolls her eyes, already knowing what we're like. She couldn't be happier that Jared and I are on track. She adores him like the son she never had and admitted after the events that she secretly hoped I would make this choice. Nanna adores him too—though she still looks at him like he is a three-course meal. I can't even blame her.

"Are we heading to the hotel together?" Mum asks. "Or are you two going to continue to stand there, making out on sacred ground?"

Jared shrugs. "I vote continue making out on sacred ground."

I grin. "Seconded. Motion passed," I chime in, laughing as Jared plants a noisy, playful kiss on my lips again, eliciting an exasperated sigh from my mother and a naughty chuckle from my nanna.

Later, the party is in full swing. We've eaten and had the speeches, and I've even had a couple of dances. When a high-pitched tinging gets my attention, I glance around. A waitress is tapping a knife on a glass.

"Single ladies, it's time for the bride to throw the bouquet!" the waitress announces. A ripple of excited chatter erupts, and my eyes widen. "If you could make your way outside of the marquee."

I look back at Jared and grin smugly. *I'm so having that bouquet.*

He raises one eyebrow and slowly shakes his head. "No."

"Oh, yeah, it's happening. I'm getting it," I tell him. I bend down and unbuckle my shoes, taking them off and passing them to him. "Hold these. I don't need any distractions."

He laughs, and I spring from my chair and follow the crowd outside, feeling the grass tickle my toes. There are about ten ladies grouped together in the middle. Heather is standing in front of them with her bouquet in her hand, squinting through the low evening sun. When she spots me, she grins and waggles her eyebrows at me.

"You'd better aim straight," I tell her as I walk past to join the group.

"I got you, boo," she replies, winking at me.

I position myself off to one side of the group, stretching my arms above my head and rolling my shoulders to loosen them. I eye the group, sussing out my competition.

That bouquet is going down!

When I look over at Jared, his eyes are narrowed at me, and he raises his hand, using two fingers to point to his eyes and then flicking them at me—the universal sign for *I'm watching you*. I chuckle and blow him a kiss as I limber up my knees too.

"Ready, ladies?" Heather calls, turning her back on us. She takes one last look over her shoulder before launching her bouquet in a perfect arc towards my face.

I squeal, reaching for it, picturing myself catching it. My insides are already fizzing with excitement, so when someone darts to the left, elbowing me, grabbing for it too, I'm too shocked to even see it coming. The girl stands on my foot, and we both land a hand on it at the same time. Heather's cousin's face is twisted in concentration and determination as she shoves and bumps me, trying to wrench it from my steely grip. We wrestle over it for a couple of seconds, and then I suddenly feel the flowers slip through my fingertips. My eyes widen in indignation. I grunt in disappointment as they're ripped away from me, and she holds them above her head in triumph.

People clap and cheer for her, and I want to kill her.

That was mine. What an absolute bitch. I've never liked her.

When she turns back to me and gives me a smug grin, I force a smile even though I know it doesn't reach my eyes.

I hope you get chicken pox on your arsehole!

Heather shrugs and raises her hands in a *wasn't meant to be* gesture, and I simmer with jealousy inside. Now that the spectacle is over, the crowd starts heading back inside the marquee again, eager for more of the free wine and canapés.

Jared strides towards me, shaking his head in mock disappointment, his eyes twinkling with amusement. "Oh well. You gave it a good go."

"Bloody muggle stole it right from my hands," I grumble under my breath.

He chuckles and steps close to me, gripping my waist and pulling me against him. I sigh and put my hands on his chest to steady myself on the uneven ground. Under my palm, I can feel his heart beating. I sigh, letting the annoyance of the bouquet go; it isn't important. What is important is that little *thump-thump* under my palm. It is the most precious thing in the world.

"I can't believe you let her take it. You had that in the bag," he teases.

I glare over at her back as she walks into the marquee, grinning proudly and waving her flowers around like a trophy.

Jared shrugs. "You had one job, Amy."

I grip his lapel and press myself closer to him, breathing him in. "I'll get the next one."

He purses his lips and nods. "Okay. But what am I supposed to do with this in the meantime?"

He removes one hand from my waist and holds it up to his chest. My eyes flick over it. On the tip of one finger, a beautiful gold ring, inset with a pink diamond, glints and sparkles in the sunshine. It's absolutely gorgeous.

My whole body jerks as I gasp in shock. I stare at it, my eyes filling with tears. "Oh my God. Are you serious?" I whisper.

He shrugs. "Well, I was. But you didn't catch it, so …"

"You'd better give it to me!" Where my hands are gripping his lapel, I give him a little stern shake.

He chuckles, his eyes glittering with amusement.

I realise what I've just done and shake my head, smoothing down his suit. "Sorry, sorry, my excitement got the better of me for a second there."

"He's gonna do it!" Nanna hisses from off to the side. "It's happening. Jeez Louise, I might actually soil myself; I'm so excited."

"Shh, Mum!" my own mother hisses.

I chuckle, and Jared and I both look to the side, seeing my mother, Nanna, Heather, and Tim all standing there, watching. They must have stayed behind because they knew this was going to happen. They're all grinning from ear to ear. My mum is crying. My nanna is waving her hand in a *get on with it* gesture. Heather gives me two thumbs-up, her face glowing with pleasure.

Jared turns back to me and smiles. "No pressure. Okay, well, here goes." He pulls back and gets down on one knee, firmly holding my left hand in his.

Before he can open his mouth, my excitement peaks again. "Yes, I'll marry you!" I squeal, bouncing on the spot.

The group laughs off to the side, and Jared beams up at me. "I didn't ask you yet."

"Sorry, sorry. Go ahead. I'm in full control again now." I press my lips together and try to breathe, smoothing my dress down with my free hand, trying to prepare myself for it.

This is it. He's going to propose. I've dreamed of this moment for months. While wedding planning with Heather, I secretly made all my own wedding decisions and stored them for one day in case Jared ever decided to pop the question.

Jared's eyes sparkle with amusement as he looks up at me, his thumb brushing over my knuckles. "Amy," he begins.

I chew my lip as a squeal escapes.

"From the second I met you, you've brought colour into my life. Before that day, I hadn't even realised that everything was just a mundane shade of grey. I love you so much. I promise I will always have your back, always support you, always be your biggest fan, and never complain if I turn up home and you've adopted a dog."

He grins, and I chuckle.

"I'm in awe of you every day. You truly do amaze me. You're weird and wonderful and just perfect. Every night, I go to sleep, thinking how lucky I am to have you. Every morning, I wake up with you and fall just a little bit deeper down that rabbit hole when you smile at me. I want to spend the rest of my life making you smile as much as you are right now."

He beams up at me and takes a deep breath before asking, "Will you marry me?"

I blink, committing each of his sweet words to memory as I nod. "Yes," I whisper as a happy tear slides down my cheek.

My bravado is gone, replaced by a quiet, humble love for him that makes my heart ache in my chest. I've never been more completely happy than in this moment.

He seems to breathe a sigh of relief as he takes the ring from his finger and slides it onto mine. My eyes drop down to it, and I feel a rush of love overwhelm me. It's perfection, just like he is. And it's mine.

He gets to his feet, pressing his lips to mine, kissing me with so much passion that it makes my knees weaken. I grin against his lips and throw my arms around his neck as he lifts me off my feet without breaking the kiss, spinning in a little circle. I hear my family whoop and holler, clapping excitedly, but I can't concentrate on anything other than Jared and the all-consuming love I feel for him. Just him.

Would you like more Jared and Amy?
How about their first meeting from Jared's point of view? You're in luck. You can get a free bonus chapter, exclusive for newsletter subscribers, at https://www.subscribepage.com/mcmbonus.

Dearest reader,

I hope you enjoyed this book!

If so, please consider leaving a spoiler-free review.

Thank you!

Hugs,

Kirsty x

OTHER BOOKS BY KIRSTY MOSELEY

SINGLE TITLES

The Boy Who Sneaks in My Bedroom Window
Poles Apart
Reasons Not to Fall in Love (Novella)

BEST FRIEND SERIES

Always You
Free Falling

GUARDED HEARTS SERIES

Guarding the Broken (Nothing Left to Lose, Part 1)
Blurring the Lines (Nothing Left to Lose, Part 2)
Enjoying the Chase
One Wild Night

FIGHTING SERIES

Fighting to Be Free
Worth Fighting For

CONNECT WITH KIRSTY MOSELEY

Be notified when Kirsty has a new release:
http://www.subscribepage.com/newreleasekirstymoseley

Website: http://www.kirstymoseley.com/

Facebook:
https://www.facebook.com/authorkirstymoseley

Twitter: https://twitter.com/KirstyEMoseley

ACKNOWLEDGEMENTS

To my husband, best friend, and biggest supporter, Lee—Thank you endlessly for always believing in me, even when I don't.

To my wonderful family—You guys are the best a girl could ask for.

To my son, Braxton—Thanks for once asking me, "Mum, why are you like this?" (a line I stole for Jared in this book. LOL.) I love you lots. You are still the best thing I've ever done in life.

To Kim Sutton, Ann Walker, and Charlotte Coles—Thank you for your invaluable feedback and help with this book. You were amazing in spotting those tiny details I overlooked, and the book is so much better because of you.

To Terrie, my PA—Girl, you are my sister from another mister, and I love you more than I love saying "dude," which is a lot!

To Ker Dukey and Natasha Preston, my personal sounding board and cheer squad—Thank you. Your support and encouragement mean more than I could ever say. Thank you for always telling me I can when I honestly don't think I can. I love your faces.

To Tash at Outlined With Love Designs—Thank you for the perfect cover. I know I was difficult, I know I'm a pain, but you never once complained and were utterly amazing in delivering the most perfect cover ever. Thank you, thank you, thank you. x

To Jovana at Unforeseen Editing—Thank you so much for all your hard work in shaping Jared and Amy's story and helping bring them to life and make them shine. x

To all the bloggers—Man, you guys are just rock stars. I'm in awe of all of you. Just … thank you for your support over the years. It honestly means the world.

To my Kirsty's Korner gang on Facebook—Thank you for keeping me entertained and grounded. Your excitement for this book made everything easier and kept me scribbling words late into the night and while sitting in the car on the school run! You guys are the best, and I feel so lucky to have you all in my group. x

And last but certainly not least, to you, dear reader—This book was a long time coming. I know it's been three years since my last release, and I just want to say thank you to each and every one of you for your patience and support. You guys make this all possible, so I owe you the biggest thanks of them all. Mwah. x

Printed in Great Britain
by Amazon